AN UNTIDY AFFAIR

A DAVID BLAISE MYSTERY

Also by MB Dabney

Short Stories

Black on Black in Black
Anthology: The Fish That Got Away

Miss Hattie Mae's Secret
Anthology: Decades of Dirt: Murder, Mystery and Mayhem
from the Crossroads of Crime

Killing Santa Claus
Anthology: Homicide for the Holidays

Callipygian
Anthology: The Fine Art of Murder

Maribeth: The Trophy Wife
Anthology: Center City Crime

The Missing Medallion
Anthology: Hoosier Hoops and Hijinks

Editor

Decades of Dirt: Murder, Mystery and Mayhem from
the Crossroads of Crime
Co-editor with Barbara Swander Miller

MURDER 20/20
Co-editor with Lillie Evans and Shari Held

AN UNTIDY AFFAIR

A DAVID BLAISE MYSTERY

Dedicated to the memory of my parents:

Carolyn M. Bell, who never got a chance to read this book but who, nevertheless, would have said it is the best book ever written, and Henry L. Dabney, whose inexhaustible work ethic remains a constant source of inspiration.

Acknowledgements

First, I thank my siblings: Marsha Jo, Pat, David, Butch and Eric — and their spouses — for their lifelong love and support.

Additionally, I thank my writer/siblings in my critique group, In Mysterious Company: Diana Catt, Michael Eldridge, Marianne Halbert, Shari Held, Brigitte Kephart, David Reddick, and Janet Williams. Their help and suggestions on this and other works throughout the years has proven invaluable. And thanks to the members of the Speed City chapter of Sisters in Crime for constant encouragement.

I browbeat several other poor souls into reading all or portions of early drafts. Such unfortunates include Dionna Allison, Terry Faherty, the Saturday Ladies Book Club in Indianapolis, Mariska Bogle, Sharyn Flanagan, and Vania Coicou Strange. Thank you, one and all.

I drew inspiration from various people at various times, including my paternal grandmother Nannie Stewart Dabney (MamaDear), Bernice Newby (Aunt Nicey), former Philly police officer Tom Cairns, Joanne Smith, Freddie (No-Last-Name. For a bus token, he'd wash my car, even in the rain), Patricia Smith, and the late Bobbie Crowder.

Seth Bengelsdorf, Shirley Johnson, Shonda McClain, and Tracey Kohl helped with some aspect of the research, while Kim and Joel Hennessy welcomed me into their Pennsylvania, home during some of the rewrites. Carolyn Phillips and Rick Helms also tolerated me during visits to their Virginia home, and inspired me for days at a time.

Writing is a lonely task but I was also inspired by fellow authors Robin Lee Lovelace, Susan Furlong, Tony Perona, Hank Phillipi Ryan, Lori Rader-Day, Solomon Jones, the late Milton McGriff, the late Kerry Kirch, Patricia Raybon, Joby Warrick, Amy Wethington, Alexis Rhone, Jess Lourey, Sheila Simmons, and the late Suzanne M. Harding.

I am especially grateful to the folks at Per Bastet Publications, designer T. Lee Harris, publicist Sara Marian Deurell and, in particular, editor Marian Allen. Thanks for making my dreams come true.

Finally, I thank my wife Angela, whose love and kindness supports me daily; and daughters Ericka, whose irreverence reminds me not to take myself too seriously, and Barbara Michelle, who is thrilled and proud that I'm a writer. Michelle's note of moral support hangs on a wall facing my desk. And there was our dog Pluto, who we lost in December 2020. Pluto would occasionally lay quietly at my feet as I wrote, while at other times, he'd just bark loudly for no apparent reason.

I owe all of you a debt of gratitude I can never repay. Thank You, from the depths of my heart.

CHAPTER I

"I think my husband's having an affair."

Many people undoubtedly call me a dick behind my back. I seem to inspire it in them. I certainly inspired my ex-fiancé. But it's a word I really hate, not so much for personal reasons; on a professional level, it's demeaning. Private dick. Gumshoe.

I much prefer private eye. Like Tom Selleck on television. Magnum, P.I. It fits.

David Blaise, P.I. Now that has a nice, solid ring to it. So, I painted it on my office door and bought business cards.

But that's where my similarity with Magnum — or Tom Selleck — ends. For one, Magnum is a fictional character and I'm not. And, unlike me, he doesn't carry a transit pass in his pocket to get around when his Ferrari is in the shop.

That's what I was doing on a warm Monday morning in May, riding SEPTA, the city transit system in Philadelphia. Fortunately, it was only a three-block walk from the transit station to my office on 52nd Street in West Philly. The street was crowded with shops and sidewalk merchants. I passed them without taking much notice but I hoped to avoid one street vendor in particular.

I wasn't that lucky.

"Yo. It's the private dick," said Mookie, a thin, dark-skinned man with some missing front teeth. He was thirty-three but looked fifty. Life had been hard on Mookie. "Car problems, huh? That why ya walkin'? I'z can get ya ah-nutter car. Better than that piece of shit ya drivin' now."

I drove a 1976 Mustang, which was new when I bought it nine years ago right after I got out of the Navy. Not the best year for the Pony car — neither in terms of performance nor aesthetics — but I wouldn't expect Mookie to understand that.

I stopped in front of his makeshift table with its assortment of video tape movies, cassette tapes, gold chains and cartons of cigarettes. Some of the stuff was legal. Most of it was not. All of it was cheap. Mookie was a hustler and made money on volume. But for a select group of clients, he could also score drugs, fake driver's licenses, and some of the best illegal auto inspection stickers available anywhere in the city.

"It's the alternator. At least that's what the repairman said." I glanced through some of his video tape movies.

"Dis here'z all da best stuff, ya know," Mookie said. "I'z only got da best."

"Hey. Where'd you get these?" I asked, picking up two movies, one by Richard Pryor and the other by Sylvester Stallone. They were in perfectly new, unopened boxes. "These two movies aren't even out yet."

"I'z got my sources," Mookie said, stepping back and holding up his hands as if he were innocent of some unspoken crime. "Imma entrepreneur."

I put the movies back on the table. "Yeah, and they send entrepreneurs like you to Graterford Prison every day."

Mookie was tiresome, but he was also a 52nd Street staple. He was a snitch for the police, saw everything that happened on the street and, for a modest price, he'd tell you what he saw. Being a snitch kept him from getting arrested for selling stolen merchandise or the occasional drugs.

Mookie stopped me as I headed off. "I'z got somethin' for ya. Just in. Straight from Europe or France or someplace like dat."

He reached under his table and pulled out a large, silk Hermès scarf with a pale silver background and a red and gold pattern that appeared to be hand-painted. "For you, it's only fifty bucks."

"I'm not buying any crap from you. It's all stolen."

"Dat hurtz, man," he said, trying without success to sound wounded. Mookie looked up the street as if he were checking to see if the coast was clear before he made a secret deal. "I'll tell ya what. Ya give me forty and we call it even. Youz know how we work. And who noz. Might give you ah chance with da lady dat owns da car. Think she'z up in your office."

Like I said, Mookie knew everything.

I turned to where he was pointing and saw a shiny, black Mercedes-Benz 380 SL roadster parked at the curb near the corner. The Benz was beautiful and an oddity in the area. I left Mookie standing there, saying nothing to him as I walked away and approached the car. It looked better up close.

Obviously new, it had light gray, leather interior with wood trim at the dash with AM/FM radio and cassette deck. It probably had power steering, windows and door locks. It was a hardtop, which was good, given that a convertible might be too tempting for thieves, but clearly it could be converted to a ragtop in warm weather. The interior was spotless, as if it was just driven off the dealer's lot. I could imagine the new car smell inside . . . a combination of the release of chemical gases, well-oiled leather and wealth.

For a moment, I stood in awe of the car but then walked the remaining sixty feet to my building, lost in thought of what it would be like to own such a car.

I intended to take the elevator to my office on the second floor but the elevator was out of order. I wasn't surprised. The building, though generally well-kept, belonged to my no-account brother-in-law. I got my corner office for a dollar a month, thanks to my handling a sensitive situation for him a year ago. It was the sort of situation I couldn't mention to my sister — or any other member of the family.

So I took the steps. To the right of the stairs on the second floor and at the end of a short hallway was my office. A sign on the wall next to the door announced me to the world.

I noticed a distinctive scent in the hallway. It was new. I considered it as I walked to my office and was surprised the scent grew stronger once I was inside the door.

My secretary, Mabelene, was already there. Mae, as she preferred to be called, often wore a fragrance, but it was never a heavy or expensive scent. Her caramel skin and curvy body wasn't that of the typical secretary. But I wasn't the typical employer. Before I even had a chance to speak, Mae indicated I had a client in my private office.

"She just got here and I didn't have a way to reach you. I told her to 'Make yourself to home' and I showed her into your office. It's been about five minutes," Mae said.

I nodded and entered my office. An attractive woman with long legs was sitting in a chair, smoking a cigarette and flicking the ashes into a small cup on the table next to her.

"Hello. I'm David Blaise. How can I help you?" I said, stopping to shake the woman's hand before I stepped around my desk to take a seat.

When I was seated, the woman stood and crossed to stand directly in front of my desk.

"My name is Elise Carmichael," she said in a low, seductive voice. "I think my husband's having an affair."

CHAPTER II

"What self-respecting man would drive a light blue Mercedes?"

"Would you mind getting me some coffee?" Elise asked, returning to her chair without waiting for my reply. Her attitude was, of course I would get her coffee.

"Mabelene, could you come in for a minute?" I said into the intercom.

At the mention of my secretary's name, Elise's eyes twinkled and she gave me an amused, condescending look, which I ignored.

Mae was immediately at the doorway.

"Would you head out to get some coffee, please? And get yourself a cup. Why don't you see Reggie at the McDonald's at the corner of Chestnut?"

Reggie, whose given name was Rhys, would be easy to spot. He'd have on a blue Oxford-cloth shirt, a tie with the Golden Arches on it, and would likely be the only white person working behind the counter. He adopted an urban persona as a way of ingratiating himself into the community and erasing most traces of his true Welsh upbringing.

Reggie was the manager. He also had a thing for black women — and for Mae in particular. She'd be able to get the coffee for free.

"I'll take mine with cream," Elise said, addressing Mae without looking up at her, as if to do so was beneath her. "Real cream. I hate the fake stuff."

Mae shot me a quizzical look and hesitated briefly but left

without comment, though I could nearly hear her unspoken expletives.

Clearly, Elise was a woman who was used to getting her way. It was easy to see why.

Tall, thin, striking and perhaps forty, she had the captivating beauty of a much younger woman. It was the type of beauty that could catch a man's eye, capture his heart, and open his fly and his wallet.

Her skin was smooth, unblemished, and a color several shades lighter than a grocery bag. She was what my grandmother would call a "high yellow," or someone who "tries to pass for white." But a white woman rarely has such full, beautiful lips. Her lipstick was a muted red, the same color she used on her fingernails.

Either she never did anything with her hands or she had had a manicure just before arriving unannounced in my office. I was betting on the former, though I had to admit either could be the case.

Her hair was as straight as hair comes, jet black and layered to her shoulders. The cut, color and style were perfect on her. When she moved her head, which she seldom did and only then for effect, her hair would fly around, then settle back into its original position.

Thanks to the influence of my ex, who lived and breathed women's clothing, and to Vogue magazines left in my apartment after we split, I developed a certain eye for women's fashion. And when it came to style, Elise definitely caught my attention. I could see her walking the fashion runways in New York, Paris or Milan, or sitting among the select group of women in the world who could wear upscale clothing and carry it off.

For her visit to my humble abode, however, she had dressed down. Her blouse was hand-painted silk. The jacket was fitted, simple and black, perhaps by an American designer. While her skirt may have come from a department store, it would have been Saks or Bergdorf. Her pointy-toed ankle boots could only have come from New York.

No longer bothering to reach over for the cup, Elise flipped her cigarette ashes on the floor. Though I said nothing, I found it irritating. But, clearly, to her, clean up was none of her concern.

I came around my sturdy, wooden desk and hiked a hip onto it. Physically speaking, I was looking down at her. Socially speaking, she was looking down on me.

"You think your husband is having an affair. Why, and what service can I provide you?" I asked her, doing my best to stay professional without showing my irritation.

"I want you to find who he's doing."

Elise looked at her partially smoked cigarette then up at me, a confused expression on her face. She glanced around quickly until I got the hint. I reached back onto my desk for an ashtray and slid it over toward her. She dropped the still-lit ciggy-butt into it and sat back in the chair.

"I can tell the SOB must have a little tramp on the side. He hasn't tried to touch me in months. He hasn't even looked."

I considered mentioning that such things were common, particularly for middle-aged men, and it didn't mean he was stepping out on her. There were lots of other explanations. But, for the moment, I decided to let her continue her quiet tirade uninterrupted.

"He sometimes works late, but when I call his office he doesn't answer. There are late business meetings he doesn't explain to me, and he doesn't offer to take me on business trips anymore. He used to say he loved having me on his arm, showing me off to his colleagues and clients, but he's stopped inviting me to his firm's business or social functions."

"What does your husband do?"

"He's a partner at a law firm downtown. One of the biggest. Watson, Whisman, Elliott and Strange. Reuben . . . that's my husband's name, Reuben Carmichael . . . is one of the first black partners in the firm. He heads the trust department. Most of the partners are a bunch of old farts. Once they all die off, he'll make managing partner. I just know it."

"And what do you do?"

She looked totally caught off guard by the question and for once seemed at a loss for words.

"Oh, I don't work," she said finally. Her toiling for wages was, apparently, unthinkable to her. "I'm too busy managing our home."

"I see," I said, though I didn't really see. I must have offended her with the question, so to break the awkwardness, I headed back around my desk and sat down. I took a pen from the wood-grain pen and pencil set on the desk and grabbed some paper, ready to take notes on the facts of her life.

"Why don't you give me some information and we'll see where it takes us," I said, but stopped as I heard Mae enter the outer office from the hallway. A moment later, she was at my door with two coffees. I looked at Elise, who glanced quickly at Mae and then back to me. Neither woman spoke.

"Why don't you leave it here on the desk," I said to Mae.

Mae put one coffee on my desk as far away from Elise as possible without appearing any ruder than she was, and handed the other cup to me. She turned toward the outer office without uttering a sound, but the set of her jaw left no doubt of the anger resting just below the surface. As she reached the door, my phone rang, interrupting the quiet of the room. I left it for Mae to answer at her desk.

"Now, where were we?" I asked Elise.

"I was telling you about my husband."

"Right. His name is Reuben Carmichael. Where do you guys live?"

"On Sedgwick Street, a block over from Carpenter Lane in West Mt. Airy, just off the Lincoln Drive."

I knew the general area. Integrated. Nice homes. A little

pricey but totally affordable on two incomes, or one very high one.

"Describe your husband for me. Do you have any recent pictures?"

Elise reached into her jacket pocket, and pulled out a white envelope. Easing out of the chair, she stood over the desk and handed it down to me. She didn't touch the coffee, didn't even look at it.

"These were taken recently while we were on vacation in the Bahamas. And there's one that's just a head shot."

I took the pictures from her and flipped through.

Reuben Carmichael was a couple of inches taller than his wife, approaching middle-age, expanding through the middle and with thinning hair. He had a round face and puffy cheeks that made him look like he had a mouth full of walnuts. His thick, graying mustache reminded me of a walrus. His shoulders slumped forward as if the world — or, in this case, an overbearing, manipulative wife — were weighing him down. He wasn't smiling in any of the photographs, an observation I mentioned.

"I don't know what his problem is," Elise said. "He just refuses to look happy, I guess."

"Thanks for the pictures. But please describe him for me. Height, weight, hair and eye color. Skin tone? That sort of thing. What's his personality? Friendly? Easy-going? Aggressive? Abusive? What?"

"He's great at work, apparently. He gets the job done, which takes balls."

I was shocked by her bluntness. She had a classy exterior but it probably didn't come from a classy upbringing.

"But around me . . . well, let's just say he leaves something to be desired. He's large, as you can see from the pictures. Six-one, two-hundred-and-twenty pounds, dark eyes, dark hair. What more can I say?" she said, shaking her head and waving her right hand as if to shoo a fly.

"If I'm going to learn if your suspicions are correct, I need to know something about his movements. His routine. Oh, and I forgot to ask. Are there any children involved?"

"No. We have no children," she said matter-of-factly. It wasn't hard for me to believe.

"Where, exactly, is Watson, Whisman located downtown?"

"Broad and Chestnut."

"How does he get to work? Does he drive? What kind of car does he have?"

Elise's expression changed immediately. She shifted in her seat, as if it caused the annoyance. With her next words, I knew it wasn't the chair that was the problem.

"It's a Mercedes 190. A Baby Benz, which is okay for some, but it's light blue. Now tell me, what self-respecting man would drive a light blue Mercedes? I hate to even get in that car with him. It's too embarrassing."

"You said you thought he was having an affair." I said, bringing the interview back to the main subject.

"He is."

"Okay, but specifically why do you think that?"

Elise rolled her eyes, as if resigning herself to describing the obvious to a dullard. It was a useless gesture, which forced me to steady my nerves. She didn't appear to have noticed my reaction. Or if she had, she didn't care.

"Like I said before," she said, irritation grating in her voice, "he's more distant and harder for me to reach, emotionally. But he also just started wearing cologne. The expensive stuff. He never did that before. I began paying attention for any stray hair or tell-tale lipstick smudge after I got into his stupid car one day when mine was being serviced. And I noticed it."

I stopped writing and leaned forward. "You noticed what?"

"The smell. There was a lingering smell inside the car. It wasn't masculine and I'd never wear something that cheap."

"Did you ask him about it?"

"Of course I did." Again, she sounded annoyed by my question, as if the situation she was in was my fault.

"How'd he respond?"

"He mumbled some lame, bullshit excuse about giving someone a ride home."

I took all the information down and considered my next move. I currently had a contract to do undercover work for SEPTA on the Broad Street Subway line during Phillies games, and I even handled a little security work at the McDonald's for a small stipend, complimentary coffee, and the occasional Big Mac, but divorce cases were my bread and butter.

Divorce cases were generally quick, easy and profitable. One-fifty a day, plus expenses. And this case had all the markings of being an easy gig.

"Okay. I'll start tomorrow."

"Good," she said, standing.

I also rose.

"I will pay you two-hundred-and-fifty dollars a day, plus any expenses you have."

"Two-fifty?" I tried to hide my surprise.

"Yes. I'm paying for results and I want them quickly," Elise said. She pulled five 100-dollar bills from her jacket pocket, and handed them to me. "This should get things going. Call me during the day at home when you have something. Let me give you the number."

I turned for a pad on the desk and she wrote down the number as she said, "I expect to hear something soon."

"I'll follow him to work in the morning and let you know what I find."

"Good plan."

"What time does he leave?" I grabbed the notepad back from her.

"Just before seven. Now," Elise said in a dismissive tone, though we were in my office, "I'll be going. You'll call when you have something."

It was phrased as a question but clearly was a statement.

"Of course." I shook her hand and she left the office without a glance at Mae. She never touched the coffee.

I gazed out the window and watched Elise walk to her car. She seemed oblivious to the attention she was getting. Mae entered the office behind me and also looked out the window.

"Glad that bitch is gone. You takin' her case?"

"It pays the bills," I said.

Mae made a sucking sound with her teeth, turned on her heels and returned to the outer office. "Believe me, that woman's trouble," she threw over her shoulder. "And sometimes the money ain't worth the trouble."

CHAPTER III

There was a tone in her voice I recognized and disliked.
Moral and judgmental.

When speaking of trouble, Mae spoke from experience.

Easy on the eyes, Mae was an attractive woman, but her choices earlier in life had somewhat hardened her. She was a former Ho and still came close to dressing like one. Her frilly and low cut blouses accentuated the ample breasts God had blessed her with. Her skirts were short and tight across the hips, generally revealing a bit of VPL — visible panty line — perhaps as an advertisement for what was underneath. I suspected when there was no VPL she wasn't wearing panties at all.

I first met Mae, then known as Baby Cakes, during a late night visit to a gentleman's club in Center City just off of 17th street. I'm told I'm not bad-looking — I'm five-foot-eleven and thin — so thin that most of my things look better when they're still on a clothes hanger — but I hadn't had a date in months. Working all-out just to make ends meet meant the prospects of getting one weren't good.

On the advice of a married client who should have known better, I had stopped at a doorway with no identification indicating what business was inside. I knocked and was allowed to enter.

Once inside, I picked from a group of four scantily clad women — two white and two black — and picked Baby Cakes to escort me to a room, which seemed like a Hollywood version of what a whorehouse should look like: red crushed velvet wallpaper, red-and-black drapes, dim fake-gold lamps.

Half-naked, Mae stood by the bed.

"Now Sugar, what can I do for you?" she said in a soft voice that nearly relieved me of an erection on the spot.

I made mindless conversation as I undressed, asking banal questions to which she gave vague answers. But just before she worked her magic, she revealed that she was a secretarial school graduate and was looking to get out of "this business."

Perhaps I felt sorry for her, or perhaps I had taken complete leave of my senses. I'm not sure. But after thirty minutes of moans and some of the best sex I have ever experienced, I told Mae I was looking for someone to handle all my clerical chores. I got dressed and handed her my business card, knowing she'd never dial the number.

I was so wrong.

Two days later she called, and against my better judgment, I hired her. So the former Baby Cakes handled my filing, secretarial and administrative work — all the things I hated and did poorly. And, the attire aside, she was working out quite well.

Mae was transfixed on something when I walked out of my office a few minutes later. She had brought in a small black-and-white television and placed it on top of a filing cabinet across from her desk. She stared at the screen, not noticing me.

"What's going on?" I asked.

She glanced quickly over her shoulder then turned back to the TV, which showed live pictures of an on-going police confrontation.

"It's MOVE. They're fighting it out with police. I'll never get to go home tonight."

Mae lived in the 6200 block of Osage Avenue in West Philadelphia, about a mile from the office and down the street from a radical urban organization called MOVE.

No acronym, just MOVE.

Group members went by the surname Africa, grew much

of their own food, hated modern appliances, and left raw meat outside to rot. They wore their hair in long unwashed dreadlocks, were militant, anti-social and prone to violent outbursts that raised the tension level of the immediate neighborhood to near-unbearable levels. The living conditions in and around the MOVE house created health and environmental problems and neighbors repeatedly pleaded for help from city officials.

But worse, at least for those living on the block, was that MOVE members were easily provoked. Given the potential for violence, one dared not test their patience.

Two weeks after Mae started working for me, I gave her a ride home from work and found the only open parking spot on the block was nearly in front of the MOVE house.

"Move the car, mothafucka," I heard as I got out of the car on the driver's side. A man with long dreadlocks approached me. He carried a machete and looked ready to use it. "Move, mothafucka!"

"Woo," I said, backing away from him as Mae moved to my side.

Looking up, I saw another man, heavily armed and standing next to a bunker at the edge of the roof of the house. Sturdy and constructed of what appeared to be railroad ties and plywood, the bunker provided a clear and unobstructed view of the street and much of the surrounding area. A shot fired from the fortified bunker could kill virtually anyone on the street while protecting the shooter.

"It's okay, David, I can make it home from here," Mae said, and headed up the street as I got back into my car.

The Osage Avenue neighbors lived in constant fear, and I could see why.

Before the current confrontation with the city, police had evacuated the neighborhood, sealed off the area and surrounded the MOVE house. With hundreds of heavily armed police officers, the city planned to evict the MOVE residents of the house by force, if need be. But the confrontation, which began at dawn, wasn't going as planned. MOVE wouldn't go peacefully, and both sides exchanged gunfire throughout the morning. MOVE had the tactical advantage due to their rooftop bunker. It withstood heavy gunfire from police and blasts from fire department water hoses.

"They're never going to force them out," Mae said, finally turning from the television screen. "I should have moved years ago."

Left unsaid was that, until she worked for me, Mae didn't have a regular income that would have allowed her to move off of Osage, which was in the middle of a lower-middle class, working neighborhood. Her prostitute's income prevented her from living anywhere except in the house left to her free and clear by her late grandmother.

"What did you do over the weekend?" I asked. "You weren't home, were you?"

"No," Mae said. "The police banged on the door Saturday and said I had to go. I went to a friend's house for a couple of nights. But she's also in this business and works a lot, not to mention she has a child. I can't stay there forever."

The expression "this business" was another one of the ways Mae talked about her former line of work.

"Maybe they'll be done by the time you leave work today," I said, trying to give her a little hope.

"Look at this," she said, pointing to the screen. "I don't think it's going to be over that soon. What am I to do?"

I headed back toward my office. "We can figure that out when the time comes. But for now, there's work to do. I got any messages?"

"Oh, yes," Mae said, following me back through the door and into my office. I rounded the desk and took my seat. It was almost comical to see her walk. The gray skirt was so tight across her hips she could hardly move her legs.

"While you had your meeting with your new client," she said, tilting her head, "you got a call from Russ Nolan at

SEPTA. He said it's urgent and for you to call him back right away."

She handed me a pink telephone memo and frowned. "What's it about? They gonna keep paying you, aren't they?"

I had an ongoing security contract with SEPTA. The regular check helped keep my business afloat and Mae away from choosing a profession where she was known as "Baby Cakes". Nolan headed SEPTA operations. We had a good rapport, but he rarely called with anything urgent.

I grabbed the phone. Mae was leaning against the doorframe, looking like she'd appreciate a quick definitive answer.

"Don't worry, Mae. I'll let you know after I get off the phone. Close my door on your way out." Mae closed the door before the call connected. "Russ Nolan, please," I said into the phone.

"Thank you," came the voice of a cheerful but disinterested telephone operator. A couple of clicks later, a heavy masculine voice I recognized answered.

"Russ Nolan."

"Hey, it's David Blaise," I said into the phone.

"You got time to come down here this morning? There's a serious and confidential matter I need to discuss."

I knew I had the time but instead I said, "Let me check my calendar. Give me a sec." Placing the phone down, I called out, "Mae, bring me my calendar, please."

Mae wore a puzzled expression on her face when she opened the door. Finger to my lips, I indicated for her to say nothing.

"Thanks, sweetheart. I appreciate it," I said to no one in particular. Then, into the phone, I said, "Russ, I can make it this morning. What time?"

"It's not an emergency," Nolan said, though it sounded otherwise, "but I'd like to see you as soon as I can. How about noon?"

I looked at Mae. *That soon?*

"Noon is perfect," I said, my tone neutral. "See you then." I hung up.

"What was that all about?" Mae inquired.

"Nothing. Don't worry about it. I'm headed down to SEPTA headquarters in about ten minutes."

She retreated to her desk and pecked on her typewriter. I had no idea what she was doing. We hadn't been that busy lately.

"I'll be back," I said, heading out. She grunted something unintelligible and kept working.

My relationship with the transit authority dated back a few years. However, I rarely ventured down to SEPTA headquarters. I preferred to keep my official business with them at arm's length. It's not that they were unpleasant to deal with. Quite the contrary. It was just that offices and meetings bored me. It was one of the reasons I opened my own business. I had an office staff of one and never called a meeting. If I had something to say, I called Mae into my office, or I walked out to her desk, took a chair, sat down and we talked. It was always easy and relaxed. No formalities.

SEPTA was all about formality, so I avoided it. Or I told myself that was the reason.

In reality, there was another reason I avoided SEPTA headquarters. And the reason had a name.

Clara.

~*~

I took the Market-Frankfort Elevated line from 52nd Street down to 8th and Market, walked up the stairs to street level and headed west to SEPTA headquarters on 9th. Once in the building, they ushered me upstairs to Nolan's office on the fifth floor.

Nolan ran the day-to-day operations of the five-county mass transit system. In high school he played basketball but lacked the talent needed for the game on the collegiate level.

In middle-age, his physical leanness was gone but he was still a pleasant man.

Years ago, when he was head of security, he hired me to the authority's police force. When I left to start my private investigations business, he steered security contracts my way. We had a good relationship.

Nolan's office was the largest in the operations division. As I strolled down the hallway, I hoped to avoid bumping into the authority's assistant security chief. As I reached my destination, I breathed a sigh of relief.

No Clara.

Greeting me at his secretary's desk, Nolan put a welcoming arm around my shoulder and pulled me into his office.

"Sit down there," he said, indicating a chair in front of his large wooden desk. Before he walked around to sit down himself, he said, "You want something to drink? Water? Soda?"

The politeness wasn't personal. It was all business formality.

"No, I'm fine. Thank you."

"You know Clara Lewis, don't you?" Nolan said, as a beautiful woman carrying a manila folder came up and took the chair next to me. I never saw her coming. She must have been standing behind the door near the corner when I entered. "Oh, I'm so sorry, Clara," Nolan continued. "You're married now. It's Lewis-Perry, isn't it? With a hyphen." To me, he sounded puzzled when he added, "I can never get used to that. Women and their names."

"Yes, of course. We've met," Clara said, extending a hand to me, which I was obliged to take. The handshake was stiff and awkward but I doubted Nolan noticed. "And yes, I'm married now," she said to Nolan, although I was sure she said it more for my benefit. "Lewis-Perry. With a hyphen. That's correct."

"Congratulations," I said and forced a smile.

She looked at me. I couldn't read the expression on her face.

"Thank you," she said.

Nolan took his chair and launched into what was on his mind, seemingly unaware of the frostiness in the room.

"We have a situation here," Nolan said. "One of our managers is missing."

"Who? Do I know him? Or her?" I asked.

"You've met him. Wilbur Stephenson. Handles security up in the North Broad Street bus depot," Nolan said. "Been here a couple of years. Was a great college athlete, way back when. Played football at Georgia Central University in Atlanta. Had a season in the NFL for the Giants but got cut after an injury. Too bad. But after he was cut, he decided to stay in New Jersey and got a job. Worked for the South Jersey transit system for years then came over here. When did you leave SEPTA? Three years ago?"

"Four. Back in the spring of eighty-one," I said.

"Yeah, right. Four years. Doesn't seem that long," Nolan said, brushing the time aside as if it were a minor annoyance. "Anyway, Stephenson's been with us a little over two years."

"And he's missing," Clara said, joining the conversation. "Hasn't shown up for four days."

"And we haven't heard from him, either," Nolan said, briefly glancing off to the side as if in thought. He didn't say more.

"Where's he live?"

"Germantown. Lives alone," Clara said. "No family around here that we know of. Had a wife, but that was before us. Heard she changed her name and moved down South somewhere."

"Have you called the police?" I asked.

"No, not yet." That was Nolan.

"Why not?" I asked.

"Saw no reason to," Nolan said. "Not sure something's wrong."

"Not sure something's wrong? You said the man hasn't been seen or heard from in four days," I said, moving forward in my seat. I looked between them. "That normal?"

Nolan shook his head no. Clara maintained a stoic expression. I shifted my position to better address them both at the same time. I couldn't believe what I was hearing. I needed to know exactly what they had and hadn't done yet.

"Have you checked the local hospitals and the coroner's office?"

"Yes. I called around this morning myself and got nothing," Nolan said. "Didn't want to alarm anyone by asking someone else to do it."

"He do this before? Go AWOL?"

"He's in my division and reports directly to me." Clara said. "He's never been a problem before. Comes to work on time, does his job and goes home. I'm following up on rumors he likes to gamble. If so, it's not been a problem before."

"There's always a first," I said to her. Clara remained emotionless. I turned back to address Nolan. "Perhaps he won some money and is living it up down there in Atlantic City with some chickie-poo, having sex and going through all the booze he can drink."

"Is that what you'd do?" Clara said. "Head down to Atlantic City?"

There was a tone in her voice I recognized and disliked. Moral and judgmental. I could almost hear her calling me a dick.

"This isn't about me," I said to her, an edge to my voice.

"No, of course not," Clara said.

In a nicer tone, I asked Nolan, "So what're you asking me to do?"

"Snoop around a little for a while. That way I can keep it inside and not alarm anyone," Nolan said. "For obvious reasons, I can't do that in-house. I figured you could handle something like this. And it was Clara's suggestion."

That caught me off guard and I paused before I turned to face her directly. "Thank you, Mrs. Lewis-Perry, for your confidence."

She inclined her head but stayed silent. I sat back in my chair and thought for a minute.

I had the new domestic case from earlier in the morning, but most of those type cases don't take long. I didn't expect Elise's case would, either. I could probably handle both at the same time, and I could use the money.

Plus, Nolan was always good to me and I wouldn't mind helping him out. It was a good business decision.

The Clara Factor was a totally different issue.

"Okay. What can you tell me about this guy?" I asked.

Nolan nodded to Clara and she opened a folder she held on her lap. She glanced through it and spoke without looking back up at me.

"White male, thirty-eight, single. Height, six-foot. Weight, a hundred-ninety pounds. His house is on Rittenhouse up in Germantown. Divorced. No kids. At least none shown here."

"Any debts, enemies or bad habits that you know of? Those probably won't be in your file, but I'm just checking," I said.

Nolan smiled and Clara closed the file, placing it on Nolan's desk.

"None that we know of," Nolan said.

"Though, of course, there are the slots in Atlantic City. It might be worth checking out," she said.

"You seem pretty sure about the gambling. You holdin' out on me?" I glanced her way.

"No. I would never withhold something important from you." There was a bite to her tone.

I turned my attention back to Nolan. "I'll do that . . . check out Atlantic City. He have a part-time job?"

"Again, don't know. But given his salary, I wouldn't be surprised if he had a little something going on the side," Nolan said. "It's not against company policy."

"You worked at SEPTA for some time, I remember seeing somewhere in our files. Isn't that how you got started? Doing some security work part-time on the side?" Clara said.

Not sure where she was going with this. "Yeah," I answered her cautiously. Then to Nolan, "What else can you give me?"

"Nothing much. He has a clean work record here. No problems at PATCO . . . the South Jersey transit system . . . that we're aware of," Nolan said. "And I think I can get you access to his house, but not today."

"I could use a key. No breaking and entering. Nothing illegal. I don't do that."

"Of course not," Clara said. "And we certainly wouldn't ask you to. You'd be on your own if you did."

"I'll head up there and look around anyway. Talk to the neighbors. See what I can see."

"Good. I really appreciate it," Nolan said. "But one more thing. I want this kept private for now . . . pretty much just between us three. I'm not sure anything's wrong but I want to keep it off the books. The board, if they were to find out, would ask why we didn't go straight to the police."

"That's reasonable, you know," I said. "Why not let the police handle it?"

"I'm not ready to do that just yet." He didn't say why and I didn't inquire further. Clara said nothing, offering no hint as to what was on her mind.

"So you're paying me under the table?" I asked, needing to be sure where the money was coming from.

Nolan thought that over before replying. "I think I can pad your security contract without much trouble or anyone noticing. Your usual hundred-and-fifty a day, plus expenses. That's as long as you don't run up a big bill."

"I'll keep that in mind."

"Send me the invoice directly, okay?" Nolan said.

"You got it."

Nolan stood, and Clara and I followed his lead. He extended a hand across the desk. "Thanks for handling this for us. It's probably nothing, but. . . ."

I took his hand. "It's no problem. I'll get on it as soon as I can. But Stephenson may have already finished his Marco Polo and come home."

"Let's hope so."

"Can I have a picture of the guy?"

"Oh, yes. I nearly forgot. Clara," Nolan said.

She reached for the folder on the desk, opened it and pulled out a color profile shot. "That's his employment picture, so it's recent," she said, handing it to me.

The picture was of a handsome man with just the beginnings of gray at the temples. He wore a brown plaid suit that he must have picked up in the seventies and a smile that looked like he'd just swallowed a canary.

I slipped the picture into my coat, wondering whether Stephenson had gotten into something over his head.

"Call me and let me know what you find out. If I'm not here, ask for Clara," Nolan said.

"Will do."

Clara and I left the office together and headed down the hall in the direction of her office. She reached her door and paused, turning back to me, but I was the first to speak.

"Clara, thanks for the recommendation. I know I probably don't deserve it after how things ended. . . ."

She held her hand up to my face to stop me. "Let's just keep this professional, shall we? What's past is in the past. I've obviously moved on. I hope you have, as well."

Someone was coming down the hallway. Clara stepped back into her office and I stepped just inside the doorway.

"I didn't mean to hurt you," I said in a low voice.

"And yet you managed to, anyway," she said, turning her back to me as she walked further into the office. "But I should have known better. You date one woman at a time but you refuse to commit to any one of them. You don't let anyone get close. It's as if you prefer being lonely and unhappy." Clara turned back to face me from across the room. "It's not a way to live, frankly. You certainly made me feel lonely, even when we were together. But it's in the past, so let's move on."

"Thanks anyway," I said, turning to leave without saying another word.

She was right about one thing. Life was lonely on the ride back up to 52nd Street.

CHAPTER IV

"They've got to put that fire out."

The Market-Frankfort El is unusual for a mass transit rail line. It starts in Northeast Philadelphia as a surface system and travels for several miles until it goes underground before the Front Street station. From there, for more than three miles through Center City, it travels underground as a subway, emerging west of 30th Street to complete the last couple of miles to the 69th Street station as elevated transit running on a track twenty feet above the surface of Market Street.

And all along the route, at ticket windows, on platforms and in transit cars, the talk was all about the MOVE confrontation on Osage Avenue. Even after I got off the El, all I heard was talk of MOVE.

"Whatz da cops gonna do?" Mookie asked as I passed his table. "Wait 'em out?"

"I don't know, Mookie." I had no earthly idea, but the confrontation was not my immediate concern. My concern was Mae.

I checked on a number of small clients in the neighborhood and got back to the office around 5:15 p.m. Mae was still there, watching the events unfold on Channel 10. One of the station's trucks was near the scene of the confrontation and had a video camera on an extended pole with a direct, unobstructed view of the top of the MOVE house.

"Anything happening yet?" I asked as I entered the office.

She turned away from the television. She looked tired, as if she hadn't taken her eyes off of the TV all day.

"No," Mae said, turning back to the TV screen. "I don't think they are talkin' to MOVE. We'll be fucked if this continues. What am I going to do tonight? I can't go home. Where do I go?"

It was almost 5:30 and I hadn't planned on staying any longer. But I also didn't intend to abandon her. As I was about to address her question, something on the screen caught my eye. Mae noticed my expression change just as I pointed at the television. "What's that going on?"

A helicopter could be seen hovering over the MOVE house. From over the side, a satchel dropped onto the roof of the MOVE house and the helicopter flew away. A moment later, the satchel exploded. Mae gasped and we both got closer to the television.

The bomb jolted the rooftop but MOVE's fortified bunker didn't collapse. The roof caught fire. It was a small blaze at first, something the nearby firefighters could easily extinguish, but no water was sprayed on the roof.

"They aren't doing anything. Why aren't they putting out the fire?" Mae asked, as if I had a clue.

"All that water they poured on the house earlier. Maybe it'll stop the fire," I said.

Mae and I watched, saying little, as the fire continued to grow without a response from the fire department. Smoke was now billowing from the roof.

"They need to put that out," she said. "My house is only a few doors down. And I don't have fire insurance."

"I'm sure they have it under control," I said. But I wasn't convinced, and I doubted I was convincing Mae.

We watched until after six when the plywood bunker and the roof were fully ablaze.

"Oh, my god. Did you see that?" I said as the bunker collapsed onto the roof and into the upper floor of the house.

"They've got to put that fire out, or it'll burn down the entire house. I hope the people get out of there."

On television, the commentators were saying much the same thing, except to note that, to their knowledge, no one had left the building.

Mae was stunned into silence as we watched. The fire, which continued to grow, was being shown on all the local stations, with the commentators babbling endlessly without having anything new or factual to say.

Firefighters turned water onto the fire by about 6:30, but the blaze was spreading by then. I pulled my desk chair into the outer office for greater comfort as we sat and watched. Soon houses up and down the block were ablaze and smoke filled the air over the scene. Mae started crying. Her house would likely be consumed.

Midway through the evening, I went downstairs for Chinese takeout and we shared eggrolls and a spicy beef dish over fried rice. But I couldn't tolerate standing there, a voyeur to a ghastly horror happening live only a mile west of the office.

It was getting late but the auto repair shop called, thankfully breaking our watch of the unfolding drama.

"Your Mustang's ready," a mechanic said over the phone. "But we'll be leaving soon."

"I'll be down right away."

I excused myself from my teary-eyed secretary and rushed out. It was dark outside but flames lit up the area only blocks away, and a thick cloud of smoke rose over the city.

In a grocery store parking lot, I found a hack I often used. Stan was an elderly pensioner who drove his bright yellow AMC Pacer as a way of making extra money.

"Where to?" he said.

"You know the guy who fixes my car? Down on Twenty-Second and Lombard."

"Yeah. I'll get you there."

It might have been faster to head down Chestnut Street, a fast-moving, three-lane one-way street heading east. But Stan, all of seventy-nine years old, hated the traffic and the speeding. So we went down Lombard through the heart of the Penn campus and then over the South Street bridge into Center City. At 22nd, he turned left and went several blocks, stopping at a large brick building on the left. A sign hanging over an open garage door pronounced the place as Bob's Auto Repair Shop. In smaller letters it said, "Experts in domestic and foreign cars."

I handed Stan five dollars, plus a three-buck tip and got out. Parked at the curb was my white Mustang with a small red trim running along the side. I went to find Bob.

The inside of the garage was like many automotive garages: dark and greasy, with tires stacked up in the corner and belts and hoses hanging on the walls. Bob, the owner, who didn't have the privilege of a last name that I knew of, walked out of his office wiping his hands on a dirty bluish-gray towel.

"Well, Mr. Detective. Here for your car, huh?" Bob asked.

Why else would I come to this hell-hole? "Yeah. It's ready, right?"

"But of course. Right out here. Let me get the paperwork first."

Bob looked over in the corner and called to someone. "Hey, Johnny. Bring me the keys to the seventy-six Mustang. I'll be in the office."

The office looked no cleaner, straighter or well-organized than any other part of the garage. Bob walked over to a wall where he kept his work orders in slots. He pulled mine out and walked back over to me.

"Yeah, well, we checked the battery but it was okay. It was the alternator. Plus we replaced the battery cable," he said, handing me the work order, as if I could understand the scribbled writing on it. "It's all right here."

Between labor and parts, it cost me $569.34. I wanted to faint. That was more than Mae's weekly salary and she was more valuable to me.

"You got more than a hundred-and-twenty-two thousand miles on this puppy. You want to trade it in for something else?" he said, looking around as if he had a car available to sell me.

"Not at the moment," I said. *I can't afford it now, thanks to you.*

"Warm weather's coming. You might want to get the air-conditioning looked at. We flush and refill. Only costs twenty-four-ninety-nine."

"Not today, but I'll think about it," I said, though it was the farthest thing from my mind.

I reached into my back jeans pocket for my wallet and credit cards. I hoped the charge wouldn't put me over my credit limit, but it went through with no problems and I signed the paperwork. I was soon on my way back to the office.

Mae, of course, had not moved since I had left. On the screen, it appeared all the houses on both sides of Osage were on fire, with the flames leaping quickly from house to house. By 10:00, I couldn't take it anymore.

"Mae, I'm tired and we can't do anything by staying here," I said.

She had cried off-and-on throughout the evening but was finally dry-eyed. "I don't know where to go."

I sighed, but accepted, as inevitable, what I had known for several hours. "You can stay in my apartment for the night until we figure out what to do next."

"I can't put you out like that," she said in a voice that indicated she was not so sure of the statement. "I don't want to impose or be a bother."

"Listen, I live alone. You know that. It'll be okay. I've got a shirt you can put on to sleep in and we can get you a toothbrush tonight and other essentials tomorrow as we figure out what to do next."

"*Really?* You won't mind?" she asked.

"It'll be okay. But it's time to get out of here. I need to lock up."

Mae's car was parked facing west on a small street around the corner. Even at this distance we could smell the smoke. The odor blanketed everything. On the street, we stopped and stared west, paralyzed by the drama.

Finally I said, "Mabelene, we need to go. We'll take my car. You can get yours tomorrow."

I unlocked the passenger side door and walked around to my side. We drove in silence the entire distance to my apartment at 40th and Lombard. I found an open parking space on the street about a block away and we walked back.

Mrs. Findley, the building owner, lived on the first floor and the aroma in the hallway outside of her apartment suggested she'd had fish for dinner. It was quiet in the hallway as we walked up the stairs and I was grateful for the silence. A Penn graduate student and his co-ed girlfriend, who apparently loved loud music and loud sex in equal measure, occupied the apartment across the hall.

My apartment opened into a long hallway, with first the living room to the right and then the kitchen. The bedroom was at the far end of the hallway. I didn't turn on the television in the living room, deciding I'd wait until after Mae was asleep to catch up on the local news. No sense in worrying her more.

I didn't have pajamas, but given our height difference — she was a very fleshy five foot three — I knew one of my shirts would be long enough for her to sleep in and preserve her modesty. We hadn't talked about sleeping arrangements so I got a blanket for myself and put it on the lumpy couch while she changed in the bathroom.

When she came out, Mae was the vision of sad loveliness. Sexy yet vulnerable. Only the middle buttons of the shirt were buttoned. As she walked down the hallway toward the living room, I realized I had probably been right that morning.

No panties.

She looked at the couch, then at me. She reached for my hand. The depth of sadness in her light brown eyes pierced my soul.

"I've lost everything, so I really don't want to be alone tonight. Please."

I intended to object as she led the way back to my bedroom, but I kept quiet until we were in the room and the lights were turned down low.

"Should we be doing this?" I gently asked.

"Shhhh," she said, placing a finger on my lips.

We had only had sex once before, on the night I first met her. And it had been amazing.

Mae kissed my cheeks and moved down to my neck as her hands unbuttoned my shirt and unbuckled my pants so quickly and expertly I barely noticed.

Man, she was good.

When she had stripped me to my boxers, she kissed my lips lightly, then with a probing tongue. We lowered ourselves onto the bed without breaking contact with our lips. But once we were lying down, I stopped her.

"I can't do this, Mae. Not tonight. I would be taking advantage of you."

"No, you wouldn't, daddy," she said, pulling at my boxers. But I pushed her away.

"Mae, no. Not tonight."

Lying on her side, she stopped and looked at me with a stunned expression that showed she rarely, if ever, was turned down for sex.

I kissed her forehead and turned over so my back was to her. I turned off the lamp beside the bed, throwing the entire room into complete darkness. She settled down, but didn't say anything.

Meanwhile, I had the worst hard-on in my life. And I had an attractive, sexy, willing, half-naked woman in bed next to me. It had been a while since that had happened.

I thought about how she'd feel and how she'd make me feel. I wanted the sex — any sort of female companionship, really.

Barely surviving on a professional level made it difficult to find the time for pursuing personal relationships. I was often alone, like a hermit, which was odd because I lived in a city with more than a million and a half people.

For several moments I considered whether I had made the right decision to bring her home with me. Then the answer became clear. Mae's soft snore filled the air.

And in that moment, I knew at least one person who probably wouldn't think I was a dick.

~*~

I woke early, in part because I had work to do and in part because Mae had pulled most of the covers off me. Easing away from her, I headed for the bathroom. In under twenty minutes, I showered and shaved, and was back in the bedroom wrapped in a towel looking for something to wear for the day.

I pulled on jeans, a white shirt and an unstructured black blazer. No tie. Not a good day for a tie. I was headed up to the Carmichael's house in West Mt. Airy.

I made a quick bowl of oatmeal, some toast and put a pot of coffee on as I wrote a note to Mae giving her the day off. She sat up in bed as I entered the bedroom with the note. The shirt she was wearing was open, exposing her chest, but she didn't seem to care.

I tried not to stare.

It was difficult.

"I hope I didn't wake you. I tried to be as quiet as I could," I said by way of apology.

"You didn't wake me. I smelled coffee. Can I have some?"

"Sure. It's in the kitchen."

"Excuse me a second," she said, getting out of bed. "I gotta go pee-pee."

Mae did not close the door and I stood to the side, leaning against the wall, so as not to see inside. She continued the conversation while she did her business.

"Thanks for letting me stay the night."

"It's no problem. How'd you sleep?"

"Okay. I was tired, I guess. I needed the rest after yesterday."

Standing there, not facing her as we talked, was distracting. I looked down at my feet and fidgeted like a little boy. "It's why I didn't wake you. Just came back to leave you a note."

"What's it say?"

"That you don't have to come to work today. You should stay here and rest if you want, then try to spend the rest of the day getting your things together and figuring out what to do next."

I heard the toilet flush followed by water flowing in the sink. Mae came out drying her hands. She seemed unembarrassed to be walking around in my apartment with virtually nothing on. No woman I had ever dated was nearly as free and uninhibited. But then, Mae and I weren't dating and none of my previous relationships had been with a former prostitute.

"I don't need the day off. I can get work done. I just need a little time this morning to figure out what's going on with my house and if there's anything left for me to get. Then I can find another place to stay."

I looked at my watch. It was 6:00 already and I needed to get going. I didn't have time for a prolonged discussion.

"Listen, I meant what I said. You should get a little more rest. You can come into the office later today. And as for a place to stay, you can stay here for a few days while we figure this out. There's no rush. And don't worry. No hanky-panky on my part."

"That was obvious last night," she joked.

"Yes, well, I didn't want to take advantage," I said, looking downward again and avoiding her eyes. "I'm headed up to Mount Airy for an assignment."

She walked over to me, placed her hand behind my head, pulled me forward and down to kiss my cheek.

"You're a sweetheart of a friend and a boss. Thanks."

"You're welcome," I said.

She had an expression on her face I couldn't read, although I could tell it was serious.

"What is it?"

She hesitated at first. "Will you come with me up to my house later today? I'd like to see if there's anything I can salvage and I don't want to do it alone."

Her vulnerability made for an awkward moment.

"Of course. It's no problem," I said as I turned to leave. "Now rest."

CHAPTER V

"I'm a private detective."
"Not a very good one."

The car rumbled to life and felt good to drive, which was a relief. I was on the street before 6:30 and stopped quickly at a convenience store to pick up the early edition of the Daily News. MOVE, with words and in pages and pages of pictures, dominated its coverage.

By 6:50, I was sitting in the 300 block of West Sedgwick Street, looking at the Carmichael's house. It was a large, white, two-story structure, with a porch and a comfortably large lot. There was a detached garage in the back, where I imagined Elise kept her Mercedes. On the street in front of the house was a light blue Baby Benz.

I was a few doors down and waiting for Reuben Carmichael to appear. If he drove by, I could follow him down the Lincoln Drive and into the city. But his wife had assured me he would take the train.

I waited only five minutes before the front door opened and out walked my target. He wore a Philadelphia lawyer's uniform — conservative, Navy blue suit, white shirt and a striped tie — and carried a leather briefcase.

I slouched in my car as he passed. He didn't appear to notice me. I looked in my rearview mirror and waited until he reached the corner before I got out and headed in that direction.

The train station was a half a block away from the corner and up a small incline. When I arrived, Carmichael was reading the morning paper and standing on the train platform with several other quiet commuters. The mood was somber.

I checked my watch. 7:08. Enough time. The ticket window in the station was open and I purchased a fare to Center City. I was back outside before the commuter train slowly rolled to a stop at precisely 7:14.

Three train cars were linked together. I didn't want to lose my target, but I also didn't want him to spot me. Carmichael boarded the second train car and I got on the first and walked back to Carmichael's car before the train moved.

As luck would have it, Carmichael settled onto an empty bench seat next to the window on the right side about a quarter of the way back. Numerous pictures of the MOVE disaster were spread across both pages of his open newspaper. He didn't look up when I took an empty bench two seats behind him.

Upsal Station was two minutes along, the next stop on the R-8 regional rail line, and several people entered the car once it stopped at the platform. I watched predictable Americans enter the crowded space. As the commuters got on, their faces showed the decision-making going on in their heads. They wanted an empty seat next to the window and once they had it, they'd prefer not to share the bench with someone sitting on the aisle. But if sharing a seat was necessary, the question was who would they prefer to sit next to? An acquaintance over a stranger, older rather than younger, a woman rather than a man, a white over a black.

There were empty seats on the train at 7:00 in the morning and I wasn't concerned about sharing mine with any of the four white people who got on at Upsal. Just a glance at a black man as they approached was enough to insure privacy until the train became too crowded closer to downtown.

So I was surprised when a woman, a striking creature of about thirty with short blond hair and a neatly tailored beige suit, chose to sit on the bench next to Reuben Carmichael. They acknowledged each other in the brief, cursory way that's common in polite American society. Then Carmichael returned to reading.

If they spoke again, I couldn't tell.

The fact that the woman sat there could mean nothing, or it could indicate something quite significant. I wasn't sure. I considered my options as we crossed over the Schuylkill River and rode past the Philadelphia Zoo. But finally I stuck with my original plan to follow Carmichael to his office in the PNC Building on Broad Street.

The train car was full by the time it reached 30th Street Station, the last stop before Suburban Station in Center City where I expected Carmichael to get off. I was readying myself for the next stop when I looked out the window and was surprised with some good luck. There, moving to get in the first car, was Freddie the Pickpocket.

Working security on the Broad Street Subway line on weekends, I often saw Freddie work his magic. He had some of the best hands in the business. I scared him off on more than one occasion, saving more than one of his targets from losing their wallets.

Freddie had a police record, but suspended sentences or probation were all he ever got.

He didn't look like a pickpocket, but that was the point. He was clean cut, in his early thirties and dressed neatly, though casually. His pants were loose, to easily allow for running, but not baggy. If you didn't look too closely, you might think he had on black dress shoes with rubber soles instead of black sneakers.

Freddie didn't see me once he was on the train and it was moving again. He didn't take a seat, either. Instead, he looked down at the newspaper he was carrying and pretended to read as he searched for a target.

People were beginning to rustle, preparing to get off at the next stop, so I knew I had a little time but not much. Three minutes at most. I got up and walked to the front of my car and crossed to the next. I was behind Freddie before he even noticed.

"Hello, Freddie," I whispered. He turned and his eyes nearly popped out of his head. "Don't say anything," I added, stopping him before he said a word. He stepped back and bumped into the commuter behind him. His escape was blocked.

I moved in closer.

"I don't care what you're doing here. I need something, so be quiet and listen," I said in a soft whisper so no one else heard. "In the car behind me, on the right sitting four seats back, is a black man sitting by the window with a young, attractive white woman next to him. You see them?"

Freddie looked over my shoulder and answered yes.

"What I want you to do is pick his pockets when he gets off at Suburban Station in a couple minutes. You think you can handle that?"

Freddie looked at me and his head moved back slightly as if the question were a foul smell that offended him. "Of course, I can."

"Good. He should be headed toward Broad and Chestnut, which is where he works. I need a wallet or a checkbook or both," I said. The train was beginning to slow down. There wasn't much time left. "Don't keep anything you take from him. I want to see it all. You got that? Do not hurt him or confront him in any way. Just pick his pocket. And above all else, *don't get caught*. Do the job and I'll have something special for you. Got it?"

The train was pulling into the station.

Freddie nodded.

"I'll meet you in that large newspaper stall in Suburban Station near the ticket windows in thirty minutes. *Be there*. Don't disappoint me and don't be late," I said, moving forward toward the front of the first car.

Once off the train, I took the first set of stairs toward the street level and was able to look back as I walked up. Carmichael and Freddie got off the train, but the woman didn't, and they came up the steps in a mass of people about forty feet behind me.

I lingered upstairs until I figured out the general direction Carmichael was headed in and then rushed to get in front of him. I didn't see it happen, but Freddie must have done his work before Carmichael exited the station, because I didn't see Freddie when we were on the street.

At the corner of 16th Street, Carmichael crossed JFK Boulevard and I followed him all the way to his office building. Nothing interesting occurred. Once he entered the building, I doubled back to Suburban Station.

Freddie was where I asked him to be, loitering in a large newspaper/book stall in the station. I bought some chewing gum and caught his eye.

"Let's get something to drink in that shop there," I said, indicating a coffee shop. There was a small booth in a corner near the back and we eased into it after getting our coffees. I was facing the front of the shop. "Okay, let me see what you got."

Freddie's newspaper was on the table. He slid it toward me. I lifted the paper and took Carmichael's black leather wallet, holding it on my lap. I had no idea how Freddie managed to get it and I didn't care.

"Good job," I said, without looking up. "Give me a sec, will you?"

I studied the contents. There was seventy-seven dollars in cash, an assortment of credit cards — American Express, Diner's Club, Wanamaker's, and Strawbridge and Clothier — a work ID and security pass for the elevator, an insurance card, and a couple of his business cards.

And finally, tucked away in a hidden fold, was a slip of paper with a local telephone number on it.

"Bingo," I said, holding it up, examining it in the light. "This might be something."

Freddie sat quietly, patiently. I pulled fifty dollars out of my wallet and handed him the bills.

"Good job. Thanks," I said. "And I think I'll need your help again in a day or two."

"Cool, man," he said.

"You'll need to get on the same train at the same time. You remember the guy, right? And the woman?"

Freddie said yes.

"I want you to tail the woman the next time and see if you can get her purse or wallet or anything that might hold identification. Can you do that?"

"It's a woman's purse. It's harder, particularly if you want it to go unnoticed. But I can handle it," he said with confidence.

"I'll also be on the train. I'll give you a nod and then you do your thing. I'll catch up with you later, same as we did today. But remember, don't do it if the risk is too great. You can't get caught. I can't emphasize that enough. Abort if you need to. Just don't get caught."

"You want me in the morning, you gotta reach me the night before."

"I can do that."

"You know how to reach me?" He seemed surprised.

"You're still over on Girard near the college, right?"

Freddie nodded and got up. "See you around." Within seconds, he was out of the shop and into the crowd in the station.

I moved the coffee cups to the side before I took out my notebook and wrote down the telephone number from Carmichael's wallet. Then, as a precaution that was probably unnecessary, I took some napkins from the table disperser and wiped down the entire wallet and everything in it. Couldn't be too careful.

I got a large envelope at a stationery store in Suburban Station, put the wallet inside and went upstairs to a courier service. It cost ten bucks to have the envelope hand delivered to Carmichael's office.

Returning downstairs, I found a bank of telephone booths. I entered and closed the door, dropped in a quarter, dialed and waited for the connection.

"Mr. Carmichael's office," said the woman who answered on the first ring. Her voice was pleasant, cheerful.

"Is Mr. Carmichael in?" I asked, knowing she would make up some excuse before passing an unidentified caller through.

"I'm sorry," she said, trying to sound genuinely sorry. "Mr. Carmichael is currently on another call. May I take a name and a number so he can return your call?"

"No. Just tell him I found his wallet in Suburban Station this morning and I've had it sent over to your office by courier."

"Oh my," she said, sounding alarmed. She rushed forward, "I think Mr. Carmichael might want to talk to you and thank. . . ."

I hung up before she finished her sentence. I had more calls to make, but I didn't want to use the same telephone booth. I went back upstairs and headed for the door.

Entering onto the street, I looked up JFK and decided to use a telephone booth in the Sheraton Hotel in the next block.

At the Sheraton, the lobby was busy, like in most hotels. I didn't immediately see where the telephones were located and was headed to the front desk until I noticed a newsstand and a beautiful young woman working there. It was a small space with a counter with newspapers, chewing gum and some candy in front, and cigarettes and other items on a wall behind the cashier.

I walked over. "Hello."

Her skin was a warm chocolate color, and she had a friendly, captivating smile that lit up her pretty face. I could get lost in her dark eyes and forget all my worries in her sensual lips. She was as cute as a co-ed and, given her age, probably was one.

"May I help you?" she asked.

"Ah, yeah. Which way to the public phones?"

"They're down that hall to the left."

"Thanks. I'll be back in a minute."

"I look forward to it," she replied with a flirt.

I left for the phones, barely able to remember who I was calling and why. But I was more focused by the time Russ Nolan at SEPTA answered my call.

"Wilbur Stephenson show up or call yet?" I asked.

"Not a word."

"Maybe one of his co-workers knows something," I suggested.

"Clara already tried. Here, take down this number. Ask for Chet. He works with Stephenson. Clara says he has a key or knows where to find one."

"If I get a key, I'll head up there this morning."

"Be careful." Nolan said.

"If I have the key and Chet's permission to enter, it wouldn't be breaking and entering." We both knew that wasn't true.

"You tell that to the police if they show up," he said.

After I finished with Nolan, I dialed the number he gave me for Chet. It was Chet who first told his boss Stephenson might be missing. We arranged to meet in two hours. Then I returned to the lobby newsstand.

"I'm back," I announced to the young woman. She looked neither surprised nor impressed. She must have men returning to her all the time.

"So it seems," she said.

"You work here long?" I looked at some of the merchandise in front of the counter as if I was interested in buying something.

"Since January. I work a couple of days a week. But with the semester ending, I hope to get more hours."

"So, you're a student," I said.

"Brilliant deduction," she said, reaching into her top at her right shoulder to adjust her bra strap. It seemed intended to draw my attention to her chest, which I tried to ignore.

"It's what I do," I said.

"What?"

"Brilliant deducting. I'm a private detective."

"Not a very good one."

I was shocked. I know it showed on my face. "I beg your pardon."

"You're not a very good detective."

"And how'd you come to that conclusion?"

"You're being followed. You notice that?" she asked.

I fought the temptation to turn around and look.

"You sure? How do you know?"

"I saw a man."

"Who? Where?"

"I don't see him now, but he was in the lobby, standing at the front desk when you came over here the first time. He followed you down the hall to the phones."

I was *stunned.* I had missed all of that, probably because I was thinking about her.

"And you don't see him now?"

"He's gone."

"Hmm. . . . What's he look like?"

"White guy in a poorly tailored blue suit. Didn't look good on him. Middle-aged, I guess. About forty, with beady eyes and short hair. Not very tall. Shorter than you. Maybe five-eight or nine."

Didn't sound like anyone I recognized. "And you're sure I was followed?"

"Absolutely. He was observing you in the same way a man interested in a woman observes her. It's the way you looked at me. Coy, but intense. Hoping I won't notice your interest but not wanting to miss anything."

She was right about that. Great observation. I got out a business card and gave it to her. "Here's my name and number. Call me if you see him again."

"David Blaise," she said, studying the card, then taking my hand from across the counter. "I'm Marie Toussaint. Nice meeting you, Mr. David Blaise, private detective."

"You have a number?" I asked. "In case I need to do some detecting for you."

"Not that you're any good at it." Her face lit with that brilliant smile as she got a pen and paper to write down her number.

Beaten by a woman in a newsstand. I needed to up my game.

CHAPTER VI

"He didna have ta go and drop that fuckin' bomb."

I took the next R-8 back to Mt. Airy to get my car but didn't stop in to see Elise because I didn't have anything yet I was willing to report.

I got in my car and turned it around, heading east on Sedgwick until I reached Germantown Avenue, where I turned right. I drove down to Chelten Avenue to get a general feel of the area and then headed for Stephenson's house. For perhaps the hundredth time, I checked the address Clara gave me. I did a pass along the narrow, one-way street, surveying the property first before finding a place to park and walking back. It was an attractive, tree-lined street with well-kept houses. Stephenson's house was a two-story structure with green shutters on all the windows. And like many older stone houses in the Philadelphia area, the exterior was made of Wissahickon schist, which contained tiny sparkles in the stone. The house looked empty as I wandered up the walk to the porch and the front door. I pushed the buzzer and waited.

No answer.

I knocked several times. Still, no answer.

His mailbox was full of letters, some fliers and a catalog but I didn't touch any of it. There are federal laws about tampering with the U.S. mail. But that wouldn't deter me. I could come back to it later if I still needed some answers.

I looked in the front windows to the right and saw nothing but a Spartan living room. Nothing was out of place. I ventured over to the windows to the left of the door, which showed another tidy, neatly decorated room. No lights were on anywhere in the house that I could tell from the front. I wandered around the side and to the back door, and looked into the kitchen. A stack of clean dishes were left to drain on the counter beside the sink.

When I got back to the front, I noticed an elderly man in a pair of pale blue polyester stretch pants and a white shirt standing in the yard next door. It didn't look as if he had ventured beyond the invisible line dividing the properties.

"May I help you, young man?" he said, a bit unsure of himself.

"Yes, well, I'm looking for Mr. Stephenson. Are you the next-door-neighbor?"

"I've lived here for fifty-five years," he said with pride.

"I work with Stephenson down at SEPTA and he's missed a couple of days of work. We're worried."

"SEPTA, huh? I worked on the old Reading Railroad for years. Retired now, you know."

"Yes, I understand," I said, trying to remain both calm and patient.

"Haven't seen him. Not unusual though. Keeps to himself a lot. Doesn't talk much to us old folks on the block. Keeps the property up, though. Talks to Mrs. Tally across the street, I reckon. Name's Roberta. She's a colored widow and the busybody type. So that explains that."

He clearly meant no offense with the racial comment so I let it drop.

"Have you seen his car? Do you know what kind of car he drives?"

"Drives a newer model, one of those Jap cars, I think. It's white," he said, turning to look up and down the street. "Don't see it now."

"Have you seen it recently? In the last several days?"

"Don't remember seeing it and don't remember not. I go

to bed early, you know," he volunteered. "Sorry I can't be of more help."

He slowly headed back toward his house.

"Thank you. You've been a big help. Let me give you a number to call me if you see him or hear anything."

Since I told him I worked at SEPTA and not that I was a private detective, I decided against giving him my business card. I took out my notebook, wrote my name and telephone number, and handed it to the gentleman. "Oh, I forgot to ask your name."

"You can call me Maxwell. Or just Max," he said.

I shook his hand. He nodded and then examined the paper as if it would provide some great revelation. I hoped his eyesight was good enough to allow him to actually read it.

"And Mrs. Tally," I said as he was going. "Which house does she live in?"

"That one there. Three-twenty-five."

"Thanks."

With nothing more to say, I offered Max a wave with my right hand and then nervously stuffed it into my pants as I walked off. I tried a few more houses before I went up to the door of Mrs. Roberta Tally.

You'd think I was expected. Probably was.

I had knocked on a lot of doors in the area. And if she was nearly the busy-body Maxwell said she was, she undoubtedly knew everything there was to know about me, including my social security number and my mother's maiden name. She was standing at the door as I walked up the steps at the front of her house.

"You must be the guy from SEPTA looking for Wil that I keep hearing about," she said, stepping out onto her porch.

Roberta Tally was a short, big-busted woman of about sixty years old, with too much makeup. She wore jeans that fit but were just a little too tight for a woman of her years.

"David Blaise," I said, extending a hand which she took. Her grip was amazingly strong. Nothing wimpy about this woman. "Have you seen or heard from him?"

"Not since Thursday night. I saw him after he got off work that night. He usually comes over for lunch on Saturdays after he gets his hair cut, but I didn't hear from him," Mrs. Tally said. She paused as if considering something and reaching a quick decision on it. "No need to stand on the porch. Why don't you come on inside?"

"Thanks." I said.

Her house was clean, orderly and organized to within an inch of its life. As far as I could tell, there wasn't a speck of dust anywhere. The over-stuffed furniture was old but well-maintained. Photos of kids growing into adulthood adorned the walls, and were discreetly situated on tables and the mantle. All testified to a comfortable, well-lived life. Judging from the many smiles in the pictures, perhaps even a happy one.

The walls were a pale blue, a shade a man would never pick. Too feminine. Since the wall color didn't seem fresh, it was obvious whose taste had always been dominant in the house.

Mrs. Tally was a formidable woman.

I sank into a comfortable, off-white sofa, and she took a matching chair across from me with the coffee table between us. There was a small bowl of blue and pink M&Ms on the table.

"Would you like some candy? Help yourself."

"No, thank you, ma'am. I appreciate it," I said. I cleared my throat and continued. "How long has Stephenson lived across the street? You mind if I take some of this down?" I added as I pulled out my notebook.

"It's no problem," she replied. "It's been about three years he's been here. Right after he moved to Philadelphia from Burlington, New Jersey, I think."

"Do you know if he was in any trouble or anything?"

"I know he needs a little money, but who doesn't? For his ex-wife, I think. Alimony or something. Not sure," she said. "I offered to help. I have the money. It's no problem. My late husband, God rest his soul, left me well provided for. But Wil is too proud to ask and he would never accept it from me anyway."

"You know where his ex lives? South Jersey?"

"No idea. He rarely talks about her. But I know she's from down South. Might have gone back there."

"He have a girlfriend?" I asked, looking up to catch her reaction.

"I tried to set him up with my daughter Brianna. They went out once but that was it. She just told me he's not her type," Mrs. Tally said, looking away, somewhat disgusted. She fidgeted in her chair. "Not her type? She ain't got no husband. Almost any man should be her type. And a nice single man like Wil. She can't be too picky."

"She give you a reason?"

"Nothing specific. Just a feeling," she said, then looked me directly in the eyes and asked seriously, "Do you think something bad's happened to him?"

"I doubt it," I lied. "He probably decided to take a last-minute vacation and failed to mention it to anyone. He'll probably turn up in a couple of days. Anyone taking care of his house?"

"I haven't seen anyone over there but you."

"Let me give you a card, okay? I'm really a private investigator and SEPTA is worried about why he hasn't shown up for work for a couple of days. They asked me to look into it."

"A detective. I see. So you don't work for SEPTA?" She seemed puzzled while she studied the card.

"They hired me, but no, I'm not an employee," I said.

She looked up as if a new idea had just popped into her head. "And are you married?"

The intensity of her stare caught me off guard and I could barely think of an answer to satisfy her and *save* me.

"Girlfriend. We're living together," I finally managed, then got back to something I nearly forgot to ask. "A minute ago you said he got his hair cut every Saturday. Any idea where?"

"He goes to a shop down on Germantown close to Chelten Avenue. It's called Charlie's Barber Shop. It's black, but Wil goes there even though he's white, and apparently likes it. Said it's the best cut in town."

I rose and headed for the front door. Mrs. Tally came along behind me. "Thanks so much for all your help," I said as I stopped at the door and turned back to her. She hesitated, not opening the door, so I reached for the handle. "And if you think of anything else, please don't forget to call me."

She smiled. "I won't forget."

I headed back to my car and sat for a few moments. I looked over my notes and began to get a picture of the man I was looking for. "Where are you, Wilbur?" Hearing nothing, I headed for the barbershop, where I hoped there'd be some answers.

~*~

It was so easy to miss Charlie's that I wondered how Wilbur Stephenson found it in the first place. Sandwiched in the middle of the block between a coffee shop and a small, woman's clothing store, there was no barber pole outside. Had the name not been stenciled on the large picture window, I might have passed it without noticing.

It had been decades since the shop was new and nearly as many since it had been thoroughly cleaned or painted. There were old posters on the walls and even older men sitting around talking trash.

There were four barber chairs, but it appeared only two had been used in recent years, including one in current use. When I entered, I was assaulted by a heated conversation on the MOVE confrontation from the previous day.

"Charlie, he dinna have ta go and drop that fuckin' bomb," a large, tall man sitting along the wall said to the barber cutting a customer's hair.

That must be the owner. Good to know.

The man sitting along the wall wore a brown suit and a white shirt that had faded to a dull shade of gray. He had apparently forgotten to put on a tie. A hat hugged his head so it was difficult to determine whether he was there for a haircut or just to talk smack.

"That's bullshit, Harlan," said Charlie, who stopped working his customer's hair and waved his hand with the scissors at the guy named Harlan.

Charlie was about seventy and wore his short, wavy and unnaturally black hair in a Process — a once-prominent African-American style for men that required a hot comb to straighten curly hair. It made hair look oily. As a style, it died out with the advent of the afro in the sixties but Charlie was keeping it alive, though it appeared he needed a touch-up.

"They should have gotten out of the house. They were shooting at police. What'd they expect?"

"There ain't no fuckin' 'cuse ta bomb ah house with innocent women and children in it, don't care what you say," said Harlan.

"How many people were killed in the house?" asked the skinny man in the barber chair just as Charlie returned to his head. The customer was at least a decade older than Charlie. And despite the white smock draped over his body that kept the clippings off his clothes, the first real indication that he was alive was that he spoke.

"Papers didn't say. Don't think nobody knows," said another barber in a white smock who sat in his own customer-less chair. "A couple of people got out. A woman and a boy. The Daily News said his name is Birdie Africa."

"And they killed all those other people and burned down the whole fuckin' neighborhood to do it," said Harlan from along the wall. "It's the white man. He's tryin' to kill all us black folks."

Activity stopped as the conversation continued.

"You're crazy, man," Charlie said. "Wilson Goode is a black man. He's the first black mayor."

"That fucka ain't no black man. If he was, he wouldna bombed that fuckin' house," Harlan said. "Shhh-it. He ain't nuthin' but a motherfuckin' house nigga. He shuckin' and jivin' and dancin' to what the white motherfucka says. Shhh-it."

"How many houses did they burn down?" said the man in Charlie's chair.

"Fifty-five or sixty, I think," said the second barber.

Charlie acknowledged me for the first time. "You need a cut? I'll be finished in a second."

"He looks like a fuckin' cop," Harlan said to the group. Then to me, he said, "You a fuckin' cop? You looks like a fuckin' cop."

"No, I'm not with the police. My name is David Blaise. I'm a private investigator and. . . ."

Harlan got up from his chair and moved toward me.

"I told you he's a motherfuckin' pig," Harlan said as he approached. "I ought to kick your sorry motherfuckin' cop ass for what you did to those people."

I held my ground, but I was sure I was about to get pounced. He was old, but he was fat enough to do some serious damage.

"Sit down, you sorry old fool, before the man kicks your ass," Charlie said in a calm manner. "Let the man alone."

The others waited as the tension slowly died down and Harlan returned to his seat, plopping down like a large, beached whale. I could breathe again.

"Now, what was you saying?" the second barber chimed in.

I cleared my throat and walked toward Charlie and away from Harlan, who was still fuming. I reached into my inside breast pocket and pulled out the picture of Wilbur Stephenson.

"Like I said, my name is Blaise. I'm investigating the disappearance of this man. Do any of you recognize him?"

They all gathered around, except Harlan, and looked at the picture which I handed to Charlie.

"What's it to ya?" Harlan said.

"You know him, Charlie," said the second barber. "That's the white boy who comes around every Saturday morning for a trim."

"Yeah, he's a regular," Charlie said, handing back the picture. "He in some sorta trouble?"

I put the picture away. "No. He's apparently missing. Hasn't showed up for work in days. No one's heard from him."

Charlie was quiet for a moment, like he was thinking to himself.

"He comes in here every Saturday morning at ten like clockwork. Likes a trim. Been a year, eighteen months," Charlie said. "Then, last Saturday, poof. He's a no-show. Never even heard from him on canceling."

Harlan was still suspicious. "And who'd ya say yaz workin' for?"

"For chrissake, Harlan. Leave it alone," Charlie snapped.

"I was hired by his employer to look into his disappearance. I'm just checking around," I said.

Harlan was about to say something but was silenced by a look from Charlie, who went back to cutting the hair of the skinny, old man in the chair.

"Didn't show up. No idea why," Charlie said.

"Was he in any trouble? Personal problems? Problems at work that he might mention?" I said.

"He's tired of that bitch he was married to picking him dry," said the second barber. "His ex."

I turned to face the other barber. "How do you mean?"

"She's always after him for money, threatening to take him to court. He can barely make it by," the second barber said. "That's what he says. But he also likes to head down to 'Lantic City and the casinos."

"He's got that new woman," Charlie said.

Charlie turned the skinny, older man around to face the mirror. He held a hand mirror to the back of the man's head, allowing the customer to see the front and back of his head reflected in the mirrors. Once the skinny man approved the cut, Charlie turned him back, found a barber brush and swept off the front of the man's smock.

"What woman?" I asked.

Charlie lowered the chair and undid the smock from his customer, making sure to shake the smock away from the guy so as not to get any loose clippings on him.

"He says he's seeing some rich broad and she's going to help him out," Charlie said.

"In what way?" I asked.

"What do *YOU* think? Money."

"Did he say anything else about her, like who she was, how he met her?"

"I don't remember him saying anything. You remember anything, Clifton?" Charlie asked the second barber.

"Nah, I don't remember he saying nothing 'bout that," Clifton said.

The skinny old man got up and reached into his pocket for a ten-dollar bill, giving it to Charlie. The barber opened a drawer to the counter in front of his mirror and dropped in the money. Then the customer gave Charlie a couple more dollars. "Here's a little something extra," he said.

"I appreciate it, Lou. I'll see you in two weeks," Charlie said, pocketing the ones.

"Not if I see you first," the skinny old man said as he walked to the door, which jingled when he opened it. The corny joke made me smile.

Charlie swept off the empty chair and looked over at the large man sitting against the wall. "Okay, Harlan. Let's go."

Harlan reluctantly rose, put his hat on the chair next to him and walked over to Charlie, dropping to the barber chair and never once looking at me. The light sparkled off the top of his hairless head. Even his sides were short. I wondered why he bothered to come in at all except to talk to the other old guys.

"He has a part-time job, though. Making a little extra cash." Charlie pulled a smock to Harlan's throat and fastened it around his thick neck.

"What kind of job?" I asked, wanting to take out my notepad but thinking better of it.

"Some sort of security. He never said what. But he says it's important."

This was the first I had heard of a second job. The barber shop crew didn't know any more than that.

"Okay, thanks," I said, getting my business card out and handing it to Charlie. "If you think of anything else, call me. That's my number."

"Ya wouldna catch me helpin' no fuckin' cop," I heard Harlan say as I walked to the door.

"Oh, shut up, Harlan. You don't know shit," Charlie responded.

CHAPTER VII

Mooching off the misery of others.

I called my apartment from a pay phone on the corner just before I got to my car. The call went straight to my answering machine.

"Mae, if you hear this, it's okay to pick up. It's me, David."

She didn't pick up. I tried the office. No answer there, either. So I headed to North Broad Street where I had agreed to meet Chet, looking in my mirror for a tail the entire way. If he was back there, he was good.

Mo's was a soul food diner just off of North Broad near the Albert Einstein Medical Center. It was a hole-in-the-wall place with over-salted, greasy, fried food that clotted so many arteries the kitchen probably had a direct line to the emergency room at the hospital only a block away.

Chet was a small, nearly invisible man with thinning hair and few distinguishing characteristics. He sat at a table along the back wall, near the counter where patrons ordered their food. I knew it was him because he was the only white person in the joint, and because he was wearing a blue jumper work suit he had described to me over the phone.

It was hard for me to imagine him being Stephenson's friend. But then, it was hard imagining him having *any* friends.

I took the seat across the table from him. "Hello," I said, extending a hand. "I'm David Blaise."

A plate of chicken wings, greens, and macaroni and cheese sat in front of Chet. The Louisiana hot sauce was nearby. Apparently, Chet's taste buds were not as dull as he appeared to be.

"I don't know where Wil is, but I can't believe he'd just take off without telling me. We worked together in New Jersey and came to SEPTA around the same time."

"What do you do?" I asked.

"I'm a bus mechanic. He does security."

"How long have you two known each other?"

"Ten years," Chet said, without hesitation.

"He have a second job?"

"Yeah. Security. Works part-time with some outfit out of Quakertown. Don't recall the name. Nothing serious, though. Stands around guarding people at big, fancy parties. Mostly in the suburbs, I think," Chet said, taking a bite of a chicken wing with hot sauce dripping off. He washed it down with water. "But that ain't what he's interested in."

"Oh? What's that?"

"He gotta girlfriend. A lady. But I think she's gotta boyfriend or something. One who gets jealous. Wil's real hush-hush about her. Said she was going to help out with some money in exchange for him helping her out with some . . . Well, you're a man. You get the picture," he said, with a mouthful of collard greens. He dipped his fork into a shallow bowl of greens, scooped up more and was ready to shovel it into his mouth. "They been seeing each other for a couple of months."

"Any idea who she is?"

He shook his head. It was a simple question but he couldn't voice a response with his mouth full.

"You know anything about her?"

He swallowed. "Nope. It's like I said. He's very hush-hush."

"You have a key to his house?" I asked.

"I know where he hides the back door key."

"Where?"

"An empty salad dressing jar buried under a bush on the right side of the house," Chet said, adding some hot sauce to his food. "Had to use it once."

"When was that?"

"A year ago, thereabouts," Chet said, taking another mouth full of greens. He chewed for a few seconds before he spoke again. "We'd been out drinking pretty heavy and I was wasted, in no shape to drive home. And I couldn't let my wife see me like that. Wilbur was going down to Atlantic City that night and said I could crash at his place. He told me where to find the key."

I considered that. "So he likes Atlantic City a lot." It was more of a statement.

"Oh, yeah. He loves it down there. Heads down to the shore every chance he gets," Chet said.

"The casinos? Where'd he go? Which ones?"

"He likes them all. Well, not all of them. Doesn't much care for the Claridge. Layout's a pain in the ass, he says, all those different floors. But Bally's, Harrah's, the Sands. He likes them all but says the Sands is the best."

"Why's that?"

He shrugged. "No reason that I know of. Says they're friendly. Maybe they give him a little more credit. Something like that."

I got up and thrust my hand across the table. He wiped his right hand quickly before grabbing mine. "Well, thanks. You've been a big help. If I find out anything, I'll let you know."

"Appreciate it," Chet said, and just as quickly returned to his food.

I left and found a telephone booth at the corner in the shadow of the hospital. I dropped a coin and dialed a contact at the phone company.

"Hey, Bubba," I said. "It's me, Davey. I need a favor."

Bubba's real name is Clarence and he supervised a group of directory assistance operators out of a building in South Philly.

"You only call me at work when you need something, Davey," he said, then paused. Finally he asked, "What is it?"

I gave him the telephone number from Carmichael's wallet. "Can you run a check on it?"

"I could get in trouble for this."

"I know," I said.

"Then why do you always ask me to run a number?" Clarence asked.

"Look, Bubba, it's real important."

"It's always important with you. I don't work for you, you know," he said, and paused again. I didn't fill the silence. Finally, he said, "Okay, I'll do it this time. But not now. I'll call you later. And remember. You promised to hook me up with your secretary."

"It didn't promise you that. And I'm no pimp," I said, a little pissed off. "I gave her your number, like I said. If she wants to call, she'll call."

"Okay," he said, sounding a little down-hearted. "I'll check in the evening when fewer people are around."

From the phone booth, I kept looking for my tail, but saw no one. I was on my way back to West Philly when I made up my mind that Marie Toussaint was wrong about my being followed. I made a mental note to see her again just to tell her how wrong she was.

~*~

I took Broad Street south to Walnut, then headed west. I wondered where Mae was as I drove. I parked in the back of the McDonald's parking lot at 52nd and Chestnut. Reggie let me park for free in addition to the security work I did once a month. It saved me the cost of parking at a meter on 52nd and the risk of getting a ticket.

For once, the elevator worked in my building and I rode smoothly to the second floor.

"I'm going to have to thank that dumb shit, Stuart," I said to myself. My brother-in-law had done something right for once.

Mae was in the office when I arrived. She had on the same skirt from the day before with one of my white shirts. "I hope you don't mind," she apologized as I entered.

"No, not at all," I said. "I called the apartment and the office several times but I didn't get you. What happened? I told you to take the day off."

"A friend from my old job found me an inexpensive room," Mae said. "But I still don't have any clothes."

"I was reading something in the paper this morning. I think I know what we can do about that. Come on."

I took her to the church at the corner of Cedar Avenue and Cobbs Creek Boulevard, three blocks west of Osage Avenue. With dozens of homes destroyed, including Mae's, there had been an outpouring of support and charity. Thousands and thousands of items of clothing had been donated to the church for the 250 people left homeless by the MOVE fire. Even from the distance, the smell of something burnt filled the nostrils.

I saw a reporter I knew from United Press International standing on the stairs outside the church. Mike Kerry had worked at UPI for a year, and I had fed him information from time to time. He was clean-cut and, in the way of most hungry reporters, very curious. With lots of book smarts, Mike was tenacious when it came to getting at the truth, but he had an almost shocking lack of street smarts.

"Hey, dude," he said as I approached, with an unexpectedly timid Mae just a few steps behind me. "What're you doing here? Trying to mooch off the misery of others?"

"I thought that's what reporters do," I said in return. He accepted the jab in good nature.

"I'm going to go on inside," Mae said to me.

"Okay, you do that," I answered and watched her weave through a crowd of people at the entrance of the church. Returning my attention to Mike, I said, "What are you doing here today?"

"Our photographer, Leonard, and I were assigned to come and interview as many of the homeless MOVE survivors as we can," he said.

"Mooching off the misery of others," I said.

"It's a job, and this is a major story," he said in a tone indicating how serious he was. "People everywhere want to know and understand what happened here. It's the top news story in every major paper in the world and will be for days. Why are *you* here?"

"You remember my secretary, Mae, who just went inside. She lived down the street from MOVE. I mentioned that to you before."

"Oh, yes. I remember now. I interviewed her earlier this year about what was happening on her block. How's she doing?"

"She's doing as best she can, under the circumstances. She lost her home. Burned to the ground, along with everything else on that block."

Mike hesitated before he asked his next question.

"You think . . . she might . . . agree to another interview? With me?"

"She might. I'll ask her."

It was a large Gothic-looking stone church in the style that Nineteenth-Century European immigrants would find comforting. I found Mae inside near rows and rows of clothes being collected and sorted. She looked my way as I walked over.

"You remember that reporter who interviewed you back in January about MOVE? That was him, I was talking to outside. Would you agree to be interviewed again?"

She looked around at many of her neighbors. It had been a trying time and they all seemed confused, milling about looking at items without having much of a purpose.

"I don't know," she said at first, backing away.

"Mae," I said, not moving to reduce the distance between us. "It'll be okay. You've met him before and you trusted him. He did okay on that last story." I paused, and then stepped a little closer. "You don't have to do it. It's okay with me. But he's just trying to do his job and tell people . . . the world . . . what happened here."

She agreed to have her picture taken on the church steps and to be interviewed. We headed that way. Once outside, I stood to the side and watched as Mike did his job.

"Miss Washington, you lived on Osage down the block from the MOVE house," Mike said, holding a small recorder up to Mae's mouth. The photographer was snapping pictures. "And you lost everything?"

"I have nothing," Mae said. "They made us move out of the house on Saturday and I haven't been back. Now it's all gone. Everything I have . . . had . . . was destroyed when they bombed MOVE."

"But the city says it will help you rebuild your life," Mike said.

"That remains to be seen," she answered.

"Why did you come down here today?"

"To get some clothes and other things. And I'm so grateful to all the people who donated stuff, because without this, I don't know what I'd do," she said.

"Who do you blame for this disaster? The city, or MOVE?"

"Right now, I don't know who's at fault. I just know I have nothing."

"Just for the record, can you please spell your first and last names for me?" he said, as the photographer took the last shots.

Mae spelled her names, which Mike recorded and wrote down. Then he clicked off the recorder. "Thank you, Miss Washington. You've been terrific and brave. I wish you the best of luck."

She nodded, and Mike and Leonard headed off to find their next interview victims.

When Mae and I left the church, she had a bag full of clothes and other basic necessities. I offered to take her to my apartment, but she insisted we go back to the office. I didn't press the issue. It was quiet the rest of the day, which was only about an hour.

"I'm closing up shop for the day. You ready to go now?" I asked as I walked out of my office at 5:30 and closed the door.

"I've been talking to my neighbors on 62nd Street all day and they say it's a mess up there. I doubt I will ever be ready."

"We don't have to do this."

"Yes, we do," she said. "I'm ready."

"We can take my car. I'll drive."

I took 52nd Street to Spruce and headed west. Osage t-boned 62nd Street, thus allowing some of its houses a clear, unobstructed view down the 6200 block of Osage and its carnage.

On nearby streets, there were media trucks from television stations from all over the country and reporters from all over the world. Everyone was wandering about, looking and waiting, though as I watched them, it appeared no one seemed to know what would happen next.

We made our way to the house of an elderly woman who had been a longtime friend of Mae's late grandmother and who, to some degree, acted as extended family to Mae. Her house faced directly down Osage and to the destruction there.

Mae clutched my arm as we walked onto the porch to look down the street. Having seen the pictures in the newspaper and video on television, I felt I was ready. But nothing, *NOTHING*, could prepare me for the devastation laid out in front of me. Mae's legs buckled and she dropped to her knees. It took a moment before I helped her up.

The street was blocked off at either end but all of Osage, on both sides, was gone. All the houses, destroyed.

I had driven down the street numerous times taking Mae home. Now, I couldn't tell where Mae's house once stood. The street looked like Berlin after a bombing during the Second World War. Of the houses, only the side walls made of brick remained, charred black and crumbling. Firefighters were still watering some of the smoking remains at the far end of the block.

Shock and gloom were evident on the faces of residents. The air was thick with the smell of smoke and death. Somewhere down the block were dead bodies, all civilians.

Visible were police vehicles and a black van with the words "Medical Examiner" written in large white letters on the side. It was in front of where the MOVE house once stood. Nearby there were also construction and excavation equipment, and a large group of city officials standing around.

"It's such a shame. All those people," said Esther, the elderly owner of the house on whose porch we stood. Turning to Mae, she took the younger woman into a long hug. "I'm so sorry, dear. I wish there was something more I could do to help. Mayor Goode promised to make you whole. But I got no idea how he plans to manage after all of this."

"Can I go down there?" Mae asked, taking a few paces toward the steps.

"No one's being allowed," Esther said, pointing down Osage. "But they are allowing some residents to walk down Pine."

Mae looked at me and it was as if her sadness, like gravity, pulled downward on the edges of her mouth and eyelids. My heart was heavy but all I could do was nod. We headed down the steps and turned right toward Pine Street. It was one block north and ran parallel to Osage.

A police officer manned the barricade at the corner of 62nd and Pine. A gaggle of reporters stood behind the barricade, waiting. I recognized Charlayne Hunter-Gault from the MacNeil-Lehrer Report and someone from NBC whose name I couldn't remember. But no one was being allowed to pass.

Then I recognized the police detective at the barricade and hoped he remembered me, and that it was a fond memory.

"Detective Thompson," I said as we approached. "What are you doing here? This a part of Major Crimes?"

"No. I'm not normally on the street doing traffic control but they needed everyone who could work to come in." He leaned on the barricade and shifted his weight from one foot to the other.

"I understand," I said, doing my best sympathetic voice. Standing all day manning the barricade couldn't be easy for a person used to moving around a lot.

"I can't let you through, Blaise," Thompson said.

It didn't work, but at least he remembered the name.

"Detective, this woman works for me. Her name is Mabelene Washington. Her house was on Osage, a couple of doors down from MOVE. Couldn't you let us at least walk down Pine? Just so she could have a look."

Thompson looked into Mae's red, puffy eyes and his expression softened. "Okay. But only down Pine. Don't go near Osage. And don't touch anything. All of this is still a crime scene, and if you get in the way, it'll be *my* ass."

He moved the police barricade to allow us through. The reporters then approached Thompson but he stood firm. No one else was allowed through.

We walked down Pine. On the south side of the street, the side closest to Osage, most of the houses were burned to the ground. Only a few near the far end of the block were still standing, but even those houses were so badly damaged they would probably face the wrecking ball. Any trees that remained were burnt stumps; the cars parked on the street were trash heaps. The siding on the houses on the north side of Pine sagged due to the intense heat from the fire.

We stopped in front of some steps that led from the sidewalk up to . . . nothing. Venturing up the steps as far as we were willing to go, we saw smoldering rubble where a structure once stood. The only vaguely recognizable feature on the property was the burnt-out frame of a window air-conditioning unit. The properties on either side of where we stood were gone — and the properties on either side of them. All were gone. The destruction was complete.

Standing and staring, Mae said this was the house directly behind her house. Looking beyond it to Osage, we saw nothing there. Her house and all her worldly possessions were totally gone, erased from existence, now just a charred foundation. I stood with her and wondered what it must be like to see your whole life destroyed. I wanted to reach over to touch her, to comfort her. But I was at a total loss for knowing what to say. So I just stood next to her and looked.

To my utter surprise, Mae didn't cry. She just turned, walked back down the steps and headed toward 62nd and Pine.

CHAPTER VIII

"See you there in fifteen."

It was good to be home. The apartment was small and normally I felt cramped and almost trapped with the loud music coming from across the hall, but for once, I found it comforting. There was a normalcy about it I needed right now because the rest of the city obviously had gone mad.

I had offered Mae the use of my apartment for a second night but she had refused, so I had taken her to the apartment of a friend.

I was concerned about Mae, but I needed to get away from Philadelphia. As I lay in bed, trying to succumb to sleep despite the noise, I planned my escape. It would come the next day in a trip to Atlantic City.

I rose early in the morning and quickly showered, dressed and was out the door. The car felt welcoming and familiar. Just before I got on the highway, I stopped for a cup of coffee that I wedged into a space between the two front seats. Driving against the traffic, I took the Schuylkill Expressway east past the exits for the Sports Complex and the Philadelphia Naval Shipyard and crossed the Walt Whitman Bridge into New Jersey. The lanes for the toll booths on the opposite side snaked back some distance as Jersey commuters fought to get into the city.

Once over the bridge, I hit Route 42 South to the Atlantic City Expressway and the fifty-minute drive to the glitzy city on the ocean.

Well, perhaps not so glitzy.

For decades, starting in the fifties, Atlantic City had spiraled downward from a fashionable coastal destination for families and tourists — and the yearly visit of the Miss America pageant — to a center of crime and urban decay that lay on the edge of the Atlantic Ocean. Businesses left, and the once popular boardwalk plunged into steep decline. Though they still had hordes of visitors, the beaches were deteriorating.

It was so bad in the mid-seventies, business interests and city fathers had conspired to convince state lawmakers that the only way out of the morass was to legalize casino gaming at the shore. Proponents of legalized gaming said if organized crime was kept out — not an easy task, state officials soon discovered — Atlantic City would rival, if not surpass, Las Vegas as a destination. The streets would literally be paved with gold and there would be enough left over to invest in better housing and schools, safer streets and improved social services.

Placed on the ballot, New Jersey voters had approved Las Vegas-style gambling.

The first casino, Harrah's, had opened in 1980 and soon others followed, like the Sands Casino Hotel, where I was headed. But the promised economic boom didn't occur. Or, it didn't occur for everyone. Atlantic City was a tale of two cities — one glitzy and glamorous, with bright lights, gaming tables, slot machines and loads of free drinks for patrons; the other depressing and teeming with the poor.

Though it was hard, I tried not to consider the stark contrast as I drove through the beautiful Jersey Pine Barrens, with the occasional stop at a toll booth. I was headed to a casino and was determined to avoid the depressing side of the city.

The expressway ended at Columbus Boulevard, which led to Atlantic Avenue, the main north-south thoroughfare through the city. I took a left onto Atlantic and a right onto Indiana Avenue, where the glamorous, 3-star Sands stood. It had more than two thousand slot machines, roughly 125 gaming tables and six restaurants, catering to every taste and appetite, from the ultra-wealthy to the nearly impoverished. The Sands, like all the casinos, didn't care. It would take anyone's money.

As I drove to the entrance, all I cared about was the valet parking.

"Will you be checking in with us today, sir?" a bright-faced young man in a uniform inquired as I exited the car. I handed him the keys as he placed a parking ticket in my hand.

"Not today. Just here for a day at the blackjack tables."

"Very good, sir," the valet said in a knowing way. He got in the car and headed for the parking lot.

According to Chet, Stephenson preferred the Sands, a fortuitous development for me. My best Atlantic City contact was at the Sands. Randall Wayne was an assistant casino manager, and in college, he was an Omega frat brother — a Que dog.

"If you ever need anything down here . . . a room, some credit, a contact . . . just call me. I'm here for you," he had said to me after the Sands opened a couple of years back.

He had hooked me up with a room several times, which was also why the Sands wasn't a particularly happy place for me. It was the site of my last weekend together with Clara.

I by-passed the hotel lobby and headed straight for the casino. The lights were bright and there were rows of slot machines. The clanging sound of quarters dropping into the one-armed bandits and the occasional bells indicating a winner filled the room. And though it was still early in the day, bus loads of little old ladies wearing hats with sun-visors sat in front of the nickel slots, hoping for miracles that would never come. The middle-aged people took up the quarter slots, keeping buckets made of sturdy cardboard nearby to hold their winnings. Only occasionally would you hear a load of coins hitting the metal trays at the bottom of the machines. But it was enough to keep people playing as they hoped to strike it rich.

The gaming tables took up the center of the room. They were populated with the more well-heeled gambler, though obviously not the high-rollers the casino bent over backwards to attract and accommodate. High-rollers occupied private areas in the casino and didn't have to mingle with the great unwashed who dominated the gaming floor.

"Would you like something to drink?" asked a pretty waitress in a short skirt.

"No, thank you. But if you could, point me in the direction of a house phone."

She stretched out a slender arm in the direction of the far wall, which led to a corridor. "Around that corner, sir. Right over there," she said in a courteous tone all Sands employees were trained to use.

"Thank you, miss."

She went on her way to offer free, watered-down drinks to other unsuspecting rubes.

At the phones, I reached into my jacket pocket and pulled out a piece of paper on which I had written Randall's extension. As I dialed, I hoped he was at his desk. I was in luck.

"Randall Wayne," came a friendly voice.

"Mad Dog. It's Snoopy."

"Snooooopy," he said, extending out the middle vowel sound. "How you doing? You coming down?"

"I'm already here," I said.

There was a pause, undoubtedly due to the shock. "Now? Why didn't you call me ahead of time?"

"It was a spur of the moment sort of thing."

"Where are you? I have to clear up a few things but I could meet you," he said.

"I'm on the gaming floor."

"Why don't you head on over to Ed's Americana. It's the restaurant on the first floor nearest to the back of the hotel, by the door to the boardwalk. The food's excellent and they're still serving breakfast."

"Sounds good. And Randall," I said before he had a chance to get off the phone, "I need a favor."

"You always do," he said.

"But this is a *big one*."

He didn't respond to that but merely said, "See you there in fifteen."

~*~

I was halfway through a Western omelet and a side order of bacon when I looked up and saw Randall approach. In a city known for its glitzy side, Randall was breathtakingly plain. Though handsomely built — he ran daily and frequented a boxing gym — Randall was not handsome. He had a look about him that prompted women to say, "Let's just be friends." He kept his hair cut extremely short, which only drew more attention to an oddly shaped, oblong head and small ears.

But his soft brown eyes undoubtedly helped reassure casino patrons that this large black man in a conservatively cut suit wasn't a threatening member of either his gender or his race.

"David," he said as he drew up a chair, "it's great to see you again."

"You too," I said as I reached for my glass of orange juice.

"Miss," Randall said to a passing waitress, "I'd like some coffee. And I'll take care of this." He indicated the food in front of me.

"Yes, sir. Right away."

"How long have you been down here?" he asked.

"Just got in. I got a couple of jobs going and I hoped you might be able to help me with one," I said.

"Lucky me." His eyes were cautious, although his voice was not.

The waitress brought Randall a pot of coffee and placed an empty cup on the table.

"That will be all," he said, acknowledging her in the dismissive way a superior does to an underling, which surprised me. I had always known Randall to be civil in all circumstances.

The waitress left the check in front of Randall and exhaled heavily. Randall ignored it. Before speaking, he poured himself some coffee.

"You want some?" he asked.

"No, I'm fine."

Randall added some sugar and cream to his cup, and stirred. Then he gave his full attention to me. "So, what is it that you need?"

"I'm investigating the disappearance of a Philadelphia guy. Works for SEPTA. They asked me to look into things."

Randall's eyebrows went up with the mention of the transit authority. "SEPTA, huh? Clara?"

"It wasn't her," I said, hoping he couldn't tell the lie. There was no need to give him all the details.

"I didn't say anything," he said as he lifted the cup to his lips. Taking a sip, he grimaced, looked at the cup as if it were some foreign object and put it back on the table.

"Well, you were going to say something, so *don't*," I said.

"What do you need from me, David?"

"I've been asking around about him . . . my missing person . . . and I found out he likes to come down to Atlantic City to gamble. He's into blackjack."

"Does he come here . . . to the Sands?"

"Apparently, it's one of his favorite spots."

"Huh. I see," Randall said, looking away for a moment as if briefly distracted by something. "And you want me to look into whether he's down here."

"Already tried that. Called and asked yesterday whether he had checked in. Nothing here, or any of the other casino hotels."

"You called them all?"

I nodded. He was surprised, but shouldn't have been. Making phone calls is one of the most basic means of investigation, though people often overlook it. Besides, I had Mae make most of the calls.

"What's his name?" Randall asked.

"Wilbur Stephenson."

"Doesn't ring a bell. But I don't remember every patron who walks through the front door. He's not a high-roller, I can tell you that. I'd remember him if he were."

"Check to see if you guys have any records on him, credit lines, when he was last here. That sort of thing."

"Is that all?" he said. Randall waited until I didn't respond, then asked, "How soon do you need it?"

"This is missing persons. Time is of the essence. Having the information yesterday would not have been too soon."

Randall grabbed the check and stood up. "I'll look and let you know. Where will you be in, say, an hour?"

"On the boardwalk."

He looked out the window facing the shore and I also turned. "My favorite saltwater taffy shop is down near the steel pier. It's called Tanya's Taffee. Catchy, huh?" he said. "Anyway, there's a bench right outside the front door. I'll meet you there in an hour."

"See you then. And thanks for picking up breakfast."

"Don't forget to leave her a tip. They don't make much here," Randall said, and then appeared amused with himself. "And don't thank me too soon. If Stephenson has no record here, breakfast might be all you get."

Randall headed off and I downed the last of my OJ.

~*~

The Atlantic City boardwalk was the longest boardwalk in the country, stretching nearly six miles from end to end. Originally intended to keep beachgoers from tracking sand into businesses along the shore, the forty-foot wide promenade was now itself a tourist destination and held scores of businesses.

It was a wonderful day to be at the shore. There was just enough breeze to cool the skin heated by the bright sun. Lazy clouds drifted by in no immediate hurry to get to wherever clouds go. As I walked, I stared at the clouds and let the salty sea air assault my nostrils.

It was early in the year, too soon to have the horde of sunbathers the beaches would see in June, July and August when school was out. The water was blue, clear and clean, and a couple of surfers rode the breaking waves.

People passed by on the boardwalk, and there were a few souls already on the sandy beach. A young couple walked hand-in-hand along the shore, letting the water wash up over their feet and ankles. An older black woman whom I saw come out of one of the casinos was collecting small seashells. And far to the right, two shirtless guys played Frisbee.

I enjoyed all the activity, having nothing better to do but people-watch as I waited for Randall. I was sitting on the bench outside Tanya's with a bag of individually wrapped pieces of taffy when Randall sauntered into view to my left. He plopped down next to me and leaned back on the bench, stretching out his legs. Dressed in his gray business suit, he looked out of place on the boardwalk.

But Atlantic City is a city of contradictions.

I offered Randall some taffy but he waved it off.

"I love this city. I love the shore," he said. "Sometimes I come out just to sit and watch the ocean."

"It's beautiful. And peaceful."

"I always took it for granted when I'd come to the shore as a kid," Randall said with a certain dreaminess to his voice. He watched in the direction of the woman collecting shells. But then, the moment was lost. He straightened on the bench and stared at me. "Let's go for a walk."

He headed down the boardwalk, away from the Sands.

"Did you find anything interesting?" I asked in a low voice so no one passing by would hear our conversation.

"Yes I did," Randall said.

"Please tell me he's registered at the hotel right now and somehow they missed it when I asked," I said.

"No such luck. But he had a registration for last weekend and never showed. Booked a room with an ocean view and a king-sized bed for Friday, Saturday and Sunday nights. It was a routine with him. He'd come down at least once a month and drop a serious dime."

"Did he come alone? You ever meet him?"

"I've never met him," Randall said, reaching into his jacket breast pocket. He pulled out two pictures and handed them to me. I studied the clear, crisp photographs. It was Stephenson, all right. One was from behind the check-in counter at the hotel as he was registering and the other was apparently taken from a security camera in the casino. In that one, Stephenson was playing blackjack.

"When were these taken?" I asked.

"Last month."

"Was he alone?"

"Can't tell. There's no one in the photos with him, but the hotel room he had is large enough for two," Randall said as we passed a Nathan's Hotdogs stand. "But there was a growing concern."

"Oh? About what?"

"Records show we extended him credit. He's into us for just under twenty grand. And on his reported salary, that's a lot."

"How do you know all that?"

"I checked around at the hotel and casino. Quietly, of course. He's a good customer and all. Friendly. Tips well. Never been in any trouble, either here or any of the other casinos. We're required to report that," Randall said. "But the debt raised some red flags, and two weeks ago we did some checking. Credit cards are maxed out. My boss, the casino manager, was going to bring it up with him last weekend, but he never showed."

"Any indication why? Did he call and cancel?"

"Not a word that I have found. I just spoke with my boss, and he told me Stephenson told him last month he was coming into some money."

"And you guys believed him?"

"No reason not to," Randall said. But then he added, "And you say he's missing?"

"Yeah."

"Think he skipped town?"

"Don't know."

"Any indication of foul play? If he's into us, he could be into others. Illegal operations, loan sharks. There are lots of ways to lose money," he said.

"Don't know. I'm still just trying to track down leads."

"But you'll let us know if you find anything, right?"

It was both a request and a plea.

"Of course," I answered, and meant it.

Randall stopped and turned around, heading back toward the hotel/casino. Apparently, we had reached the end of the confidential stuff he might have been fired for telling me.

We walked for a moment in silence as I considered the information. Stephenson's money problems and increasing debt raised the possibility that he had met a violent end.

Randall apparently had other things on his mind.

"So, David, what happened with you and Clara?" he inquired.

I felt heat rise again and it wasn't from the warmth of the sun. I was caught totally off guard but shouldn't have been.

Randall and I were tight frat brothers in college, but lost contact when I entered the Navy and he continued in school to get his MBA. Years later we re-acquainted because he still lived in the area — and we both knew Clara.

"Just didn't work out. She wanted. . . ."

"Commitment?" he interrupted. "And it was more than you were willing to give."

"She tell you that?" I reached over to grab his arm and we stopped. I turned him toward me.

"It was obvious, David. You love being alone, wallowing in your own solitude and misery."

It was a harsh assessment but, given his perspective, not an altogether inaccurate one. I lived alone, generally worked alone and rarely reached out to old friends, except in cases such as this one — when I needed a favor. It was not so much a matter of choice as it was of habit. But Randall wouldn't know that.

"It's not like that," I said, although I knew I sounded lame.

We started walking again.

"Then what?" He pressed on.

"It just wasn't our time. She decided to move on."

"The guy. You know, the one she married. Eli Perry. He's a drip," Randall said. He paused for a few breaths then added, "They did it down here, ya know. Got married. It was at First Baptist."

I knew, but I wasn't invited. I wouldn't have gone, anyway. "You go to the wedding?"

"Of course. She's a friend. And I gave them some sort of wedding gift. A toaster, maybe. Not sure."

The conversation lagged and we both searched for a neutral topic for the last few moments we'd be together. Nothing came to mind before we stopped in front of the door to the Sands.

"You got everything you need?" Randall asked. "I gotta get back to work."

"Yeah. I'm just going to walk through to get to my car," I said.

"You park here? Give me the ticket so I can validate." I handed him the ticket as he pulled out a pen and then scribbled an unreadable signature on the small piece of paper. He handed it back with a certain triumph. "There. That should do it."

"Thanks, Randall."

"I'll see you around, David."

And he was off. I headed for the door and to the same young valet who took my car earlier. He again greeted me cheerfully, as if he remembered me, though I doubted he did.

~*~

Driving back through the Pine Barrens, I tried to focus on the trees and enjoy their beauty. But my mind was elsewhere, and it wasn't on work. I needed to get Clara out of my head—focus on my jobs. And I knew a place that would help me do both.

Once back in Center City, I headed over to a dive on 13th Street just off Arch, near City Hall. The block had three strip clubs and thus enjoyed a steady stream of city workers as daytime customers. That came in handy when working domestic cases and you needed to obtain official information in unofficial ways, and at unofficial times.

I bellied up to the bar. There was a mirror behind the bar with a shelf under it holding virtually every brand of liquor. The array of bottles were reflected in the mirror.

"Blaise. How ya doing?" asked the bartender who wiped large hands on his white apron as he approached.

"Hey, Imamu. What's up?" I said.

"Whatever you order. What'll it be?" he asked.

"Gin and tonic."

"You want a twist?"

"Not today."

Few people knew Imamu was born Lawrence Peterson. He changed his name, he once said, because Lawrence was a slave name used by whites to hold down blacks. Everyone in the bar, black or white, addressed him as Imamu. But that probably didn't matter much to his employer, who I knew wrote out his paychecks to Lawrence Peterson.

Probably didn't matter much to the IRS, either.

Imamu grabbed a bottle of Gordon's gin and returned with a glass. He poured a generous portion.

"What's goin' on with you today?" he said. "You still got

them women problems?"

"We all got women problems," slurred a slightly drunk man two bar stools down. "They always tryin' ta take over."

I nodded to the man, who downed his drink, flipped some bills on the bar and headed out. I was glad he left. I wasn't up for scintillating conversation with a drunk.

"Yeah, something like that," I said to Imamu before I took a sip of the gin.

"You still thinking 'bout that ex-girlfriend of yours?"

"Some."

"Man, you have *got* to move on," he said.

My left elbow rested on the bar as I rubbed my forehead. I had heard all this before, of course. But it didn't cure my predicament. I was working a case for my ex, and everywhere I went seemed to remind me of that fact.

I took the glass and finished the drink. Imamu poured more gin.

"Man, you gotta get out more. That's the way I see it. Play the field. I'm surprised you aren't beating women off with a stick."

I smiled at the idea. I'm not classically handsome but I'm no Quasimodo.

"Tell me about it."

Another customer called and Imamu left. I was alone with my thoughts again. Clara was the past and would stay that way — by choice. I couldn't allow her to distract me from the cases I had to handle.

"Imamu, I need your help on something," I said when he returned.

"What is it?" he asked.

"You know Freddie Aldridge, right?"

"Yeah, little Freddie. Lives over on Girard. Comes in here sometimes and tries to work, if you know what I mean. I kick his sorry ass out."

"You know how to get in touch with him?"

Suspicion played across Imamu's face for a brief moment and he concentrated on wiping the bar in front of me, although it didn't need it. "I can reach him."

"Tonight?"

Another pause before a slow and uncertain "yeah" escaped his lips.

"Tell him I need him tomorrow morning per our earlier arrangement. He'll know what I mean. You can do that, get him tonight?"

"I'll handle it," he said.

I reached for my wallet and dropped some bills on the bar for the drinks, plus a little extra for the call to Freddie. "Thanks for everything, including the advice. I'll take you up on it."

CHAPTER IX

The only problem was, what to do with him.

I awoke in a pleasant mood. Not having Mae around was one less distraction and, overnight, I had decided to put the previous day's events behind me.

I dressed hurriedly, putting on a pair of gray slacks, a blue polo shirt and a blue jacket. I picked up some coffee and a paper at a convenience store and at 6:50 in the morning was on Sedgwick waiting for Carmichael to leave his house and head for the commuter train.

Things went as I thought. As the three-car train arrived, Carmichael moved to sit in front of the second car. I managed to get on the train first and took a seat near the back facing forward. Carmichael took the same seat as two days earlier. At the next stop, Upsal, the same white woman got on and sat next to him.

This was more than a coincidence.

When the train reached 30th Street Station twenty-five minutes later, Freddie was on the platform and got onto the first rail car. As the train moved forward again, I gave Freddie the slightest of nods indicating that the plan was to move forward.

Carmichael and I got off at Suburban Station while Freddie and the woman continued on. It would be only a matter of time before I had some answers regarding her.

Thanks to my talk with Bubba, my telephone company contact, I already knew the name and address of the person whose telephone number Carmichael kept hidden in his wallet. With any luck, Freddie would confirm the information with what he found in the woman's purse.

My plan to gloat with Marie when I saw her at the Sheraton later in the morning went out the window when I first picked up Carmichael at the Carpenter rail station, because I also picked up my tail. A white male, roughly forty, in a poorly fitting dark suit, got on with me at Carpenter and off at Suburban Station. That was not conclusive, but I planned to stay in public places and around lots of people until I heard from Freddie. Then, if my stalker happened to pass by, I would have him.

The only problem was, what to do with him. I couldn't risk confronting him, or even letting him know I was on to him. But I did need to know who he was and who he was working for. And, for my safety, the sooner I could answer those questions the better.

~*~

I waited nearly forty-five minutes before Freddie showed. He was dressed in a long, light-weight coat which I knew concealed his ill-gotten gains. Instead of the coffee shop in Suburban Station, I opted for a restaurant on the lower level of the Sheraton Hotel. It was dark, a little off the beaten path and was more likely to expose the foot surveillance I was now sure I had.

On the trip through the hotel lobby, I walked past the newsstand, giving Marie a wink but saying nothing. In the restaurant, I took a seat in a booth near the back. I faced the rear and instructed Freddie to be on the lookout for foot traffic, though it would be difficult to see because of the dim lighting.

I described who to look for.

"Cops?" Freddie asked.

"I don't think so. He was following me, not you," I said.

A waitress in a maroon uniform took our orders — an omelet for me, some bacon, eggs and toast for Freddie — poured coffee and brought orange juice. We engaged in meaningless chit-chat while waiting on the food.

"I see the guy you mentioned. He's passed three times," Freddie said when we were halfway through the meal. In his profession, he had to keep a very watchful eye. "Not a cop, though. Too obvious. Even when cops want to be obvious, they aren't this obvious."

"Okay. Let me see what you've got," I finally said. From some hidden recess in his coat, Freddie pulled out a Navy blue handbag with a long strap that had been neatly cut. He handed it over. How he had managed to get the purse amazed me. "Nice job, Freddie."

"The way she wore it, she was begging for someone to steal it. I'm just glad I got there first," he said.

I opened her wallet and took out the ID. Carolyn B. Adams, who lived in a pricey condo just off Main Street in Manayunk. Staring out from her driver's license was a pretty woman, age thirty-one, five-foot-four, blue eyes and blond hair. I suspected the hair color wasn't natural and the 110-pound weight listed was a bit of wishful thinking, though not by much.

There was an assortment of personal care items in the handbag — makeup, eyeliner, mascara, blush, lipstick, a small bottle of sweet pink fingernail polish. I also saw a little loose coin discarded in the bottom of the handbag but most of her money was in a small purse, along with pictures and credit cards. One particular photograph caught my attention, but I decided to examine it more closely later.

Amongst the paper debris was Carmichael's business card. Her business cards showed she was a men's sportswear buyer for the Strawbridge and Clothier department store.

I opened her checkbook and flipped through the check registry. She made a large deposit every two weeks, which was undoubtedly from Strawbridge's. The sum was impressive but she couldn't afford that condo on that salary. However, there wasn't a large monthly outlay that would cover housing. She apparently wasn't paying rent.

The handbag answered a lot of questions about her. But what it didn't explain was why she drove twenty minutes out of her way each morning to ride into town sitting next to Reuben Carmichael.

"You need me anymore?" Freddie asked after a while. Our plates were empty and what remained of the coffee was cold.

"Maybe." I'd been considering how to handle my situation. A plan came to mind but I wasn't sure if Freddie would agree. "I think I can use your help. And there'd be something in it for you."

"Besides what you already owe me?" Freddie eyed me with suspicion but I had his full attention. I paid him for grabbing the purse. "Is it dangerous?"

I wasn't sure, so I lied. "I doubt it."

Freddie's profession required he size up people quickly and correctly, and I was certain he was sizing me up by my answer. I was sure he knew I was lying. But then, I saw his shoulder relax a little. He would accept the challenge.

"Okay. What is it?" Freddie asked.

"The guy who was so interested in me. You think he might recognize you?"

"Probably not in here. It's dark. He'd just know you were in here talking to someone."

"But he could have seen you from before," I said, but then stopped to think a moment. "We'll have to risk it."

I outlined my simple plan and he accepted.

"Shouldn't be too hard. When?" he asked.

"As soon as you can. Just be careful."

"I'm always careful, you know that. Have to be in my line of work." There was a pause before he moved his hand around to indicate the remains of the food on the table. "You taking care of this?"

"Yes."

"You know where to find me if you need me," he said and eased out of the booth and out of the restaurant.

I contemplated what to do with the handbag and how to dispose of it. Certainly, Adams wasn't getting it back. That would draw too much attention to the theft, as if more attention were needed. There's lots of crime in Philadelphia and people like Freddie, if they're talented, can make a lively living. But both Adams and Carmichael being crime victims in the same week and getting their property back might seem too much of a coincidence.

None of that was foremost in my mind. I pulled out the photograph I took from the handbag and studied it again.

It was taken at a fancy, black-tie event. Carmichael was in a tux sitting at a table full of plates and empty water glasses. His arm was around Adams, who wore a satiny red dress. Flanking Adams on the other side was Elise Carmichael in a black dress. All three were smiling at the camera.

~*~

I left the restaurant and went upstairs and onto JFK Boulevard. I kept her case and dumped the handbag in the first trash container I found on the street. There was a First Pennsylvania Bank at 15th Street across from City Hall and I needed to get a cash advance. I planned to pay Mae early but I didn't have that much money in my checking account.

Thank you, credit cards.

I walked slowly, pausing to look in the window of a travel agency as if I was interested in a trip to Greece. But the stop allowed me to see the street behind me reflected in the glass, and to see if my tail was there.

The bank had large posters in the windows announcing new higher interest rates for certificates of deposit. I went straight to the first open teller, handed over my credit card and asked for the cash advance.

The teller, a matronly woman who would have looked a little less matronly if she ever smiled, transferred money from my card to my checking account with speed and efficiency. I didn't think my shadow followed me into the bank but I didn't want to look around to be sure.

I didn't see him when I headed out back up JFK.

I knew I should get back to work. I had two urgent cases and I wouldn't get any closer to solving them by stopping by the Sheraton Hotel and flirting with Marie, but I couldn't resist. I no longer made the occasional late night trip to a gentleman's club, and I had only been out on a date twice in the last year, both at the urging of my match-making grandmother. They both lasted through dinner but not long after that.

I'm not the best conversationalist.

Talking to Marie was different. She was extremely easy on the eyes, quick-witted and funny. And, for some reason, she was getting under my skin. So until I suffered the inevitable crash and burn, I wanted to find her and flirt.

When I arrived in the hotel lobby, Marie was talking to a salesman refilling some of her already burgeoning supplies of gum, candy and potato chips. I lingered nearby for about ten minutes.

"Mr. Detective, how are you this morning?" she asked as I approached. "Made any deductions lately?"

"You were right about me being followed."

"I know. You must be quite popular. So, why's he following you?"

"Don't know. But I intend to get some answers. You see him again? And be careful when you look."

She looked around the hotel. "He's not here. When you see him next, why not just confront him and see what he wants?"

Civilians! They never understood how things work. It's amazing more innocent people aren't injured or killed out of pure ignorance.

"Can't do that. Too many unknown variables. I'd like to know who he is and who he works for and whether he's be armed before I confront him."

"You could just shoot him, couldn't you, with your gun, if he threatened you?" she asked, standing back and arranging candy on the counter.

Shock showed in my face. "I rarely carry a piece."

Now she was shocked. "You *don't* carry a gun? I thought all detectives carried a concealed. They do in the movies."

"This isn't the movies. This is real life," I said. "And I didn't say I never carry a gun. I just don't have one now."

A playful smirk appeared on Marie's face. "Then how can a big, strong man such as yourself protect me from all the horrors that often happen in this lobby, if you don't have a gun?" she said with mock humor.

I looked around to survey the peaceful surroundings and was about to remark that Marie could take care of herself when I saw something that caught my breath. Entering through the front doors of the hotel, laughing and talking, were Reuben Carmichael and Carolyn B. Adams. *Together.*

They were headed toward the front desk.

"Damn, why don't I have a camera when I need it?" I said looking around. I was walking away from Marie when she spoke up.

"I have a camera," she said.

It stopped me dead in my tracks.

"*What?*"

"I said I have a camera."

"Where? With you? Right now? What kind is it?"

"It's in the back here, with my stuff," she said, pointing over her shoulder to a door in the back of the stall. Marie turned and opened the door to the back. "I have a photography class. It's later today so I brought my camera with me. It's a Nikon, 35-millimeter."

Carmichael and Adams were standing at the front desk, apparently checking in. Time was running out.

"Can you get come clear pictures of that couple at the front desk?"

"It'll be in black and white. That's all the film I have with me today."

"Doesn't matter," I said hurriedly. "Just take the pictures. Hide in back if you can."

Marie grabbed the camera and I moved out of her line of sight. She was partially hidden in the back room when the camera went *click, click, click* in rapid succession.

"So, I'm helping with a case, huh? What do I get out of this?" she asked. More clicks.

"Depends. Nothing, if the pictures don't turn out," I said.

"Oh, they'll turn out, all right," Marie said with confidence.

I ignored her sureness because I had another thought in mind. "Then how about dinner? Tonight. After your class."

She stopped taking pictures and lowered the camera to look at me. "I accept."

"Good. Now *take* the damned pictures."

Marie caught them at the counter and heading together toward the elevator. Though it was discreet, she was still taking pictures when they entered the elevator alone and Carmichael's hand slipped down from Adams' waist to her butt.

"This is incredible. Truly incredible," I said. "When can I see the pictures?"

"Not until I get to school this afternoon and develop them."

"That's too late. I need them right away."

"I can't leave, Sherlock," she said.

"Damn." Then I had another idea. "Can I have the film?"

"I don't know of any film developing companies that can get it back to you today," she said.

"Someone owes me a favor," I said.

She took the film out of the camera and handed it to me as I leaned over the counter and kissed her cheek. I handed her ten dollars and pointed to some of the film hanging on pegs on the back wall of the stall.

"Here. Buy some film there to replace what we just used."

As I began to leave, she said, "I've got some pictures on that roll. I need them for class today."

"I'll have the prints and bring the negatives to you before you go to class."

In the business lobby of the building in the next block, I called upstairs to Mike, my trusted UPI contact. Their offices had a darkroom.

"Mike, this is David Blaise. I need a favor."

"What is it?" There was caution in his voice.

"Can your photographer develop some film for me? It's really urgent."

"When?"

"Now."

"I don't know. I'd have to ask him. He might be busy," Mike said.

"Please. I really need this," I said. Then I played my only card. "I helped you out, remember? With the interview."

"Hold on," he said and the line was quiet for more than thirty seconds. When Mike returned, he said, "Leonard says he has the time if you can get it here fast."

"I'm in the lobby. I'll bring the film right up. Which floor?"

"Fourth. At the end of the hall on the east end. You'll see the sign."

"I'll be there in a minute. Thanks."

~*~

UPI's darkroom door was closed and a heavy black curtain was draped over the entire doorway, shutting out any possible light from the outside. The interior lighting was a weird amber color. I stood next to Leonard the photographer as he developed the film and made prints of the shots I wanted. They were in black and white, as Marie said, but they were clear and in sharp focus. They were so good I wondered why she was taking a photography class.

"She's talented," Leonard commented. "Not professional level, mind you, but these are very good. She's got talent."

When he finished, I took the black-and-white prints and the negatives and headed out, intending to go directly back to the hotel. But, to my total surprise, Freddie was in the lobby of UPI's building, standing by the large glass window near the revolving door. He didn't seem startled when I got off the elevator.

"Took you long enough," he said.

"What are you doing here? How'd you know where I was? I was going to call you tonight."

"Your little friend over at the newsstand told me you were here."

That concerned me a little. "You keeping tabs on me?"

"Don't flatter yourself. I saw you with her not long ago and thought she might know where you were. I wanted to get in touch with you fast."

"You got it already?"

He smiled and pulled a slip of paper out of his pants pocket. He looked at it, then back to me. "It was a piece of cake. He watched you for a few seconds talking to your little friend, then he left. I followed him until he got to his car. It was parked illegally in the alleyway behind this building."

"He didn't see you, did he?"

"I don't think so," Freddie said, handing me the piece of paper. He recited what he had written down. "Black Ford sedan with Pennsylvania plates, license number ERD-079. I didn't get the expiration date but I didn't think you would need that. I think it was some sort of company car. No obvious markings on it, though."

"Thanks." I folded the paper, put it in my jacket pocket and pulled out a twenty. I passed it to him and we walked outside together, standing at the top of some stairs about to go our separate ways.

"You remember this favor the next time you see me in a subway station," Freddie said.

He looked serious, but I was serious, too. I owed him nothing for breaking the law. I had just paid him for services rendered. "This wasn't a favor. You got paid, so no promises, Freddie. We square?"

"Yep," he said. "But you let me know if you need anything else."

"I'll do that."

He headed right and I headed left, back toward the Sheraton and Marie.

She was busy sorting newspapers in front of the stand when I arrived. "Here are the negatives," I said, handing her an envelope from my breast pocket. "I assumed you want to make your own prints."

"How'd the shots turn out?" she asked.

"Excellent. Clear as a bell. He said you're very good for an amateur." Marie couldn't contain a smile filled with pride, and I couldn't blame her. "I'll pick you up on campus at seven-thirty, okay?"

"That's fine. I'll just be getting out of class at seven-thirty, so I might be a few minutes. See you then," Marie said.

CHAPTER X

I was tired of playing games.

I knew what I needed to do next, though at first I hesitated. I bid Marie good-bye and headed down the hallway to the pay phones. I dropped the coins and waited for the phone to ring.

"Hello," came Elise's voice.

"Mrs. Carmichael. It's David Blaise, the detective."

There was a pause for recognition on her end, followed by a short, "I see."

She didn't say anything else, even to inquire about any progress on the case.

"I have to be up that way. Can I see you in an hour?"

"An hour? That's not much time."

"I guess not, but it's the only time I have today and you'll want to have this information."

"Couldn't you just give it to me over the telephone?" she asked.

"That's not how it works. Besides, it wouldn't be safe." I said.

Elise apparently resigned herself. "All right, then. But we have to make it short. I have other priorities. I'll see you in an hour." She hung up before I had a chance to respond.

As I rode the commuter train to Mt. Airy, I considered how the meeting would go with such a temperamental client. I didn't know her well, but I was sure one could never be totally prepared for Elise Carmichael.

It was a quick walk from the train station. I passed my car as I approached the house. Elise's car was in the driveway.

"Is that your Mustang there, Mr. Blaise?" she said as she opened the heavy, hand-carved wooden door with frosted leaded glass inlaid in the top half. She was dressed all in black — flats, slacks that showed a well-toned figure, and a short-sleeved top. Her black hair was pulled back and tied in the type of bun worn by ballerinas. She resembled Audrey Hepburn in the 1954 version of the film, "Sabrina."

She just couldn't pull off the air of innocence Audrey had.

"I noticed the car today and two days ago. Not very inconspicuous, I'd say. But my husband's an idiot," she said. "I doubt he noticed it. Come in, won't you?"

Said the spider to the fly.

She stepped back and allowed me into the house.

It was expensive and decorated to display their wealth. The house opened into a large foyer with a marble tile floor. A round mahogany table with a large vase filled with fresh cut flowers sat in the middle of the foyer under a massive crystal chandelier. Directly ahead were stairs leading to the second floor. To the right was a formal living room with a black Steinway sitting in front of a window. The draperies were open to display the room's elegance to the outside world.

To the left of the foyer was the library, and that's where we headed. There were floor-to-ceiling walnut bookshelves, their contents' colorful spines facing outward.

"May I have a look?" I said as I entered the library.

"Be my guest," Elise said, making a wide sweeping arc with her arm and figuratively opening the room for my inspection.

I walked around the room slowly, taking in title after impressive title. Many were first editions that looked like they were never opened. Others, such as a couple by Judith Krantz, indicated Elise might have read them.

The room was comfortable enough, but it was hard to imagine anyone would linger in the library unless they totally loved the look and smell of old books. There was an Indian rug on the hard-wood floor and a desk with an electronic word processing computer sitting to the side.

Elise ushered me over to a dark blue sofa with colorful African pillows at its ends. It was a way of culturally diversifying an otherwise Euro-centric room. On a table in front of us was a silver serving tray with a crystal decanter and three matching glasses.

"Water," Elise asked, pouring herself a glass. She didn't wait for my reply before pouring me one. "Now, what have you got for me?"

"I followed your husband to work twice this week and I must sadly report it is what you suspected. I believe your husband is having an affair," I said, watching for her reaction.

There was a sudden intake of breath and she sat back on the couch, as if to absorb the shocking news. But I didn't believe her fake reaction.

"You have proof?" she asked.

"Yes," I said.

I took out the envelope with the black-and-white prints. I handed her the envelope and waited while she opened it and looked inside. There were more than a dozen shots of her husband in the hotel lobby with his mistress.

"When were these taken?"

"This morning."

"Where?"

"The Sheraton Hotel downtown, on John F. Kennedy Boulevard."

"And this is the woman?"

"Yes," I replied.

"Who *is* she?"

"Carolyn Adams. She's a buyer for Strawbridge's downtown," I said. I was tired of playing games. "But I think you already know all that." She looked at me with piercing eyes. "When you came to me, you didn't just suspect your husband was having an affair. You knew. And you knew with whom."

Elise got up and crossed to the window. "How could you say that?"

I could almost imagine her tilting her head back, raising her arm and placing the back of her hand to her forehead. It was a move popular in old movies.

"You knew because of this." I didn't stand when I pulled the picture I took from Adams' purse from my jacket pocket, the picture of all of them together. I dropped it on the table with the crystal water decanter, careful not to get it wet.

Elise walked back and picked it up. She was surprised and it showed. "Where did you get this?" she said with an urgency in her voice.

"It doesn't matter. What matters is that you've been lying to me and I want to know why."

She stood speechless for a moment before accepting the truth. She sat back down on the couch with a certain resignation.

"You're right. I knew. I've known for some time," she said, her head down. She appeared to be looking at her expensive black shoes.

"That still doesn't answer why," I said.

She finally looked directly at me. Her tone softened and there was a pleading sincerity in her voice that was always lacking before.

"Because I wanted proof. We haven't had a happy marriage for a number of years. We keep up appearances," she said, indicating around the room, "for his career and our social standing. But I'm tired and I want out. So I hired you to get the proof I need to divorce him."

"You handed me five hundred dollars. That's a lot of money for proof of something you already know."

"Not for the evidence I need," she said.

"How did you come to suspect an affair in the first place?" I asked.

"I was telling you the truth before, in the beginning. I had some suspicions at first," she said in a moment of honesty. "And, well, I have met the little *tramp*. A couple of times at social events. I think that's how they met. She's divorced. Lives in a nice condo and has a lot of nice clothes. I know she gets a discount from her job at Strawbridge's, which would explain a lot of the clothing but *that condo?* There's no way she can afford that. She commented once that she isn't getting any money from her ex, but she has to be getting money from somewhere. Well, that somewhere is *MY* husband. I just know it."

"How are you so sure?" I asked. "There could be other explanations."

Elsie rose and walked over to the desk, opened a drawer on the right side and pulled out some papers. When she returned, she had a check book and banking statements from the Philadelphia Savings Fund Society.

"I think he started the affair about a year ago. I've checked all our joint checking and savings accounts. Look at them. Take them with you if you'd like. There isn't any money missing," she said. "Obviously, he's funding her lifestyle with money I'm unaware of."

I quickly looked at the account summaries but there was too much information for me to determine anything without a more thorough and detailed examination.

"Okay, then. What is it you really want me to do?"

"I plan to file for divorce as soon as I can. But I can't until I know where the money is, some of which I'm entitled to," she said. "I want you to find where he's keeping his . . . *our* . . . money."

"You know, of course, I'm a private investigator, not a forensic accountant."

"But it's there somewhere, and I need you to find it," she said, moving closer to me on the couch and placing her hand on my thigh just above my knee. It was an intimate gesture and was designed to be. *"Please!"*

I thought for a second. I had a source at PSFS and, if the other accounts were there, she could find them. Asking might cause some complications, but it couldn't be avoided. It was a starting point, at least.

I reached for the glass of water and took a sip. It was cool going down. I imagined Elise put out the decanter and the cold water as soon as she knew I was coming. And I truly liked the glass in my hand. It had a heavy bottom and felt good.

"I'll do it on one condition," I said.

She pulled away from me on the couch and returned to her more standoffish countenance. "What might that be?"

Everything with her was an act, of course. But for the first time I considered how incredibly exhausting it must be to *be* her. I couldn't do it. Most people couldn't — and wouldn't want to.

"You can't lie to me anymore. You lie to me again and I'm done."

She agreed without any discussion.

"Okay, then," I said. "Tell me everything."

CHAPTER XI

I was disappointed with the first words out of her mouth.

The Philadelphia College of Textiles & Science had one of the most beautiful college campuses in the country for a school in an urban setting. Situated on a hundred acres on the edge of Fairmount Park in the East Falls section, Textiles was fifteen minutes from Center City, and though at the busy intersection of Henry Avenue and School House Lane, felt completely removed from the hullabaloo of downtown.

I parked outside a building on Henry just before 7:30, and five minutes later Marie came out. She had on jeans and a "We Are the World" t-shirt. But when I saw her, my thoughts were not at all on humanitarian aid to Africa.

"How was your class?" I asked as she got in the car.

"Wonderful. And the pictures turned out good, so thank you," she said. "Where are we going? I'm hungry."

"How about some place in Manayunk? Not that far away."

"Sounds great." She smiled.

Pulling into a parking lot and turning the car around, we went back to School House Lane and then to Ridge Avenue. At the bottom of the hill, we took a right onto Main Street.

It was the middle of the week, but it was still hard to find a parking spot. I got lucky, however, when a car pulled out and I found a space on Main just before Rector. The walk to a corner bistro allowed me a chance to scope out the building at Main and Rector where Carolyn Adams lived. The restaurant was on

Main and, once inside, I took a seat facing the front window, which offered a direct view of the front of Adams' building.

The restaurant, the Main Street Bistro and Grill, was an upscale establishment in a neighborhood with lots of upscale competition. Attractive people populated the open bar, with men in business suits but without ties on ordering drinks to impress slender, attractive, single ladies. Both sexes were on the prowl, visibly sizing up their victims.

Like most eating places on the upper reaches of Manayunk, the bistro was a pick-up joint for well-heeled, well-educated Center City professionals, though it was hard to see how anyone could find a meaningful relationship in such surroundings.

And it seemed only pretty people were allowed inside.

We had been sitting for only about a minute when an attractive young man approached. I looked up when he arrived. At least he worked there.

"May I interest you in something from the bar?" he asked.

Marie looked at me but didn't speak. I was uncertain, and apparently, so was she. "No, not right now. Perhaps later," I said.

We quickly decided on an appetizer of potato skins, followed by something called an Oriental chicken salad for her and fajitas for me. Like most American restaurants, the bistro liked to take essentially ethnic foods and Americanize them to fit American taste buds.

Finally, just before the main course arrived, we ordered a pitcher of beer to share. Domestic.

"Tell me. How'd you become a private detective?" she asked while we waited for our food.

"When I got out of the Navy, I didn't know what I wanted to do. I kicked around for a while and finally landed a job for SEPTA police. All I did was dress up in a uniform and walk around a lot. But in time, I was out of uniform and doing some investigative work . . . property damage, vandalism, mostly.

That's when I began taking small investigative jobs on the side. After I while, I decided to do it full time. I got a detective's license and set up shop. SEPTA, of course, was my first client. I still do contract work for them, though mostly just weekends."

"What are you working on now? Or can't you tell me?"

"I have two big cases at the moment that are going to pay the bills for a while. One involves a missing person and the other is about infidelity. I can't say any more about either case," I said.

I was grateful when she didn't probe.

"Where are you from, originally?" she asked.

"Philadelphia. I have two brothers and one sister, Valerie, who's married to a jerk. All of them live in North Philly. I don't want to get into my brothers. But my sister, well, I enjoy being with her. We're close. Unfortunately, I have to deal with her husband, too. Regularly. He owns the building where my office is located. But I see her . . . and him . . . once a week when I have Sunday night dinner with my grandmother. She's lived in North Philly since before the beginning of recorded history. Sunday night dinner is a tradition that probably goes back that far." I chuckled, and she joined in on my laughter.

"And your parents? They are also part of the Sunday night tradition?"

Before I had a chance to answer — or evade the question — our beer arrived and I poured us each a glass. I took a sip of the golden brew. Enjoying the cool taste flowing down my throat allowed me a few extra seconds to steel myself for my answer.

"My dad died of a heart attack right after I left for the Navy. My mom died of heartache about a year later."

"Oh, I'm so sorry," she said as the pitch in her voice dropped.

"It's okay. You didn't kill them." I hoped the comment lightened an otherwise heavy subject. Not sure if I succeeded.

"So, you're close to your grandmother and sister," Marie said. "Why do you live and work on the other side of town?"

"When I got back from the Navy, I wanted to get away from all the family drama. West Philadelphia was the perfect choice. Rarely does one of them ever venture west of Thirtieth Street."

Marie laughed at that, tilting her head back and briefly closing her eyes. It was a hearty laugh from deep inside, and it brought a smile to my face. By the time she settled down, the food had arrived and we ate. The pitcher of beer mellowed us.

"None of my family had ever left North Philadelphia, at least until I left the military," I said.

"You go to college?" she asked.

"Temple. And I lived at Seventeenth and Columbia Avenue, uh, Cecil B. Moore now. I could walk to most of my classes."

"What'd you take? Criminal justice?"

"You might think so, but no," I said. "I majored in history but switched to political science when I discovered the only job I could get with a history degree was teaching history to kids."

"And with political science?"

"I thought I'd go to law school. Temple, maybe Penn. My grades were good enough for the Ivy League but my wallet wasn't. So after college, I joined the military. Thought I'd attend law school after I finished my tour of duty. But when I got out, I had no job and no money. So I went to work. And that's about it."

There was no more probing as we ate for a while. But as we finished, I decided to take the initiative.

"What about you, Marie? And what about school? I thought the semester ended earlier this month," I said.

"The spring semester did. But Textiles has a three-week semester in May before the start of summer school in June. It's called a Maymester."

"How's that work?"

"You can take one class for three credit hours. It meets every day, five days a week for three hours each day. It's intense but you can knock off a class easier that way."

"It's ambitious."

"I guess," she said, adding no further comment.

"And that's your photography class?"

"Yes. It's not my major. It's an elective, but I've always liked photography and decided I might as well get some credit for it," Marie said.

"Makes sense. Tell me more about you."

"Like what? You deduced I was a student, which was brilliant on your part, as I said before," she said and smiled at her own joke. "Next year is my senior year. I'm majoring in textile design with an eye on working for a clothing wholesaler when I finish school."

As she spoke about her life, I thought I saw my mysterious tail enter Adams' building. It was quick and it was dark outside, so I couldn't be sure. I didn't see the Ford but that didn't mean anything. Why was this guy following me?

Marie noticed my sudden inattentiveness. "Are you with me here?"

"Uh, yes. Sorry," I said, looking up, probably sounding like a person caught sleeping in church. "It's hard sometimes to turn off work."

"Did you see something?" Marie asked, and turned in her seat to look around.

"No. It's nothing, I'm sure," I said. It would be best to change the subject. "You have any brothers or sisters?"

"Only child. And no cousins around, either. Just me, my mom and my dad. They live in Downingtown but I couldn't stand it anymore, being alone in that house with just my parents. So I moved into the city and live on-campus. I wanted to be around people and not have to drive forty minutes on the Expressway to find them."

"I can understand that." I smiled, though I often preferred to be alone.

We didn't have dessert and I managed to appear attentive, at least I think I did, while I still kept an eye on the front of the building across the street. I didn't see anyone I even marginally recognized go in or come out.

After dinner, we walked up Main Street, looking into shops for about thirty minutes before Marie said she needed to get home to study. Finals were coming.

Back in the car, it was a quick trip to campus.

I pulled up outside her well-lit building, and like the gentleman my grandmother trained me to be, I got out of the car and opened her door. But I was disappointed with the first words out of her mouth.

"You don't need to walk me to the door. I'll make it okay."

"Certainly. But you can never be too sure. A man in a trench coat might jump out and flash you," I said, trying to be funny.

"I'll take my chances," she said with a twinkle in her eyes. "Thanks for the dinner and the company, even though you were distracted half the time."

"I'm sorry about that. Occupational hazard, I guess," I said, knowing this would probably be my last chance with this beautiful young woman.

Marie leaned in and kissed me. Her body pressed tightly against mine. Her tongue entered my mouth and danced around with a hungry lust that couldn't be denied. In only a moment, I was lost in her lips. The kiss seemed to last an hour, although it was over in only seconds. Then she backed away.

Marie had surprised me again. Her gaze held mine.

"I really do have a lot of studying. It'll be different next time, I promise."

"Talk to you soon," I said.

"You'd better," Marie said as she turned to go. She looked back over her shoulder as she reached the door. Then she smiled and was gone.

Driving back to my apartment, I contemplated whether a trip to a gentleman's club was needed or whether a cold shower would suffice.

In the end, I opted for the latter.

~*~

It was a fitful night and I was glad when the first rays of sunlight peeked through the closed blinds on my windows. I had decided the night before there was little reason to follow Carmichael again. Finding his money would take a different tack. I decided to concentrate on the Stephenson case, at least through the morning hours.

I was already out of bed when the alarm went off at seven, the first time all week I had been able to stay in bed past six and enjoy it. Padding into the kitchen, I fixed oatmeal and toast and ate it quietly as I watched the "Today" show on television. Then I showered and dressed for the day.

Since the weekend, it had been hot and sunny. For once, it was overcast and cool, but I figured my normal jacket with tan slacks would be enough.

I went to the car at about quarter to eight. I considered taking a drive by Osage Avenue but decided against it. They had pulled eleven bodies from the MOVE house over the two previous days, including four children. No one was sure how many more people were in the house at the time of the bombing, but the city, which had endured a week of negative news coverage from around the world, was hoping the last of the bodies had been found and recovered.

I made my way up to Germantown, and Stephenson's house was exactly as I remembered seeing it last — empty. At that early hour, even the neighbors weren't out and didn't seem to be watching the house.

I went to the right side, where there was a long row of bushes. I felt around until I came across a jar with a key in it. Chet had said it was a key to the back door, not the front. The house had a wooden deck on the back and I climbed the steps to reach the back door. Unlocking the storm door was no difficulty, but the main door was a problem. I stood there exposed jiggling the locks, trying everything until there was a sudden click. The door was a little sticky in the frame but opened with a small shove of my shoulder.

The kitchen was neat and clean. No unwashed dishes, or pots and pans. It was the kitchen of an orderly man, not the kitchen of a man planning to abandon it.

I went through the house, observing but not touching or disturbing anything except what little dust was on the floors. I used the back stairs to reach the second story and checked the master bedroom and bathroom. Clothes were hanging in the closet or folded in dresser drawers. All his personal items and toiletries — razor, deodorant, cologne, toothbrush, hairbrush — were in the places I'd expect. The only thing out of place was an unfolded bath towel on the bathroom counter. It was dry.

And there were no signs of the towel's owner.

I went down the front steps and looked around the living room but there was nothing telling there. Then I headed to the dining room and it wasn't what I expected. It must have been where he worked when he was at home, because the room was in total disarray.

One chair was pulled up to the head of the dining room table, which was piled high with books, magazines, papers, newspaper clippings, calendars and yellow legal pads full of notes. In the corner was a small table with wheels. It held a typewriter. When he wanted to type something, he could just wheel it over to the table.

He must have eaten at times in that room, too. A wadded up paper napkin sat on an inexpensive white plate with a few crumbs still on it. Next to it were an unwashed knife and fork. Sitting on an empty legal pad was an expensive-looking high ball glass. It left a ring on the pad of paper, damage he clearly didn't want to befall his cherry wood table.

I sat down in the chair, with its back to the kitchen, and was amazed at how comfortable it was. He must have spent a lot of time in it.

There was so much information scattered about the table that, at first, it was hard figuring out what he was up to. But then a pattern began to emerge.

He had been taking notes about corruption in Atlanta roughly fifteen years earlier. There were several old newspaper clippings from Atlanta and someplace in Alabama about a prostitution ring involving football players and others. I checked the articles to see if there was an obvious connection with Stephenson but I saw none.

What I *did* see were several hand-written notations referring to someone with the initials LMS. It was written on more than one page in the legal pads and in the margin of at least one newspaper article he had clipped out.

I looked at the article and something about it rang some distant bell but I couldn't tell what. Though I knew it could be lifting evidence from a potential crime scene, I quickly folded the article and slipped it into my jacket pocket. I would examine it more closely later.

I reached for his calendar and flipped through several pages. I saw several meetings penciled in with an LMS, including on last Friday morning, presumably the day he disappeared. It didn't say what the meeting was about or where.

Who was this LMS, and what did Stephenson want with him? Did they have business together? I didn't see anything to indicate who LMS was, only that he existed. But finding LMS was key. It might explain Stephenson's disappearance.

I heard a sudden noise. In the kitchen.

I had probably left the back door unlocked. A stupid mistake. I seemed to be making lots of mistakes lately and I couldn't blame them all on Marie for distracting me; I had made mistakes before I met her.

I rose from the chair and turned toward the kitchen. There was a flash of movement and suddenly my vision filled with multi-colored lights.

Then everything went black.

CHAPTER XII

"You gettin' some of the nookie now, huh?"

Ahhhh. My head. It was killing me. I heard someone talking but didn't want to open my eyes to see who.

"He's coming around, sergeant." It was a strange voice. And an unfamiliar one.

I opened my eyes and things slowly began to come into focus.

"Can you see me? Lie still. How many fingers do you see?" said the man with the strange, unfamiliar voice.

I saw two fingers and said so. He nodded to someone else. I tried to move, but it was hard. I was lying on the floor.

I moved my lips. "Can I get up?" It was my voice but it sounded hoarse, barely recognizable and distant.

Two men, including the man with the voice, helped me into a chair. If I tried to go any further I was sure I'd fall. My knees were shaky, my head throbbed and I felt like I'd been hit by a SEPTA bus.

The room was rotating, but I recognized the Stephenson dining room. It was full of people — EMTs, uniformed police officers and, most likely, non-uniformed officers. And then, standing to the side, was someone I recognized: Detective John Thompson, last seen standing guard on a barricade at 62nd and Pine streets.

It was the EMTs who helped me into the chair but it was probably the person someone called sergeant who was staring down at me. I didn't recognize him, but my head throbbed so I wasn't sure of many things.

What I wouldn't give for a couple of aspirin.

"He looks like he's in some discomfort. Can you guys give him something for his head?" Thompson said to one of the rescue workers.

"Here. Hold this to the back of your head," a guy in a blue EMT uniform said as he handed me a cold plastic pack.

The man I didn't recognize spoke up.

"I'm Sergeant Ryan Gregory of the Detective Division and this is Detective Thompson," Gregory said, indicating Thompson. Gregory was a tall man with a strong, square jaw and a Marine Corp crew cut. He had on a black suit and probably liked to wear the same color every day. He was a larger version of Jack Webb from TV's *Dragnet*.

"You're trespassing in this house after breaking and entering," he said.

"I didn't break-in. I had a key."

"Blaise. What are you doing here?" It was Thompson, who moved into my direct field of vision again. He used a stern, questioning voice without the confrontational tone Gregory had used. But it was also clear he wanted answers.

"Why are you guys here?"

"We're investigating a missing persons case . . . the case of Wilbur Stephenson . . . and it seems you're involved, Mr. Blaise. You were caught breaking into his house." It was Gregory again.

"I told you. I didn't break-in. I had a key."

"That's not what the neighbors said when they alerted the police. They said someone was breaking in."

"They were wrong," I said, protesting, although somewhat weakly.

"Blaise, what do you know about Wilbur Stephenson's disappearance?" Thompson asked.

"He hadn't shown up for work for several days and I was asked to look into it. Quietly."

"Why?" Gregory demanded loudly and I winced.

Softer, Thompson asked, "By whom? What's your interest in this?"

"He works at SEPTA and a supervisor over there asked me to look into his disappearance."

"How long have you been on the case?" Thompson asked.

"Monday, though I didn't get started until the next day."

"I have you on breaking and entering, burglary, theft, possibly an accessory to murder if Stephenson's dead, and anything else I want to charge you with, Mr. Blaise. So you had better come up with some answers I want to hear before I drag your sorry ass downtown," Gregory virtually shouted. Spittle hit my face.

"I have no idea what you're talking about," I tried not to appear angry as I used my sleeve to wipe the side of my face.

"But you're here, in his house and. . . . " Gregory said before Thompson interrupted him.

"Ryan, let me handle this for a second, please," he said respectfully in a voice that was personal rather than professional. They must have worked together for some time for Thompson to take such a familiar tone during a questioning.

To me, he said, "What have you found out?"

"Nothing much. I've found no trace of him. When was his disappearance reported to the police?"

"Last night," Thompson said.

"Stephenson apparently hasn't been seen for a week now. But I saw some. . . . "

I stopped as I looked at the table, then around the room. The table was clear. None of the stuff I saw earlier was there, or anywhere else in the room.

"Where's the stuff on the table? What'd you do with it?" I asked.

"What stuff?" It was Gregory again.

"When I got here, there was all this material on the table. Legal pads, newspaper articles, other stuff. Stephenson was looking into something. I don't know what it was."

"You probably stole it." Gregory said. Even Thompson looked at him with a puzzled expression. Gregory was needlessly antagonizing me like some rabid dog.

"How could I have stolen anything? I was hit in the head from behind and I'm still here."

"I don't think that means anything," Gregory said.

"I have a knot on the back of my *head*," I said.

"Did you get a good look at any of the stuff you said was on the table?" Thompson said.

"Not really," I lied. I was beginning to recover my senses.

"Did you see who hit you?"

"No. I was sitting at the table and was about to look at a calendar when I thought I heard noise coming from the kitchen behind me," I said, turning sharply to look back. It was a mistake. A sharp pain radiated from the spot where I'd been hit and I thought my head would fall off. "*Ahhhh.*"

"Just sit still," Thompson said, touching my shoulder softly. "A couple more questions and then you can go. Did you notice any evidence of a forced entry once you were inside?"

"No."

"No sign of Stephenson, either, I suppose?" Thompson said.

"No."

"Any signs of foul play? Signs of a struggle or anything?"

"No. Nothing. The place was neat and orderly except in here," I said.

Thompson backed away. "We're going to have the lab tech boys check the room for prints, although I suspect we won't find anything other than yours and our missing person's. That's not good for you but it doesn't prove anything and we don't have anything to hold you on." Gregory was about to interrupt but Thompson continued. "You feelin' all right?"

"Yeah, but my head's killing me."

"It'll be fine. Good for the soul," Thompson said. "But listen, Blaise. This is a police matter, so leave it to the police. Don't get in the way. And don't go out of town. Got it? We may want to interview you again."

What he didn't say was I was their only lead in a missing person case and I might be the reason the person was missing. They weren't arresting me, but I wasn't off the hook, either.

"I understand." I said.

"Glad we have an understanding," Thompson said.

"Can I go now?"

Thompson looked at the EMTs, who gave a quick nod.

"You got a car here? You feel up to driving?" Thompson asked.

"That's a nasty bump on your head," Gregory said in a sarcastic tone without a hint of concern. "You should have it looked at."

"I can drive," I said to Thompson, ignoring Gregory.

"Okay, go. But stay close," Thompson said.

"And Mr. Private Detective, watch out for strangers creeping up on you. They might take your head completely off next time," Gregory said.

"Thanks for the advice," I said, and left.

All the neighbors on the block, including the old man from next door and Mrs. Tally from across the street, were out watching all the police activity. Scores of eyes followed me as I walked to my car. I was certain I'd be the subject of street gossip for some time.

~*~

I was back in the office nearly an hour later. I stopped on the way to buy a big bottle of aspirin.

"You don't look good, boss," Mae said as I entered. She was wearing clothes I had never seen before. The frilly white blouse with red dots revealed ample cleavage, while the black linen pants could not have been tighter if they tried. They had to be at least one size too small and it was a wonder she could inhale, let alone sit.

"It hasn't been a good start to the day. How you doing?" I asked as I walked into my office. She followed. "Those some of the clothes you got from the church?"

"They look okay, don't they? They don't look trashy or used, do they?" she said, turning around for me to get a full view of her. "I don't want to look like a homeless person."

But you are a homeless person, I wanted to say but didn't. It would be cruel.

"You look fine. Better than me, certainly," I said as I sat behind my desk.

I immediately took the aspirin bottle out of my pocket and struggled with the child-resistant top. It wouldn't have been a problem four years ago, before the Tylenol scare.

"In answer to your question, I'm doing okay," she said. After a moment of watching me struggle, she reached for the bottle. "Here, let me do that." In a flash, she had the bottle top off. "That report you were after is sitting on your desk."

In the clutter of my desk was a manila folder marked *confidential* across the top. I was sure Mae had read it and marked it to make it appear important. She did things like that.

"You want some water?" she asked.

"Water would be wonderful."

Mae turned on her new high heel shoes and was about to leave when she swung back around to me.

"I forget," she said, approaching the desk again. "You got a message from a young woman, or at least she sounded like a young woman. Seemed unsure. Didn't want to leave a name but I pressed her."

"Who was it?"

"She said her name was Marie." That information hung in the air, but I could see she was curious.

"So she called," I said, pausing to consider the implications. "What was the message?"

"Nothing. Only that she called. Didn't say more," Mae said. Now the curiosity was getting to her. "You got a girlfriend? A hot date? Don't you hold out on me now."

"It's nothing. She's a nice young woman I met at a hotel in Center City," I said and instantly regretted saying hotel.

"A *hotel*? She in this business?"

"No," I said, perhaps a little too strongly. "She works in a newsstand in a hotel lobby. It's how we met."

"How old is she?"

"No idea. Didn't think to ask."

"What were you doing in the hotel?"

"Who are you, my mother? I was doing surveillance in the Carmichael case."

"And she's calling you now?" Mae said, placing her hands on her hips and slightly shaking her head to indicate disbelief.

"We went on a date last night. And that's all I'm saying. You need to get back to work."

Hands no longer on her hips, Mae stared back at me with an expression I couldn't read. "You gettin' some of the nookie now, huh?"

"No, I'm not getting any of the nookie," I said in a rush of embarrassed impatience. I had no intention of discussing it with her. "And could you please get me that water now?"

Mae turned and was leaving as I heard her say, to herself as much as to me, "You better be gettin' some nookie. You really need some."

I opened the folder after she left. Inside was a report from SEPTA police on my tail. I had called Clara with the license plate number of the person following me. They traced the car back to one of the largest detective agencies in town, The

Henderson Group. The car was assigned to a guy named Simon Balcombe, who apparently was the guy following me.

I knew the Henderson agency, of course. Who in the business didn't? It was a large agency with big corporate firms as clients, providing all manner of security for outrageous fees. But it didn't make sense that someone from Henderson would be following me.

Mae entered, placed the glass of water on the desk without comment and left. I kept reading the report. Then I noticed something interesting.

Among the agency's specialties was pre-divorce investigations, particularly in messy cases. And while security companies rarely advertised their clients, among the firms known to have contracts with Henderson was Watson, Whisman, Elliott and Strange.

Reuben Carmichael must know Elise had retained me. But how could he know that? And when did he find out? I picked up my shadow on the ride downtown on SEPTA the day after I met Elise for the first time.

I took my aspirin, followed by a couple of deep breaths, and thought about that for a while.

"If they're on to me, I'd better speed up the search for Carmichael's money," I said aloud. "I've got to see an accountant today."

~*~

I nearly forgot the newspaper clipping in my pocket and was surprised Gregory hadn't rummaged through my pockets while I was unconscious. He would have found it.

I pulled it out. It was a photostatic copy of an article in an Atlanta newspaper dating back to October 1969.

ATLANTA (UPI) — State and federal law enforcement officials are investigating reports a fraternity house provided members of the Georgia Central University football team with numerous financial favors, including cars, women and cash.

The probe started after local police were called to the scene of a wild fraternity party last week in which several members of the football team were witnessed having sexual intercourse with a number of prostitutes.

The team members were immediately suspended pending the outcome of the investigation.

"We want to get to the bottom of this," the school said in a press release. "If any of our players were involved in any illegal or immoral activity, we will take immediate and drastic action."

College athletes are not allowed to accept financial rewards for participating in college sports or they risk losing their amateur status, and their schools could be suspended or banned from participation in NCAA events.

But experts familiar with collegiate sports say there are ways of getting around the ban. One way is to funnel the money through fraternities.

"I see this all the time," said Tim Drake, who studies college sports for the Chicago-based Tooley Foundation, a not-for-profit group committed to improving sports participation at all levels. "It is rampant on campuses across the country."

Police were called to the Gamma Phi fraternity house after neighbors complained of loud noise. When police arrived, they found large amounts of money and drugs in the rooms where two hookers were performing sexual acts with at least 12 athletes.

The women were taken into custody and charged with performing immoral acts. Their names have not been released. Officials are also investigating whether more women were involved.

"We intend to find all these hookers and get them off the streets. We cannot have them corrupting the morals of our fine college players," a police official said.

What was so important about this article and how did it tie into Stephenson's disappearance? And why only knock me out? Why not permanently silence me?

The phone rang, interrupting my thoughts.

"David Blaise," I said into the phone.

"David, this is Mike Kerry over at UPI," he said in little more than a whisper. "I need some help with something."

"What is it?"

"I don't want to say over the phone. Can you meet me?"

"Sure. When and where?"

"I'm downtown and getting stonewalled by police on something that's about to break," he said. "On the way back to the office, I have to stop and pick up a couple of newspapers at the newsstand in the Sheraton Hotel. I can meet you there in fifteen minutes."

"I'll be there."

I stopped by Mae's desk as I was heading out. "I'm running downtown to meet a contact. Hold down the fort." I purposely didn't mention it would be at a hotel newsstand.

Parking in Center City can be problematic at times so I left the Mustang in the McDonald's parking lot and took the Market-Frankfort El to Suburban Station. It was a short walk back to the lobby of the Sheraton Hotel. I hoped Marie would be there.

"Couldn't wait to see me again, I guess," she said.

"I'm returning your call, just doing it in person."

"Likely story," she mocked.

"Actually, I'm meeting someone here," I said.

"Who?"

"A guy who called and wanted a quick meeting before

heading in to work. He was the one who suggested this location."

Mike walked through the hotel's front doors and came over to the newsstand. Seeing Mike, Marie reached behind the counter and picked up two copies of the Philadelphia Inquirer and three copies of The Daily News. She handed him the papers.

"Thanks, Marie," Mike said.

"You two know each other?" I asked.

"You jealous?" she asked with a quizzical look.

"No. Just surprised."

"We have a contract for papers from the newsstand each day," Mike said. "Someone from the office comes over to pick them up, once in the early morning and once later in the day. I was on my way into the office so I had to stop by."

"I see. So why'd you want to meet me here?" I asked.

"Co-incidental," Mike said. "But I need your help with something."

"If it's personal, then perhaps we should move over here," I said, directing him away from the stand and more into the lobby.

"It's not personal. We can stand here," he said. To Marie, he added, "You don't mind, do you?"

"Of course not," Marie said. "Don't mind me."

"They found a body. The police did," Mike said.

"Where? When?"

"On Osage. Early today."

"But they knew they might find more MOVE bodies from the bombing," Marie ventured.

"The police believe they've recovered all the bodies from the MOVE house. This was down the block in a property that should have been empty," Mike said. "Everyone thought all the houses on the block were evacuated."

"Someone from MOVE?" I asked.

"No one is officially confirming there was a body, let alone speculating who it might be. But from what little I know, they don't believe it was someone from MOVE. All MOVE members are accounted for," Mike said.

"Everyone on the block was evacuated last weekend before the bombing. Police went door-to-door and were sure no one was in any of the houses. My secretary lives on that block and told me." I stopped and scratched my head. "This means they'll have to question all the people who lost homes to figure out who it might be. Maybe Mae knows something."

"The body was found downstairs, probably in the basement. If police knocked on the door and no one answered, they'd have moved on," Mike said. "But finding the body isn't the strangest thing."

"What is?" Marie said.

"Whoever it is was shot several times," he said.

It took a moment for the full impact of that information to register. *They were shot*. "What was the address?" I asked.

"They're not sure yet. It's such a mess up there, as you'd expect. They're trying to pin down which property it is and then check tax records to see who owns it," he said.

"What do you want me to do?" I said.

"You have police contacts. I thought maybe you could ask around and get a little more information than I have. Unofficially of course," Mike said. "I don't think AP or any of the newspapers know this yet. This is hot, and I want to get a jumpstart on the story."

"I know some folks, but I'm not sure how much I can help. I'll make some calls and get back with you."

"Thanks, dude. I owe you. But I gotta run," Mike said and headed for the exit. "Call me if you get anything."

Once I was alone with Marie, I faced her completely. "I'm sorry for conducting business in front of you."

"*That* was business. I was right. You aren't good at this."

"Let me make it up to you," I said, ignoring her jab.

"Dinner again. Maybe the weekend."

"Can't Saturday night. I already have plans. But Sunday could work," she said.

"Won't you be focused on classes for Monday?" I asked and nervously scratched the side of my face.

"Yes, but I also have to eat," she said. Then she paused as if remembering something. "Uh, you said you eat with your grandmother on Sundays."

"You're right. How stupid of me! Another time then."

"I'm still okay for this Sunday night."

That caught me off guard. "You're willing to eat dinner at my grandmother's house on what will be only our second date? I wouldn't wish that on anyone — even someone I had dated for years."

"Yes. But she seems sweet. At least you made her sound that way. I'd like to meet her," Marie said. "I assume I'd get a good, home-cooked meal and I wouldn't be eating alone on a Sunday evening."

"What about your parents in Downingtown?"

"Like I said, I wouldn't be eating alone."

I don't know why but I agreed, knowing this would certainly kill my chances with Marie.

"I'll pick you up before six," I said.

"Sounds good."

"I have to get going."

"Call me and we'll make the final arrangements."

I left and headed for Suburban Station.

It had been an exhausting week but a fruitful one. I was back in the office before Mae left for the day. She was cleaning off her desk when I walked into the door.

"What have you got going on for the weekend?" I inquired. I sat in a chair across from her desk in order to continue the conversation.

"Nothing much. Hanging out with a girlfriend mostly. And you?"

"Phillies games this weekend against the Dodgers. I'm not doing any security work tonight. Too tired. But I'll probably do some SEPTA security tomorrow night and for Sunday's afternoon game."

She finished and turned to face me like a stern taskmaster. "That's three nights in a row without some loving. When are you going to get yourself a life?"

"Well," I said, although with a little hesitation, "the woman who called earlier this morning. . . ."

"I remember," Mae said, a twinkle in her eyes. "She's the one who didn't give you nookie last night."

"We're going to have dinner together. On Sunday night."

Mae walked over and slapped me hard on the shoulder. "Are you *fuckin'* insane? You have Sunday dinners with your family. You're *not* taking her to meet your family. On the second date? That's a recipe for disaster."

"I thought the same thing. But she said she wanted to go. She said my grandmother sounded 'sweet'."

Mae headed for the door. "You'd better watch out for that girl. She could be a stalker."

"Ah, Mabelene," I said, before she could leave. I hesitated at first, unsure of whether to mention that a body was found on Osage. But then decided to take the plunge. "I heard today, and this is unconfirmed, that the body of a man was found in a house down the block from MOVE."

"Which house? Was it a MOVE member?"

"Not sure of which house but my source said the cops doubt they were in MOVE," I said. "You have any ideas who it could be?"

"Why would I know?"

"You live on that block. I thought maybe you saw something."

Mae thought for a moment, then leaned hands down on my desk. "There is a house down there. . . ." she said, stopping and standing straight once more. ". . . There was a house down the block, I should say, that was mostly abandoned. Near the corner. Drug addicts got in there sometimes but the block captain is pretty good at getting them out. Could be one of them. That would be my guess."

This seemed like a dead end and I let it go. But there was one more thing I needed to bring up before she left. "I'm going to need you to check on some things down in City Hall on Monday. Okay?"

"No problem, boss."

"It's just that I'd like it if you dressed, well, a little more conservatively, that's all."

She turned and struck a pose exactly the way a Hollywood director would stereotypically cast a black prostitute — hands on hips, hips cocked, head tilted to one side. The voice more guttural, mock-insulted and as if she had forgotten every grammar lesson she had ever learned. It was almost comical.

"Are ya sayin' I don't noz how ta dress? I noz that ain't what ya sayin'."

"You're right. That's not what I'm saying. Sorry I said anything. Have a good weekend."

She strutted to the door, mumbling below her breath. "*Damn* right. I know how to dress proper. And you better not forget it."

And with that, she was gone.

Before I left the office, I got a friend in the police department to officially confirm a body was found in another home on Osage. The dead man wasn't involved in the MOVE confrontation and police were not sure how or when he got inside the house.

"We're sure it was a male but aren't sure of his race, because the body was badly burned in the fire," said my source, an officer named Ian, who worked in a deputy commissioner's office. "An autopsy's scheduled for Monday. That should determine the cause and manner of death. But it could take time. And my boss said a positive identification might take a while. They'll have a dental on the guy but without knowing whose dental records to look for, it'll be hard to ID him."

I called Mike at UPI and gave him the details. His story hit the wires within an hour and the next morning made the front page of newspapers across the country. He had scooped the world.

And I had another debt to collect at some later date.

CHAPTER XIII

"He specifically asked for Baby Cakes?"

Saturday was a good day to run, particularly on the Kelly Drive along the Schuylkill River. At nine in the morning, I drove up to the Art Museum, parked on the back side and made my way to the drive. It was a cool, partly cloudy morning, but I decided I'd still wear shorts and a light-weight t-shirt and brave the temperature.

While running wasn't a regular habit, it was enjoyable. It was another activity I shared with the fictional Thomas Sullivan Magnum.

I stretched at the beginning of Boathouse Row, then started a light run. I gathered steam as I reached the end of the Row as it curved to the right and continued along the river.

The Schuylkill was full of private rowers, which wasn't the case the previous weekend because of the Dad Vail Regatta. But it also meant River Drive was open for runners like me and the occasional biker.

I continued for nearly four miles to the Falls Bridge and considered crossing over the river and returning down West River Drive. There were fewer cars on the west side of the river, but somehow I missed the view. So I returned the way I came, stopping at the intersection with Fountain Green Drive and walking the last mile back to Boathouse Row as a cool down.

My heart rate was back to normal by the time I reached my car and fished for my keys. As I did, I noticed a white envelope on the driver's seat. I remembered locking the car and the door was still locked, which meant someone — a real pro — had unlocked the door, left something behind and relocked it. Regardless of what was in the envelope, he was telling me he could get to me at any time.

I looked around but saw nothing suspicious. I was a bit shaken but opened the door, got the envelope and opened it to see a type-written note.

There was no signature.

Getting knocked in the head yesterday wasn't enough for you? Well, back off. You're in way over your head. If you don't, you won't wake up next time. And the cash advance you got to cover your whore's salary probably won't be enough to get Baby Cakes out of jail.

I got in the car and raced home, finding a parking spot right in front. I ran up the stairs, two at a time, and reached for the telephone as soon as I entered my apartment. There was a blinking light on the answering machine indicating a new message. I pushed playback and listened. My heart sank when I heard the voice.

"David. It's Mabelene. I'm in a little trouble. I'm in jail downtown and I need you to bail me out. Please. You're the only one I can call."

I changed out of my sweaty clothes, showered quickly and got into jeans and a white dress shirt. It was only a twenty-minute drive to the jail. When I arrived, I was directed to a tired-looking overweight man with a blue officer's shirt stretched across his massive belly. It was so tight the buttons nearly popped out. He was reading the Philadelphia Daily News. Pictures of the MOVE debacle still dominated the front page. But he was reading in the back, undoubtedly the coverage of the Phillies' 10-5 win last night over Los Angeles. He didn't look up as I approached.

"I'm here for Mabelene Washington."

The officer slowly put the paper down as if to consider my request. But he reached over for the files and leafed through until he found her paperwork.

"Huh, prostitution," he said, then looked up at me as he passed judgment. "Bail is set at twenty-five thousand dollars with a ten percent cash bond. You can go pay down there," he said, pointing down the hall before returning to the newspaper.

I leaned against a drab green wall, with police officers and the occasional malcontent passing by, as I waited for Mae's release. When she came, she looked as I feared — high heels, a very short, strapless black dress with sparkles, a long wig with blond streaks. No wonder she was arrested for prostitution. She looked the part.

She walked slowly, head down, as she approached. She clearly didn't want to look directly at me. I decided it could wait, but we would have to talk.

There was a silence between us as we headed for my car. Outside, I opened the car door for her to slide in, shut the door and walked to the other side. I sat for a while before I put the key into the ignition but I didn't look her way. I just stared out the front of the car.

"Okay. What happened? I thought you gave up working."

"I needed the money, and I know Rita. She runs a good, safe business. Never has legal problems. She pays top dollar for that," Mae said. She reached over to touch my arm and without thinking, I pulled slightly away. I could tell she was about to cry.

"I'm so sorry about this," Mae said. "I don't know what to say but I promise, I will pay you back."

I fired up the engine and pulled away, heading back to West Philadelphia by way of Walnut Street. I didn't speak at all until after we crossed the bridge over the Schuylkill River near 30th Street. "Are you hungry?"

"I'm starving but I didn't want to ask."

"We can go somewhere. But you have *got* to take off that wig." I was serious but she chuckled at the remark. Even I softened a little inside.

We stopped at a restaurant at 38th Street near the Penn campus, and got a table near the back. No sense in drawing more attention to ourselves than necessary. I ordered a hamburger and fries. Mae ordered chicken fried steak, a salad and apple pie for dessert. It was already an expensive day and it was going to get worse.

"So, tell me what happened," I said as we waited for the food.

"After MOVE, Rita called me to see if I needed anything. She was the one who helped me get the apartment. I pay on a weekly basis," Mae said.

"And that was in exchange for you returning to work?"

"No, that wasn't part of it. But she said some of my old customers had been asking for me. Well, one, really."

The salad came and the conversation cooled while she ate. They must not feed people in the Big House. She wasn't just hungry. She was ravenous.

"You had a customer who wanted to see you, you were saying," I commented as she finished the last of the salad.

"That's what Rita said. And he wanted it to be on Friday night," Mae said, popping a cherry tomato into her mouth. "So after Rita asked all week, I agreed to work a little over the weekend. I didn't have anything else to do. My house was burnt to the ground."

"So what you're saying is that boredom is your excuse," I said.

"David, I'm not trying to make excuses. I just did it, okay?"

The main course arrived. I couldn't understand why anyone would want to eat a chicken-fried steak. It was breaded and deep-fried until the outside was crunchy, and served with mashed potatoes and gravy — more food that was unhealthy. Completing the meal was a medley of over-cooked vegetables. There was not a single nutritional calorie on the plate.

"What time did you get there?"

She cut a bit of the steak, dipped it into the potatoes and gravy and put it in her mouth. At least she was enjoying it.

"Around nine-thirty. I had a quick customer at ten. He wanted a local. Didn't take long."

I ate the hamburger. It tasted okay, but I had had better — and cheaper.

"Did the guy who wanted to see you come?"

"Yes. A little after eleven."

"Did you remember him?"

"Yes, of course. His name's Simon. Mr. Simon. He's the one who started calling me Baby Cakes."

I was about to put a French fry into my mouth and stopped in mid-motion. "Is Simon his first or last name?"

"I don't know. It might be his first but I never asked."

"*Baby Cakes*? He specifically asked for Baby Cakes?" I asked.

"Yeah," Mae said. "It's because of my butt. He likes to slap my ass."

That was more detail than I desired, so I moved on. "And, you are sure this guy's not a cop?"

"*Absolutely*. Before I quit this business, he came around a lot. Couple times a month. Saw some other girls, but mostly asked for me."

We were both eating again.

"What's he look like?"

"Average white guy. Okay body. Nothing to write home about in terms of looks, but who cares? Good tipper."

I saw the waitress and stopped her. "Could I have more napkins and another Coke, please?"

"Me, too," Mae said, quickly before the woman left our table.

"So he comes in. . . . "

"Yes. He asks for me and I'm just finishing up another customer, so Rita puts him in another empty room to wait. After I was finished, I went in to see him. He said he missed me and begged again for my phone number but I wouldn't give it to him."

"Had he asked that before?"

"Yes, but I never do that," Mae said with emphasis. "So we do our thing. He's a little nasty boy. Likes some kinky stuff, but not too kinky."

"Mae, I don't need to know the intimate details."

She gave me a look like I was some sort of prude but also didn't comment on it. "When he's done, he drops me a nice tip and leaves. I thought that was it."

"It wasn't?"

The waitress returned with more napkins and Cokes in both hands. She had a strange expression when she looked at Mae and then me but, of course, she didn't say anything. She set the drinks down and departed.

"A little after midnight, the police came in and said I solicited sex for money from a guy. They arrest me, put me in handcuffs, dump me in the back of a patrol car and took me downtown," Mae said.

"What about the others? They arrest anybody else? What about Rita?"

"It was just me."

I swallowed hard. "Come again?"

"I was the only one arrested."

"Weren't there other girls there?"

"Yes. There were four other girls but nothing happened to them. Only me," she said.

I was nearly done eating. Reaching for the Coke, I took a sip and sat back in my seat. I could barely believe what she told me. But then again, it added up.

"Since it wasn't a cop who caught you, they don't have anything on you. I'm a little surprised the judge didn't just throw it out to begin with," I said. "You have a lawyer there when you went to court?"

"Public defender. She was a raw rookie, though. Probably just out of law school and on her first case. Didn't know much," Mae said. "But before the cops arrested me, Rita promised to get her lawyer to handle the case."

I wanted to say it hadn't happened but held my tongue on that subject. "I'm sure this will be thrown out."

"How are you so sure? You're no lawyer," she said with concern rising in her voice.

I stopped the passing waitress and asked for the check when she delivered the dessert. She returned with a plate of French apple pie with ice cream and two spoons. "You might want to share," the waitress said.

I said thanks and let it drop. Then I turned my full attention to Mae, a.k.a Baby Cakes.

"I'm sure, because this isn't about you at all. It's about harassing me."

"What? *You*?! How is this about you?"

I reminded her about the incident in Stephenson's house the day before. And I explained about the note in the car and how it directly implied she was in jail — and used her play name.

"Someone is trying to tell me to lay off. I must be getting close to something, but I don't know what it is. That's why I need you down in City Hall on Monday. You think you can still do that?"

"You tell me what you need me to do down there and I'll get it done," she said with determination. She apparently was beginning to see the gravity of the situation. "I want to help."

"By the way, that guy, your customer, I think he's a detective named Simon Balcombe who works for The Henderson Group."

"Why would he want to set me up like that? And Rita? Was she in on it? I've trusted her for years."

"I don't know why, but I intend to find out," I said. "And as for your friend Rita, you could have been set up without her knowledge or help. But I'd stay away from gentlemen's clubs if I were you, even Rita's."

She agreed to that but she had said that before. I hoped this time she'd follow through.

I paid the check and we left the restaurant. I drove her home, which, in this case, was an efficiency on the second floor of a three-story brick building off of 59th Street. It wasn't the high rent district but it looked clean and reasonably maintained. There was a small area in front for grass and a few flowers, which were cramped and battling the odds of staying alive in the coming months.

Out of a mixture of curiosity and concern for her safety, I walked her upstairs. She thanked me again for bailing her out — *and* for not firing her. It wasn't too hard. I liked Mae.

Plus, I gave her a chance before and it seemed to work out. I hated the office duties and she did it well. And generally without serious complaint.

I did, however, have a lingering question and thought it was finally time to ask it.

"Why did you give up the business . . . come work for me in the first place, Mae?"

I was leaning against a wall with faded blue paint, though I wasn't sure it would have looked any better when it was new. Mae unlocked her door and nudged it open slightly, then turned to face me. It was several more heart beats before she spoke.

Though she was upbeat most of the time, Mae's shoulders slumped slightly and she looked at the grimy tile floor before she spoke.

"I was already thinking of getting out of this business before the night you showed up," she said. "I took your card and immediately forgot about it for the rest of the evening, *and* for most of the next night. You still with me?"

"Yes," I said. I was fascinated, but had no idea where the story was going. She briefly looked up at me, then down again and finished the story.

"That night something happened for the first time. A guy came in with a gun. He robbed everyone. Rita, all us girls. He pointed a gun at my face and took all our money. You have any idea how terrifying that is?" Mae asked.

I shook my head. "What happened? You call the police? File a report?"

"*Hell no*! Not officially," she said, straightening up slightly.

"Rita actually called a couple of guys she knows downtown. But no official report. She couldn't do that. They'd have to shut down the business," she said. "It was unofficial but there were more police patrolling nearby after that. I had had enough, though. It's a dangerous business. You meet all types. But you convince yourself you enjoy it. I liked the instant cash. But it wasn't worth the risk. I called you the next day."

Mae's eyes began to water and I took my cue. "I'll see you at work on Monday."

As I turned to leave, she reached out and pulled me into a hug. It was long, tight and sincere. "I'm so sorry. I really am," she sobbed into my shoulder. "I won't do it again. I promise."

Finally pulling away and hoping she didn't notice my embarrassment, I smiled and left Mae to her tears and her thoughts.

I needed to get my mind off of Mae and her troubles as I drove home, so I concentrated on work.

Sending Mae to City Hall on Monday to work on the Carmichael case might help keep her out of harm's way. I hoped so. It was going to be hard enough for me to protect myself. I generally don't carry a gun but come Monday, when I got back to work, I'd have one on me.

CHAPTER XIV

"Why are you here?"

It was a short, five-minute drive from Mae's place to my own. I entered my apartment, dropped the keys on a table and went to the kitchen in search of a drink. A soda would do fine but something harder would be better.

I flipped on the television and had settled on the couch with a glass of Crown Royal nearby when there was a tentative knock at the door. It was as if whoever it was hoped I wasn't home, or that I wouldn't hear the door. I had had enough intrusions into my life in one day but curiosity got the best of me. I went to the door, opened it and there stood, of all people, Clara.

I froze in surprise for an awkward moment.

"Well, aren't you gonna invite me in?" she said finally.

"Yes, of course," I said, stepping back to allow her to enter.

It wasn't just Clara's sudden and unannounced arrival that caught my breath. She was stunning in jeans and a well-tailored jacket worn to downplay her hippy-ness. It was Saturday casual wear, something fashionably appropriate for shopping at Bloomingdale's in the King of Prussia Mall.

What I didn't understand was why she was standing in my living room.

Clara walked around the room, doing a full circle as if appraising it. She touched the back of the couch, ran her hand across the surface of the desk, looked at pictures without touching them, and glanced at the television set as she passed it. I watched her reaction when she noticed the single glass of whiskey on the table.

"Drinking alone?" she asked. I was still standing near the door when she abruptly turned to face me.

"It's been a hard day," I said, approaching the table and taking my drink. "You like some?"

"No," she said but quickly added, "You still like Coke, don't you? I'll take that, if you have any."

I headed for the kitchen, glass of Crown Royal still in my hand. The counter was a mess and I put the glass down as I looked around for something clean to offer her. I found an old Mason jar sitting alone on a shelf and knew it was my only option. The ice from the freezer made a tumbling sound in the bottom of the Mason jar at the same moment I heard Clara speaking from the other room.

"You haven't changed, David. Everything looks like it did the last time I was here."

I didn't know what to make of the comment, though I suspected she was inspecting the room for any female influences and finding none. I walked out of the kitchen with the jar and a can of soda. She was standing in the middle of the room staring at a framed wall poster from a Covent Garden production of the play EQUUS. The poster was a gift from her. She had bought it while on a trip to London and framed it herself when she returned.

"You want to have a seat?" I said, motioning her to the couch as I poured the drink. She sat and crossed her legs. The hesitancy she displayed when she originally entered the apartment was gone, replaced with a certain smug self-satisfaction.

I handed her the soda and retreated to the chair at the desk. I had left my whiskey in the kitchen and would have gone back to get it but I had a question first.

"Why are you here, Clara?"

I also wanted to know why she was without her husband, but I didn't ask that.

She took a sip from the Mason jar and placed the drink on the table in front of her. "Wilbur Stephenson. I wanted to know what progress you're making."

We both knew that was a lie. There was absolutely no reason for her to come down on a Saturday to my apartment — which she had not visited once in the eighteen months since we broke up — to ask me about a professional matter that could have waited until a phone call on Monday morning.

I ignored the elephant in the room and rolled my chair over toward the coffee table. I went with the easy part — the trip to Atlantic City.

"How is Randall, by the way?" she said when I finished.

"He's fine," I said. But I assumed she probably already knew, so I directed the conversation back to the subject at hand. "I checked around and found no evidence of Stephenson being down there. He had a reservation for a stay last week, but was a no-show."

"Did you talk to his friend Chet? He was the one who had a key or knew how to get one."

"Chet helped. Told me where to find the key."

"You get in the house? You learn anything?" Clara asked in rapid fire, uncrossing her legs and sitting forward as she did.

"I learned Wilbur must be into something."

"Like what?" Her arms were apart and her hands open, as if the gesture would entice me to provide greater clarity.

"I don't know. The house was clean. Everything in its place. Didn't look like he was planning on leaving or skipping town," I said, sure that my answer disappointed. "But in the dining room, there were papers all over the table. He was working on something, or for *someone*. It appeared to have something to do with when he was back in college."

"What did the papers say?"

"I don't know. I was trying to figure that out when I was attacked."

Clara moved to the very edge of her seat. "Attacked? What do you mean?"

"Someone must have followed me into the house. Snuck up on me and hit me from behind. Cold-cocked me. I was out when the police arrived."

"The *police*? Was anything taken?"

She didn't ask how I was or whether I was hurt. Her concern was obviously elsewhere. I didn't say anything at first, allowing her questions to hang in the air. I leaned forward, eying her closely, and she sat back on the couch, moving away from me.

"Why are you here, Clara?"

"I told you. Because I wanted to know what's happened to Burt."

"*Burt*? Wilbur Stephenson, you mean? The guy who works for you?"

She looked at her wrist and rose quickly from the couch. "I just noticed it's late. I've got to go."

I got up and grabbed her arm. "You aren't wearing a watch, Clara. How can you know the time? My clock is in the kitchen." She tried to pull away but I held firm. "Why are you here? There's something you aren't telling me."

She struggled again, not saying a word.

It wasn't until Clara finally relaxed her arm that I let go. She dropped back down on the couch. She didn't look at me at first. There was a long silence which I finally ended.

"I've talked to a number of people about Stephenson and you're the only one who's called him anything other than Wil or Wilbur. What was he to you?"

Clara didn't look up but she deflated like a balloon.

"Burt was a good manager and . . . a good friend."

There was more, but getting it out of her was going to take

a lot. I didn't know if I wanted to invest that sort of energy or time.

"Did the police contact you?" I asked.

She shook her head no. "They talked to Russ a day or so ago."

"They told me to lay off. The police. That's what they said after I was attacked. They said I should lay off the case."

Her eyes searched mine. "Are you?"

"Not if you don't want me to," I said. "You have any idea what he was doing or what he was into?"

"No."

"Clara, you're hiding something. Whatever it is, you need to tell me. I can't help you . . . I can't do anything until you level with me."

Finally, she looked up, her eyes watery, though she managed to hold her composure.

"When you and I . . ." she paused, "stopped seeing each other, there was a time when Burt and I . . ." again she paused, ". . . dated. I know it was wrong. We worked together. But he was what I needed at the time. He was open and giving in ways you weren't. Burt was considerate and caring," she said, and then looked around the apartment. "And he was neat."

She reached for her soda and I wished I hadn't left the whiskey on the counter in the kitchen. She regained her forcefulness to address me directly.

"You didn't want me. You just wanted the *idea* of me. You were fine with your solitary work and your Sunday dinners with your dysfunctional family. I was just someone to have around so your grandmother would stop trying to fix you up. But I wanted more than that. More for me. More for both of us."

I stood and paced around the room. It was like we were replaying the same scene again from more than a year earlier.

"I tried to give you what you needed."

"You think you did, David, but you didn't. It's not what you do. You always hold back. I never knew what you were thinking, or what you felt in your heart."

I stopped pacing. I was across the room, as if the physical distance would help me win this old argument. But I knew it wouldn't. Nothing would.

"This is getting us nowhere, rehashing the past," I said. "Let's just focus on the case, okay?"

She retreated into herself and nodded, and I settled again in the chair.

"How long did you see each other?" I asked.

"A couple of months. Until I got back on my feet emotionally," she said. "And by then I was feeling guilty about sleeping with a guy who worked for me."

How odd, I thought to myself, that you were concerned about the ethical issues of sleeping with a subordinate but not the moral ones. "Did anyone at work know about your relationship? And what about Russ. Did he know?"

"I don't think so. Nobody knew, though Chet may have guessed later on."

I didn't want to go back into the past but I decided to say what was on my mind.

"Is that why you recommended me for this job, to rub my nose in it?"

"*Good heavens, no*, David. How could you even think that?" she said with vehemence, looking at me squarely. "I recommended you because you could handle the case, and do it discreetly. And that's what we needed."

"What's *he* to you now?"

Again there was a pause as she rose, pacing the room. Her back was to me when she spoke.

"I've made some mistakes, David. With you. Perhaps with Wilbur. But I definitely made a mistake in getting married. It was what I thought I wanted and needed at the time. But, now, I'm not so sure." Turning to face me again, she probed my eyes and undoubtedly saw she hadn't totally answered my question.

"We really are just friends, Burt and I, if that's what you are asking. He's someone I can call on and talk to."

"And he didn't tell you anything about what he was doing?"

"I knew he was busy on something and keeping some things in his house, but he wouldn't tell me anything. And I do know he was seeing someone, and it wasn't his ex-wife," Clara said.

"Do you know where the ex is?"

"Burt rarely had anything to say about her and when he did, it wasn't nice," Clara said. "She left New Jersey after the divorce and maybe headed back down South, but I don't know for sure where."

"Why'd you come here, Clara?"

"Because I wanted you to reassure me that everything's going to be okay. Despite our past history, I needed someone I can trust and can turn to. That's why I came."

I stood and walked to her, taking her hands. "I'll do the best I can, of course. I can't do more than that."

She didn't say a word, but threw her arms around my neck and buried her face on my chest. The tears came quickly.

CHAPTER XV

A spry woman of eighty, thin to the point of being frail....

I was glad to see Sunday come. There was a promise of regularity to it that I welcomed. Through the afternoon, the day didn't disappoint, despite the Phillies' loss. The game ended on time, shortly after four, and I didn't have any trouble as I rode the Broad Street subway and patrolled several platforms in search of pickpockets.

I called Marie before I headed home. She said she'd be ready at six for dinner. I had just enough time to get to my apartment, make a quick change of my clothes and head out again. It promised to be an eventful time.

Marie was already outside in the parking lot when I pulled up. "You sure you want to do this?" I asked as I opened the car door for her to slide in. "There's still time to back out."

"Did you tell your grandmother you were bringing company?"

"Of course. Wouldn't spring something like that on her unexpected."

"What did she say?"

"Nothing, really." I hoped she'd let it drop.

"Then we go." She grinned at me.

I drove and prayed most of the way.

Grammy Taylor lived in North Philadelphia, not far from Broad Street. Her house was a brick-front townhouse nearly indistinguishable from all the other townhouses on the block, except that her house was next to a vacant lot. The lot had once held a townhouse, of course, but at some point the occupants moved out and it was left vacant. In time, the abandoned property morphed into a crack house, where my efforts to evacuate the addicts resulted in their setting the place on fire. Once the remaining structure was torn down, the lot was left vacant, with overgrown weeds and trash thrown everywhere.

Since no one was sure who owned the property, the city did nothing to clean it up. And while I hated how it made the neighborhood look, it was better than my having to constantly chase off druggies camping out in a vacant house.

Like all the other houses in the block, Grammy Taylor's had one front window on the first floor, and two windows facing the street on the second and third levels. Her bedroom was on the second floor, and my no-account brothers had bedrooms on the third.

As it was not in their nature, I doubted they would show up for Sunday dinner. They generally didn't. When they did show, it was late, and typically they were drunk. As I drove up Broad Street with Marie, I prayed for their continued absence.

I parked several doors from the house and we walked the rest of the way. As I was about to knock, Grammy Taylor opened the door.

"Come on in, child. We been waitin' for you," she said after giving me a hug. "Food's gonna get cold."

I entered and Marie followed, though slowly at first. Once inside, I turned to bring Marie to my side and to make the introductions.

"Grammy Taylor, this is my friend Marie Toussaint. Marie, this is my Grammy Taylor."

"Nice to meet you, my dear," Grammy said, taking her hand.

"And you, as well. David speaks of you often," Marie said.

"Davey does, does he?" she said.

Grammy Taylor was a spry woman of eighty, thin to the point of being frail, but she walked without a cane or assistance. The color of her gray hair was approaching blue and she wore a white ruffled apron over a spring dress that was the color of sunshine.

We headed through a narrow living room toward the dining room, where the table was already set for seven. The place settings were somewhat formal, certainly a greater formality than Marie had expected.

My sister Valerie came out of the kitchen carrying a plate of scallions, sliced tomatoes and cucumbers, and placed it on the table. A man followed her with a bowl of corn.

"A friend? Davey hasn't brought a quote-unquote friend to dinner in some time," Valerie was saying to her husband, unaware that I had just walked up.

When Marie had agreed to dinner at Grammy Taylor's house, I knew such a comment would be coming. I was still annoyed when I heard it, although I brushed it aside.

"Valerie, this is Marie. Marie, this is my big mouth younger sister, Valerie and her husband, Stuart Thomas."

Stuart tried unsuccessfully to be discreet as he took Marie in, but there was unmasked desire in his eyes.

What an asshole!

"And those two over there are our twins, Cora and Cody," Valerie said of my niece and nephew who entered from the kitchen. They ignored Marie in the way seven-year-old children do as they focus on what they want at the moment. But their mother would have none of it. "Children, say hello to Miss Marie."

Cora and Cody chimed in with a quick hello. And they took a liking to Marie instantly.

"I'm gonna be a fireman when I get big," young Cody said.

"He always says that," Cora chimed in, having heard it too many times before.

"And so you will be a fireman," Stuart said to his son, while giving a disapproving eye to Cora.

"Let's all sit down before the food gets any colder," Grammy Taylor interrupted. "Stuart, you sit down there."

Grammy Taylor took the end of the table closest to the kitchen, while Stuart sat at the opposite end. It put Stuart as far away from Grammy Taylor as physically possible. She grew up in an age when good manners were an expectation, not optional behavior. She was a church-going, relentlessly proper, unfailingly polite woman. But she didn't like Stuart any more than I did. Random seating assignments at the table were as rude as she would ever be toward him.

Marie and I sat on one side of the table, with me closest to my grandmother, and across the table from Valerie, who was flanked by her children.

Grammy Taylor looked over the top of her glasses down to Stuart as a cue to say grace, which he did with an economy of words rarely heard at a Sunday dinner in a Black household. When he finished, Grammy Taylor visited him with a stern expression of her displeasure at his disappointing offering to God.

Marie reached for her fork and quickly stopped, showing her embarrassment. No one else was moving.

By tradition at Sunday dinners, everyone at the table said a Bible verse after the food was blessed and before we ate. I had forgotten to share that piece of information with Marie, so I leaned and whispered, "I'm sorry I failed to mention this. You can just go with 'Jesus wept,' like the kids."

From his end of the table, Stuart would go first, with my grandmother at the other end going last. Stuart mumbled a verse which I didn't recognize and was followed by Valerie and the kids reciting the briefest verse in the Bible.

Marie smiled and gave my hand a gentle, reassuring squeeze. Then she spoke.

"'But the fruit of the spirit is love, joy, peace, patience, kindness, goodness, faithfulness, gentleness and self-control. Against these there is no law,'" Marie said, citing directly the book of Galatians. "Amen."

Grammy Taylor said nothing but her eyes lit up with a smile. That said it all.

Sunday evening dinners involved a weekly rotation of baked ham, fried chicken, roasted turkey, pot roast or lamb. It was a week for ham, just like at Easter or on Christmas. Also on the rotating menu was corn; greens; mashed, baked, fried or boiled potatoes; macaroni and cheese; a plate of slice vegetables; freshly baked rolls and some sort of fruit pie. On holidays, there was also ice cream.

Grammy Taylor insisted that, as Marie was our guest, I serve her first, with Valerie handling the children at the same time.

"How long have you two been seeing each other?" Valerie asked before she added, "Cora, be careful. You're getting the corn all over yourself."

Amused by the question and enjoying my discomfort, Marie allowed me to answer. "Seeing each other is not totally accurate. We only met this week. On Tuesday."

Stuart spooned some corn into his mouth and then addressed Marie. "And in less than a week you're willing to meet his family? It was years before I was invited."

I wished it were longer, but there's no accounting for Valerie's taste.

"David talked about how much he loves Sunday dinners and I never had that with my family. It sounded interesting and I wanted to see what I was missing," Marie said.

There was a sweetness to her earnest comment.

"Grammy, could you pass the pepper, please," I said, hoping to deflect the conversation a little. I dashed the potatoes once with pepper and put the shaker down. "Marie is a student at Textiles and works at a newsstand at the Sheraton Hotel downtown. I met her there."

"What are you studying?" Grammy Taylor asked.

"Textile design. I'm about to start my last year."

"What will you do after that? Move to New York?" Stuart asked.

"My parents hope not. They'd like me to stay in the Philadelphia area."

"Where do your parents live, dear?" Grammy Taylor asked.

"Downingtown, in Chester County. We've lived there since before I could remember."

"And your parents, what do they do?" Grammy Taylor asked as she reached for the bowl of corn.

"My mom works for a dentist near home and my dad does environmental research for a consulting firm near the University of Pennsylvania. I think it's connected to the university in some way."

Marie seemed to be able to handle her own. As long as it didn't get too personal, things would be okay.

By the time dinner was over, Marie had totally won over my grandmother and sister. What Stuart thought was unimportant. Somehow, over warmed peach cobbler, Marie managed to charm them all with how a newsstand was run.

"Davey, will you help me clear the dessert dishes?" Grammy Taylor said after everyone had finished.

Knowing it was a command not a question, I dutifully helped her collect the dessert plates, silverware and napkins, leaving the glasses for someone else. But everyone knew I was being ushered into the kitchen for a reason. The glasses would wait.

I put all the cloth napkins in a laundry basket situated near the basement door.

The sink was still full of dinnerware, which my grandmother liked to completely rinse before loading them into the dishwasher. She was loading dishes as she edged toward what was on her mind.

"Allen couldn't make it tonight. He said he had something to take care of," she said.

Of course he did, and on a Sunday night, no less. Allen, the youngest of my brothers, was perhaps the laziest person alive. But that he managed to find some activity to occupy himself on a Sunday night was neither surprising nor unexpected. His continued mooching off of Grammy Taylor was an unspoken sore point in the family, but not with Valerie. She threw it up in his face virtually every time she saw him.

That was the reason Allen tended to miss Sunday dinners. Valerie.

"Davey, hand me those dishes, there," Grammy Taylor said, pointing to a stack on the counter. As she continued loading, she got to the point. "Can't you find something for Allen to do, some work?"

"Like what, Grammy? We've had this conversation so many times. He doesn't have any of the skills necessary to be an investigator. More to the point, he doesn't want to do it. I can't just hire him to do nothing, even if I wanted to. I don't have the money for that."

"What about office work? He could do your filing," she said, loading some flatware.

"I have a person who does all my clerical work, and I barely have enough money to pay her. Anyway, he'd never do it. I asked him about it before I hired Mae."

"You hired a stranger before you hired your own family," she said.

"I had to. He got indignant. He said, 'I'd never do that. I'm a man. That's women's work.'"

Grammy Taylor stood still before she spoke again. There was sternness in her posture and in her voice. "Davey, he's family, and we help family. Your brother-in-law helped you when you needed it."

That she brought up Stuart, even without mentioning him by name, indicated her desperation. It also suggested she knew of his past transgressions. I, of course, never told her. But I could tell she knew.

I also knew I stood a better shot at getting my lazy brother a job than I had of winning any argument with my grandmother. We both knew that.

"I'll do what I can," I said as I turned to leave the kitchen. Stopping at the door, I looked back. "But no promises."

"Okay. No promises," she said. Her expression softened and she continued before I got out the door. "Now tell me what's going on with this new friend, Marie. She seems like a wonderful young lady. I like her."

I was her prey and she was far from ready to release me. I was going to be in the kitchen for a while.

When the evening was finally over shortly before 8:30, Marie hugged my grandmother and promised to come to dinner again.

"You're always welcome in my home," Grammy Taylor said. She stood on the stoop and watched as we walked to the car. I waved to my grandmother as I closed the passenger side door once Marie was inside.

"You were quiet most of the evening, which doesn't seem normal for you," Marie said to me as I turned right onto Broad Street and headed toward Center City.

"It didn't seem like you needed my help. You totally killed them. They love you, probably more than they love me."

"I'm sure that's not true. But I did enjoy myself."

"I'm glad," I said, with both honesty and relief.

"What did your grandmother want to talk to you about in the kitchen?"

"Family stuff, mostly."

"I'll bet," she said, looking my way. Even in the darkness I could read the sarcasm in her eyes.

We rode in silence for a few minutes as I worked up some courage. "I know it's getting late and you have a full day tomorrow, but would you like to stop for some coffee or something?"

I hoped I didn't sound too needy, pathetic or desperate. I enjoyed being with her and wanted her around a little longer. The next words out of her mouth would tell.

"No, I don't think so," she said.

My chest fell along with my hopes.

"But, David, do you know what I would like?"

I turned again to face her in the darkness, hoping light from the street lamps didn't betray the sadness on my face.

"I'd love to see your apartment."

She smiled and I drove a little faster as we headed toward West Philly.

CHAPTER XVI

Of the Seven Deadly Sins, he most closely personified sloth. . . .

It was early — the clock said 6:11 — when I felt Marie stir next to me in bed. I opened my eyes and attempted to shake some of the sleepiness from my brain.

"David, I need you to get me downtown by seven. I have to open the newsstand," she said.

Last night, she had mentioned she needed to be downtown in the morning but that was *before* we got into full-contact sport.

Marie leaned over to kiss my face and reached under the covers to grab my cock. It was erect, which was surprising, given the workout it had had overnight.

"Hmmm, you're ready again. Let me take some of the pressure off," Marie said. And with that, her head was under the covers.

Later, we showered together, and it was difficult for me to keep the grin off my face.

At the stroke of 7:00, I got Marie to work. She was smartly dressed in jeans and one of my white shirts with the collar open. I promised to call her later in the day.

Though it was still early for me, I went straight to the office. I was there for an hour before I heard the front door open, signaling Mae's arrival.

"Hey, sweet cheeks. I'm in here," I said playfully. My feet were up on my desk, a cup of coffee nearby. I rarely made sexual references to Mae and she wore a surprised look when she came into my office. Her brows were furrowed and she looked as if she was about to speak when she noticed my smile.

"Either you won some money at the slots over the weekend or you got some nookie," she said.

"I'm still broke."

And with that, she smiled.

"Okay, we've got work to do," I said, dropping my feet to the floor and straightening up. "You ready to head downtown?"

"What do you need?"

"Go get a pad and I'll tell you."

Mae went out and was back in seconds.

"I need you to go to the county assessor's office and search the tax records for who owns the property at 600 Rector Street in Manayunk, Unit Number Three. It's a condo. We need to know ownership and how long they've owned it. And *this* is important: Find out who owns the mortgage, if there's any record of that. There's got to be a money trail somewhere.

"All of this is for the Carmichael case," I said. "But I might have you look into something on the Stephenson case, too. So call me when you have something from the assessor's office and definitely by noon. Okay?"

"Got it. You *are* buying my lunch if I'm staying down there, aren't you? You know I gotta eat lunch to keep up my strength," Mae said.

"Just keep the receipt so we can file the paperwork."

"You mean so *I* can file the paperwork," she corrected me.

I nodded and she left.

~*~

I still wasn't sure why it mattered, but I decided to go to the Philadelphia Free Library on Logan Circle to do research on that prostitution case in 1969 in Atlanta. Since Stephenson was so interested in it, there must be something there.

Before I left for downtown, I called my brother Allen.

"Allen, this is Dave."

"Davey, what's going on?"

"I thought we could talk."

"About what?" he said, sounding cautious.

I waited for a second, not knowing what to say next. "This and that."

More silence. I could almost *hear* him thinking.

"Grammy Taylor put you up to this, didn't she? Last night."

I wanted to deny it but also knew it was of no use. We had been in this situation before — and all because of our grandmother.

"Yes. But we don't see each other that often. You miss Sunday dinners a lot and I thought it would be good to talk, just to catch up on things."

"Like what things?" he asked.

Okay. He had me. We shared few, if any interests, and he would never give me many details of what he was up to these days. As for me, Allen didn't care what cases I was working on or who I dated.

"Perhaps it's a bad idea. I guess I'll just let you get back to doing whatever you're doing," I said.

"I need a ride downtown," he said. "Can you come get me? We can talk then."

"Right now? You're at the house?"

"Of course, I'm at the house. You called here. Remember? I thought you were a better private dick than that," he said, needling me. "And you said you wanted to talk. So let's talk."

"Yeah, yeah. All right," I said as I glanced at my watch. I know he could hear the impatience in my voice and for once I didn't care. This little side trip would cut into my time at the library, particularly if he wanted to go somewhere out of the way.

"I'll be there in twenty minutes. But be ready to go. I have something I need to get done this morning."

"Thanks, Davey. I appreciate it."

Save it, I wanted to say. "Oh, where am I taking you?"

"You can drop me off near Logan Circle," he said.

And I couldn't help but smile.

An even bigger smile spread across my face twenty minutes later when I pulled up in front of the house.

Allen was two inches taller than me, fifty pounds heavier and attractive to women who like the Bad Boy type. His typical dress was casual. And of the Seven Deadly Sins, he most closely personified sloth, although most women of his acquaintance would probably put lust at the top of the list.

So I was awe-struck when he came out wearing well-pressed gray slacks and an ill-fitting Navy blue blazer with the word "SECURITY" stitched in yellow across the breast pocket. I had a hard time finding words once he was in the Mustang.

"Security? Where?" I asked.

"Just drive, okay? Take me to Logan Circle. I want to get a hot dog before I start, and I don't want to be late."

I put the car in gear and we headed off, turning south on Broad Street in the direction of Center City. "You gonna tell me where?"

"The Franklin Institute. I got the job last week."

Amazing. The Franklin Institute was across the Ben Franklin Parkway from the Free Library, which is where I was originally headed. I turned to face him in the car. "And you didn't tell Grammy Taylor? Or even Valerie, just to get her off your back?"

"You know, it's easy for you. Nobody knows what you do but everybody assumes you're okay. They put all this pressure on me to be like you. But I ain't you. I don't want to be like you," he said.

The words sounded bitter but his tone did not. I was grateful for small miracles.

Broad Street at any point is a busy street. There are dozens of traffic lights from the county line on the north end all the way down to City Hall, and nearly an equal number from City Hall to the Sports Complex in South Philly.

So traffic was slow, but it allowed for more time to talk.

"How'd you get out of the house every day without Grammy Taylor noticing?"

"I've been spending a lot of time at this girl Renee's house. She lives off of Ogontz and she's been giving me a ride every day," he said. "Everybody always expects me to fail. I wanted to show I could handle a regular job before I told anybody in the family."

I could almost feel a smile in Allen's voice when he turned to me. "Now, all the pressure will be back on you . . . on you movin' back to North Philly and findin' a woman. They ain't got over you losing Clara yet."

A wonderful evening with Marie had helped me get over my last encounter with Clara, but now it was back in my face. I lost focus for a moment and didn't see the car until it flashed in front of me.

"Dave, watch that blue car up there!" Allen yelled.

I hit the brakes and swerved to the right to avoid a blue sedan that cut me off.

"Idiot," I yelled but they probably couldn't hear me.

The near collision happened so fast I didn't have time to look at the license plate as the car sped off, but I could tell it had Jersey plates and there was only one occupant.

Once I regained my composure, I turned my attention back to Allen. "Everybody's worried about you, that you're drifting aimlessly. And that you're mooching off your grandmother."

"Don't lecture me. I'm getting my act together," he said. "And besides, Renee is giving me a little help. She helped me get the job."

"You should bring her around sometime. Maybe one Sunday night at dinner."

"Don't think that's gonna happen anytime soon," he said cheerfully. "You're on your own there."

We had just crossed Vine Street and I was about to say something when I noticed a police car riding close to my bumper. Getting someone off your bumper can lead to violence, so it's best to proceed slowly. With any other tailgater, I'd tap the brakes a couple of times very quickly to get them to back off. I couldn't do that with the police, and certainly not when they put on their flashers.

I pulled over. Two officers, both white and one on each side, got out of the patrol car and walked up cautiously, each with one hand on the butt of his gun.

Not a good sign.

I rolled down my window. "Is there a problem, officers?"

"Sir, would you mind stepping out of the car, please? Both of you, please," said the officer closest to me. "Right now!"

At no time should a black man mess with a Philadelphia police officer. And with the botched MOVE bombing the previous week, which created an international scandal for the city and the police department — for several days straight, images of bombed out houses made the front pages of every major newspaper in every country from Afghanistan to Zimbabwe — police were on edge.

I nodded quickly to Allen and opened my door.

As soon as I was out of the car, the officer grabbed my arm, spun me around and threw me on my car. The same happened to Allen on the other side.

"Spread 'em. Spread 'em, now," the officer barked.

I tried to question him, but he shoved me hard back onto the car again. I spread my arms and legs, and was quickly and thoroughly patted down. They took our identification from our pockets.

"Officers, what's this about?" I asked. Allen said nothing but looked at me with both surprise and suspicion.

We were both handcuffed and placed facing the street on the passenger side of the car. It seemed like the whole world was passing by to witness, yet again, two black men in police handcuffs. I felt humiliated, but I refused to bow my head down, as if not doing so would lessen the humiliation.

The shorter of the two officers, the one who was driving the patrol car, approached me with a no-nonsense expression made all the more menacing by his close-shaven head. He looked lean and mean, the type of guy who joined the force just to constantly face situations where he'd have to prove his manhood.

A badge over his breast pocket identified him as Anderson.

"Where'd you get this car?" Officer Anderson said.

I was puzzled. "It's my car. I have the registration and insurance information in the glove compartment."

The other officer, whose name, apparently, was McCallahan, pushed past us, opened the passenger side door and reached into the glove compartment, fishing through the debris that was inside. He tossed unused plastic straws, napkins from fast food restaurants, ketchup packets and all sorts of papers onto the seat or the floor until he found the documents.

"What are your names?" Officer Anderson said, bringing our attention back to him.

"David Blaise. My ID was in my pants pocket. You have it now, right there." I inclined my head in the general direction of our wallets.

Allen also responded with his name and with nothing more. Anderson looked at him and the uniform and moved closer. "And where do you think you're going?"

"My job," Allen said. "I work security at the Franklin Institute science museum on the Parkway."

Anderson stood between us and the car. "We got an urgent police report saying a car matching this description and with this license plate was stolen this morning by a guy matching your description," he said, indicating me.

At that, even Allen looked over at me.

"The police bulletin says the man was armed and dangerous." Anderson continued.

"This is my car. I didn't report it stolen." But I was glad I didn't have my gun. Though registered, it would escalate this situation.

McCallahan looked over all my paperwork then up at his partner. "The car registration and auto insurance are here and everything looks in order. It's all current."

"Check their ID and we'll see," Anderson said to McCallahan, who reached for the wallets. "If you are who you say you are and this is truly your car, why would it be reported stolen by an armed man?"

I didn't immediately have an answer for him. I was baffled. It made no sense.

But then something caught my eye. A car, similar to the one with New Jersey plates that cut me off only minutes earlier, was driving by. It slowed and the occupant looked over at us.

It was *Balcombe*. My stalker.

The police officers were facing us and had their backs to traffic in the street. They didn't see Balcombe point his fingers directly at me as if he were cocking and firing a gun. He sped away quickly and my heart nearly stopped as the implications became clear.

"Officer Anderson, isn't it?" I said, "I have no idea who would do something like that."

"It all checks out, Henry. They are who they say they are. And the car apparently does belong to him," McCallahan said a few moments later.

"Filing a false police report is a serious thing, you know," Officer Anderson said.

"Yes, I know that," I said. "And obviously I didn't do it."

The officers looked at each other as if that thought had never occurred to them. They seemed at a loss as to what to do next. Then Anderson said, "I'm going to call downtown and check this out. Don't you move. Understand?"

I answered for us both. "We understand."

Officer Anderson walked back to the patrol car with a swagger and got inside. He reached for the car radio and spent several minutes talking to some invisible person somewhere inside the police department bureaucracy.

"This happen to you often?" Allen asked me. He had apparently missed seeing Balcombe.

"It's a first. And I need to get to the bottom of it," I said.

"Davey, you really need to get another job," he said.

"Are you going to be late?"

"Not if we get out of here in a hurry. But I won't have time for a hot dog first," Allen said.

Officer Anderson finished talking in the police car and returned to us.

"You fellas don't have any drugs in there, do ya?" Anderson said, pointing to the interior of the Mustang when he returned.

"No, officer."

Anderson grabbed me with the same level of firmness as before and turned me around. "Uncuff 'em, Joe. They check out downtown. Must have been a false report."

~*~

Allen said virtually nothing to me for the remaining drive to the Franklin Institute.

"I'm sorry, Allen, I don't know what happened there. I hope you get inside on time," I said.

"I should be okay," he said, looking one last time at his watch. He had glanced at it every 60 seconds or so for about five minutes.

I dropped him off in front of the museum on 20th Street and he rushed inside. Then I drove back around the block and found a metered parking space on the Parkway in front of the Youth Study Center, which was a block from the library and across the Parkway from the science museum.

Like other buildings nearby, the Free Library was a Grecian structure with Doric columns at the front entrance that stand two stories tall. Inside the entrance was a large open space with marble floors. From a second-story balcony that ran along the sides, I could see directly down into the massive lobby area.

The borrowing library was to the right on the first floor and an information desk was to the left of the entrance.

"I'm looking for newspapers on file," I said to the person at the information desk.

"Microfilm is in the research area on the second floor," she said, pointing to the stairs at the opposite end. Halfway up the wide staircase, the steps split, with some heading up to the left and some to the right.

At the second floor research desk, I was directed to local newspapers of the time. The library didn't carry copies of out-of-town papers, such as the Atlanta Journal-Constitution, but I assumed if the story in Atlanta had NCAA implications, some reports might appear in local papers, particularly in the Philadelphia Bulletin. Though the Bulletin closed in early 1982, it was probably the best paper in the city in the late sixties.

I flipped through old Bulletins first, and after an hour of searching, hit the jackpot. There was a series of articles on football players at Georgia Central frequenting prostitutes; several players were thrown off the team, while others were suspended for varying lengths of time. Their names were listed, and I wrote them down, but Stephenson, who was probably at the school at the time, wasn't one of them.

The NCAA considered placing the school on probation for two years, but the probation and threatened fine were never imposed.

What was exciting, however, was one of the first articles written by the Associated Press. It named the two prostitutes at the party and revealed the names of two other women, both from Alabama, whom police were looking to question. They reportedly were at the party, but left before police arrived.

One was named Lula Mae Stobe.

Stephenson must have found his LMS.

CHAPTER XVII

"Looks like you have a pest problem."

I was at my desk finishing a Big Mac and waiting for another call from Mae when there was a soft knock at the front door of the office. After the unsettling encounter with the police, thanks to the suspected help of my stalker, I didn't want to be bothered, but I knew it was of no use.

"Come on in," I shouted, hoping the two, all-beef patties didn't muffle my voice too much.

The door opened and Mookie scuffled in.

Oh shit, I thought. *What do you want?*

"Mr. Private Dick, how ya doin' taday?"

"I've been better, Mookie. How can I help you?"

"Question is, howz can I help you?"

I was in no mood to play games. But it appeared whatever Mookie wanted, I was going to have to drag it out of him. I took one last bite of the cold burger, wrapped up the rest in a napkin and stuffed it into the bag with the remaining French fries. It all went into the trash.

"Get to the point, will you, Mookie? What do you want?"

"Dere's been dis white dude askin' lots of questions 'bout ya up and down the street?"

Another time that would have been only mildly interesting. But given that Balcombe and the Henderson Group were up to something, it did get a rise out of me.

"What's he look like?" I asked.

The man Mookie described had to be Balcombe. I was going to have to meet this guy. And have a gun handy.

"When did you see him?" I asked.

"Some last week, some taday? He was really into who owned dis building."

"Today?"

"Bout an hour ago, just before ya got back."

"What did he want to know? Who was he asking?"

"He ask everybody. He wanta know your habits . . . when youz come and go . . . what kinda clients you had. He ask't me what cases youz workin' on, and who you're workin' for now."

Mookie wouldn't know much about my business, nor would anyone else on the block. But it was interesting to know Balcombe was so interested.

"What you tell him?"

"I tell him I don't noz whoz you workin' for, 'cept dat lady in the Benz," Mookie said.

I sat up in my seat. Mookie had mentioned an actual case.

"What did he say to that?"

"Nuthin'. Pay me a twenty and dat was it. I tried to sell 'im some cassettes."

"You took the money?"

"I ain't noz fool," he said.

Apparently not, I thought.

"You let me know if he comes around again, okay?"

Mookie agreed. "Don't you worry. Iz take care of ya."

After Mookie left, the telephone rang almost immediately.

"David Blaise," I said into the phone. It was past noon and I was expecting another call from Mae.

"Mr. Blaise. This is Mrs. Findley, at the apartment. I hate to bother you but you need to come home right away." She was an old lady and easily spooked, but she sounded off the chart.

"What's going on, Mrs. Findley?"

"The police are everywhere up in your apartment. You had a break-in."

"I'll be right there."

~*~

There were two patrol cars and an unmarked police cruiser in front of the apartment when I arrived ten minutes later. Once I made my way upstairs, I saw officials in the hallway talking to Mrs. Findley and taking notes. They said little to me except to inform me that officers were waiting for me in the apartment.

I walked in and there stood Detective Thompson and his easy-to-dislike partner, Sergeant Ryan Gregory.

"Looks like you have a pest problem, Blaise," Gregory said in a tone that showed his pleasure at the situation.

The place was a complete mess. The sofa cushions were all over the floor. Records and cassette tapes, normally stacked carefully in a corner cabinet, were flung about. Some of the vinyl albums were out of their protective covers, carelessly stepped on by whoever went through the place.

Lamps were overturned, stereo equipment knocked over, newspapers and magazines were scattered across the floor. I walked down the hall to the bedroom. The bedding and the mattress were pulled off the bed, with the mattress lying partially off the box springs. All the drawers in the dresser were open. Clothes from the dresser and the closet were everywhere.

I continued an inspection of the apartment. None of it was any better than what I'd already seen.

I returned to the living room, picked up some cushions and put them back on the sofa, where I sat. Thompson, who had followed me to the bedroom and back again to the living room, pulled up a chair to face me. He hadn't said a word the entire time.

I was perplexed, but only partly because of the break-in.

"What are you guys doing here? This is just a break-in, a standard burglary, which unfortunately happens all the time in Philadelphia. It's not the sort of thing you would investigate," I said.

Gregory walked over, smug, arrogant and gleeful in my misery.

I hated him.

"You're why we're here, Blaise. You're a person of interest in a major missing person's case," Gregory said. "And if something big happens, like a burglary, or, heaven forbid, a shooting where you end up dead, it concerns us. It concerns us a lot. That's why we're here."

"Good to know your position on my well-being, sergeant," I responded, but was sorry I said it. I didn't want to give him the satisfaction of knowing I was concerned about my own well-being. After all, I never told the police about the threatening note from Balcombe, nor about the stolen car report he apparently orchestrated.

"You notice anything missing?" Thompson asked.

"No."

But two things struck me. There were no signs of forced entry. It was a professional job and they could get into my apartment or office as easily as they got into my car. Second, the place was a mess but it didn't appear anything was stolen.

Thompson must have concluded that as well.

"Looks to me as if someone was looking for something specific," he said. "You have any idea who it might be or what they are looking for?"

"You got me," I said.

"And soon they may get you, too, Blaise," Gregory said. A look from Thompson ended any other comment.

"What cases are you working, other than the Stephenson case, which, as I recall, we advised you to back away from?" Thompson said.

"Just a routine domestic case. A cheating hubby."

"At the Stephenson house last week, you said the attacker cleaned up the dining room where we found you. Took everything." Thompson said.

"That's right," I said.

"Perhaps he didn't get everything. Perhaps he thinks you kept something and are hiding it. Perhaps he thinks it's in your apartment," he offered.

"I don't have anything. I was attacked before I could even begin to think of taking anything," I said. "And if someone thinks I have something, I have no idea what it is. Besides, if they thought I had something, they'd probably communicate with me first, then break in. Wouldn't you think?"

Thompson rose and put away his notebook. "Our job here is done," Thompson said and headed for the door.

As he joined his partner, Gregory stopped and sneered at me. "Looks like you should get a different line of work, Mr. Private Investigator."

They collected the other officers and left me to clean up, which I didn't have the energy or the desire to do. Fortunately, Mrs. Findley was standing in the doorway.

"Would you close the door for me please," I said to her. "I need a little privacy."

"Oh, I almost forgot. Parker from across the hall said he found this this morning in the hallway. It's apparently for you," Mrs. Findley said, handing me a plain white envelope.

"Thanks," I replied, and she closed the door after her.

I opened the envelope to find a handwritten note.

Sorry I missed you this morning, Blaise. I tried your office, your apartment and even tried to catch you on Broad Street. I'll get you next time.

Again, it was unsigned.

With that, I put my head back on the couch and closed out the rest of the world for a while.

~*~

I straightened up some of the mess in the apartment with a promise to myself to finish the job in the evening. I didn't want Marie to see my apartment this way.

She called but I kept the conversation short. I didn't mention the break-in, of course. No sense in worrying a woman I'd like to spend the night with again. Knowing I had a break-in in my apartment might put a damper on things.

"When are you going to try to take your shirt off my back?" she said.

I laughed. Marie did have a way of making me smile.

"I thought you had school this afternoon or evening."

"I do, but later I'm free," Marie said.

"I got work to do. Maybe tomorrow we can talk."

Silence. Then, "Is this a brush-off?"

"Absolutely not," I said with an edgy cheerfulness in my voice. "You know you'll see me at least once more. You're wearing my favorite shirt."

Somehow, I knew she smiled.

I promised to call the next day and we hung up.

I drove back to the office mid-afternoon and Mae was already there.

"Where have you been? I've been calling you all day," she said. Then, more to herself than me, "Have me downtown doing stuff for you, making me promise to call you all the time, and you off gallivanting somewhere doing God Knows What. Probably with that new girl of yours."

"Mae, it's been a tough day for me. Just let me know what you got."

She stood over my desk with a notebook full of scribbles.

"Tough for *you*? I was the one who had to. . . ."

"*Mabelene, please!* What did you learn?"

"What's wrong with you?" She stomped her foot and tossed the notebook on the desk.

I knew we wouldn't get anywhere until I told her what had happened, and I needed someone to confide in. "I got pulled over this morning by the police for stealing my own car and someone broke into my apartment. I just got back in the office from home."

She sat down in the chair in front of my desk, concern showing on her face. "What? When?"

"The break-in? Sometime today. This morning, after I left," I said.

"Are you all right? I mean, you look okay, but was anything stolen? How did you find out?" she asked. "Nobody's hurt?"

"I'm fine. No one got hurt. No one was in the apartment at the time."

"Not even . . ." she said and stopped before she finished the question. "Good," she said in relief.

"My landlady called to say the police were there."

"Was anything taken?"

"Nothing that I can tell. The place was . . . is . . . a mess. But I didn't notice anything missing."

"Then what did they want?"

"Don't know."

"And what about the police. Why they stop you?"

"Routine, I think. They thought I was a different guy." I wasn't ready to tell her more, but I was ready to get back to business. "Now, tell me what you learned downtown."

She cleared her throat.

"Unit Three at 600 Rector Street is owned by a corporation called Branch Limited. Branch also owns Unit Four in the building, and I think some other properties in the city but I haven't been able to run all those down yet. Unit Three has a mortgage through a local bank, PSFS."

"Where is Branch Limited located?"

"The address is listed as a post office box at the Thirtieth Street Post Office. There's an escrow account at the bank and since the taxes are paid regularly and on time by the bank, there was no other information, other than the P.O. box, on the location."

I got up and walked around the desk, then turned back to look out the window.

"No record on who owns Branch Limited, I assume," I said as I looked out.

"No, there wasn't."

I turned back. "When was it purchased and for how much?"

"Now that is interesting. Unit Four was first purchased five years ago for a-hundred-and-ten-thousand dollars. Unit Three was bought only eighteen months ago for three-hundred-thousand," Mae said.

"The price of those properties has skyrocketed," I said. "But that whole area along the river in Manayunk is getting more and more popular. Prices were bound to increase."

I looked at Mae closely; she seemed different. More relaxed, despite having spent so much time in City Hall.

"You okay?" I asked.

"I got a call from Rita's lawyer who called the DA's office on my behalf. They dropped all the charges against me," she said.

I closed the distance between us and gave her a hug.

"That's great. What happened?"

"It was like you said. It was a set-up without police being directly involved. It would have been hard in court. So, they dropped the charges."

"That's wonderful." I said. "Now Mae, you got lucky this time. You started working for me because you said you wanted to get out of 'this business.' You have to decide, are you going to be a Ho or not? Because I can't keep bailing you out. I can't afford it."

"I know, I know. I promise, I'm through," she said. "And I will pay you back."

I waved my hand and shook my head to sidestep the topic. "I'm not worried about that. I'm just glad it's all over."

"Okay. But I have some other news that might interest you."

"Enlighten me." I moved back around my desk and sat down. Mae also took a less formal posture and sat down on the office couch.

"They finished the autopsy on the body found down the block from the MOVE house."

I raised an eyebrow and she knew she had my attention.

"They worked it up over the weekend," she said. "So, listen, he was shot in the chest and head. They pulled two thirty-eight slugs out of him. Same gun. They think he was shot at close range. No smoke in the lungs, so he was already dead at the time of the fire."

"That makes sense. He was shot in the head. That would have done it," I said.

"The body was badly burned, but they know he was a male, forties, maybe fifty, no identification on him and his clothes were burned up. They're assuming he was unmarried; he didn't have a ring. They're checking for dental records."

"Could they tell how long he'd been there?"

"Not with certainty, but they thought not long. Probably only a matter of days."

"How'd you get all this?"

She gave me a sexy, knowing smile. "I know someone in the Medical Examiner's Office."

"You don't mean . . . " I stopped and let it go. "Good work. Thanks. And, Mae, one more thing. Mookie says some white guy has been asking around about me. And with the break-in in my apartment, I think you should be more careful."

Mae headed out the door, stopped briefly as if thinking about something, then went to her desk. She returned with her purse. Mae fished through its depths and came up with a can of pepper spray, which she deposited on my desk, and some brass knuckles which she put on and demonstrated.

"I'm ready for any sorry-assed white man sneaking around here."

I grinned up at her. She was probably right. Because she scared the hell out of me.

CHAPTER XVIII

"Chico, set me up again. A double, this time."

After I closed and locked the office, wishing I had a bit more security, I headed downtown for drinks with my accountant at the restaurant called Bogart's. It was attached to the upscale Latham Hotel on the corner of 17th and Chestnut streets.

Bogart's was dark and intimate and generally not crowded. It wasn't, when I arrived. The bar was well-stocked with the best spirits and the service was outstanding, whether for drinks or for dinner.

My accountant, Leslie King, was one of the most punctual people I had ever met and he was already sitting at the bar when I arrived, only three minutes late. He had a glass with a dark, amber liquid inside. He liked his drinks neat.

"What can I get you?" asked the bartender as I pulled up a stool next to Leslie.

"A beer. Domestic. What've you got?"

"Miller?"

"That sounds good. And put it on his tab," I said, pointing a finger at Leslie.

The bartender left to get the beer as Leslie said, "I'm just going to bill you for it later, you know."

"And I'll write it off on my taxes, which you prepare. So it'll be a win-win for us both."

He shook his head in disbelief as the beer arrived, and we clicked bottle-to-glass in a salute.

"I need to know how off-shore accounts are set up," I said.

"You looking to go off-shore? Hide a little income from Uncle Sam?" Leslie said. "I'd advise against it."

"Why?"

"Because if you do any official business in the United States, the federal government will probably find you," he said, taking another sip and looking at the bartender. "Chico, set me up again. A double, this time."

He then turned his attention back to me.

"But, okay. It's simple. The Cayman Islands are a very popular destination right now. You can set it up in your own name or another name if you'd like. A dummy corporation, for example. You ship money down there into the account, either by wire from another account, or take it in person. And when you want the money, you have it wired back from the account."

"You can pay mortgages or taxes or deposit it into an account up here?" I asked.

"Definitely. It's a way of hiding the source of the income," Leslie said. "Criminals do it all the time. But like I said, Uncle Sam's looking to make sure taxes get paid. He's looking at the banks, where he can, and looking for wire transfers of taxable money. And if those taxes aren't paid, he's got you."

"But you can do it . . . hide income from someone else, say a spouse, who is unaware that the account exists," I said.

Leslie nodded. "Rich people, particularly rich men, do it all the time."

I downed the last of my beer and slid off the stool. "Thanks, pal. That's all I needed to know."

"You going already? You only had one."

"I got work to do."

"I understand." He was drinking too much too fast, and getting drunk. "Hey, we need to talk about your 1985 taxes."

"I'll make an appointment and come in," I said. As I reached the door, I said to myself, "Just not when you're drunk."

~*~

I had a headache as I headed home. It was stress-related, I was sure. The day had started well — waking up with Marie in bed — but it had been a hard day. My apartment door had a new lock, though I doubted it would make a difference, and all I wanted to do was grab a quick pizza and do nothing in front of the television.

As a bonus, I had some leftover pie from my Grammy Taylor's house.

I climbed the stairs, warm pizza box in one hand and door keys in the other, hoping not to have another interruption of my personal space.

No luck there. But fortunately, it wasn't my stalker.

Taped on the door just above the new lock was a SEPTA business card. In a very un-businesslike fuchsia ink, Clara had written, "Call me Re: Stephenson update." She added a telephone number, which I assumed was her home number because it wasn't the number printed on the card. I pulled the card off and stuck it in my pocket.

Perhaps facing the stalker in the close confines of my apartment building hallway would have been a better situation than calling Clara.

Once I was in the apartment, I placed the pizza on the kitchen table, and took two pieces from the box before heading back into the living room.

A light flashed on the answering machine. Four unanswered messages. I played them back. The last two were from Clara. I knew I couldn't deal with her now. The stress would be too much.

I ate the pizza and washed it down with Coke. Afterwards, I took a cold shower and headed to bed. I'd deal with Clara tomorrow.

CHAPTER XIX

Elise made it sound both sexual and dangerous

It was shortly after eight in the morning and I was already in the office trying to get an early start. If things were going as normal, Carmichael would just be arriving at work, having left home more than an hour earlier, so there wouldn't be a problem calling Elise at home. As I reached for the phone, it rang.

I was startled at first — I rarely got calls early in the day — but picked it up before the second ring.

And speak of the devil.

"Have you made any progress on my case, Mr. Blaise?" Elise asked.

Even in professional situations, I preferred being called David. Many times when someone called me "Mr. Blaise" they intended it as an insult, such as when Sgt. Gregory used it. Though I must admit, Marie made Mr. Blaise sound playful and sexual. Elise, on the other hand, made it sound both sexual and *dangerous*.

Fortunately, hearing it from her reminded me to stay on guard.

"Yes, I have, and I was about to call. But I'd rather not do this on the phone," I said, not mentioning my phone was probably bugged by the Henderson Group. "I could come up."

"No. I have a sorority meeting at the Hershey Hotel this morning. I could stop by your office on the way in. Say, at nine-thirty."

"Sounds great. See you then."

Mae arrived on time, but I decided not to mention that a client was coming in. No need to piss her off so early in the morning.

Elise had set the time, but showed up late, as if to remind me who was in charge and who was paying the bills. But when she arrived, even I was impressed with what she had on.

It was a Jersey print wrap dress intended to show off her figure. Once the observer, particularly a male observer, had admired her narrow waist and full chest, the expensive high-heel sandals would draw attention to her beautiful legs.

I wondered whether all women attending sorority meetings arrived in similar attire. If so, I'd consider crashing the party.

My office door was open when she arrived, and she glided past Mae's desk without slowing down and came to stand directly in front of mine.

"So, what have you got?" she said without preamble.

I rose and walked around the desk, indicating one of two chairs in front for her to sit in. I took the other.

"Elise, would you like something to drink? Coffee, perhaps?"

She paused at the question and looked at my open office door. Then she turned to me but spoke in a voice clearly loud enough for Mae to hear.

"I think I'll have coffee."

I called Mae in and, just as she entered, Elise changed subjects. She took a conversational tone, as if we were friends just sitting around gossiping.

"You know, I saw the nameplate on your desk which says your last name is Washington. Is that right?" Elise said to Mae, then took a quick glance at me and then back to Mae. "I read in the papers over the weekend that the police raided a whore house and arrested some poor prostitute named Mae Washington," she said, placing a lot of emphasis on the last name. Her focus sharpened on Mae as she continued, "Did you see that? I know it must have come as a shock that some *whore* had the same name as you. I feel so sorry for you, but it's such a common name you'd have to expect something like that."

Turning back to me, she said, "I know you would never hire someone who worked in this business. I don't see why anyone would degrade themselves like that. It's so distasteful and dirty." She spit the words out.

I could tell Mae was about to strangle Elise so I intervened. "If I remember correctly, Elise, you like your coffee with cream. Real cream."

"Oh, you delightful man. You remember everything," Elise said, flirting, reaching over to touch my arm.

"Not everything," Mae put in as she turned to leave. She shot me a glance over her shoulder when she reached the door.

"Now, what have you got for me?" Elise said.

"I have confirmed where his mistress. . . ."

"His slut," she interrupted.

". . . where Carolyn Adams lives. It's in Manayunk and it's a condo, which she doesn't apparently pay for. It, and another unit in the building, is owned by a shell company called Branch Limited."

"That son-of-a-bitch," she said with such vehemence it surprised and shocked me, forcing me back in my chair. "Branch is my maiden name. The bastard used my maiden name to hide money from *ME*. Boy, am I ever going to screw his butt to the wall and squeeze his balls in the divorce. Where *is* the money?"

"Elise, you need to hold on a minute," I said, trying to calm her down. "Branch is based in the Caymans and has a post office box in Philadelphia, but I don't yet know who owns the company. We have to take this one step at a time."

"No! I'm not going to calm down. I want my money. What's next, then?"

"I need to find out who owns the company and to whom money is transferred. There has to be an account somewhere," I said. "If I was him and I was hiding a separate account from you, I wouldn't necessarily use a different bank from what I used for our joint account. Where do you bank?"

"We've always banked at PSFS. It's the oldest bank in the city," she said off-handedly.

This is perfect, I thought. I could probably get the information I wanted at PSFS. Another bank would be infinitely more difficult.

"How many accounts do you have? Do you have the account numbers?"

"Of course I have the account numbers," she said. I could tell she was getting bored with me as she reached for her purse. I retrieved some paper and a pen from my desk. She handed me a small booklet from her bag that contained a place for all her account numbers. "There are two savings accounts . . . it is a savings bank, you know . . . and our checking account. We also have a couple of certificates of deposit, but I don't have those numbers."

"Don't worry. If they're at PSFS, I think I can find them," I said as wrote down the numbers, then handed the booklet back to her.

She looked at the Cartier Tank watch on her wrist and abruptly stood.

"I'm sorry, but you've taken up enough of my time. You're going to make me late," Elise said. She reached into her purse again and took out an envelope, thrusting it into my hands. "This should cover what you've done so far. There will be more, of course, when you have more information and you finish the job. Give me a call."

Elise left, passing Mae coming into my office as she exited. "Miss Washington," she said with a forced politeness. It was dismissive and was intended to be.

"That stupid, ignorant bitch," Mae said, spitting out the words as if they left a bad taste in her mouth. She slammed the coffee cups down with such force the lid partially came off and coffee spilled onto some of the papers on my desk. "I should snatch that fuckin' wig off that nappy-headed Ho and kick her pretentious, uppity black ass."

"Shhhh . . . Mae, please," I said, looking to make sure the front door was closed. "She's paying the bills."

"I don't care what that Ho's doing. I'm sick and tired of her black ass."

"You got some napkins to wipe this up?" I indicated the spill.

She got some napkins and cleaned up the mess.

"I bet the men love to tap that Ho's big ass. The uppity ones are always the freaks, believe me. And I bet you a hundred bucks the Ho does it for free."

I looked at Mae, snatching the wet napkins from her hands. It was one thing not to like the woman. I didn't particularly care for her. But it was another thing altogether to keep referring to her as a prostitute — and in the worst possible way.

"I understand your feelings toward our client, Mae, but I can't have you talking about her in that way . . . and using that tone . . . in the office." I threw the napkins into the trash.

"Why the *fuck* not? She's a Ho. Or at least used to be."

"What are you talking about? Elise Carmichael is not a . . . a, uh, prostitute."

"Yes she is. All Hos wear wigs. And that's a Ho's wig," she said.

"A lot of people . . . women . . . who are not prostitutes wear wigs for a variety of good reasons. Some like the look. Some wear them to cover thinning hair. Performers wear them. Some cancer survivors wear them. There are any number of reasons to wear a wig," I pointed out, re-arranging things on the desk.

"And being a Ho is one of them." Mae shook her head and visited me with an expression one might give a naïve child. "She all but said it to your face."

"Said what? What the *hell* are you talking about?"

"The bitch was trying to put me in my place with all that shit from the Inquirer. She knew it was me and she was calling me a Ho. And that's okay. I've been called worse," Mae said. "But she called it 'this business.' I have never heard anyone but a Ho refer to prostitution as 'this business.' *Never.*"

I stopped to think, walking to the window to look out. I saw Elise crossing the street, literally stopping traffic. Then I remembered. She had said, "I know you would never hire someone who worked in this business."

I didn't remember going back to my chair to sit down.

"See. What I tell you?" Mae said.

I looked up at Mae and finally began to think clearly. "Just because she used that terminology doesn't mean she *is* or *was* a prostitute," I said, as I weakly tried to convince myself. I put my elbow on the desk, and rested my chin on my left hand.

It was a long time before either of us spoke again. But finally Mae said, "You need me for anything else, boss?"

"No, that's okay." Mae was headed to her desk when I changed my mind. "On second thought, get my sister Valerie on the phone. Her number's on file. She works at the PSFS branch at 30th and Market. Across from the post office."

I took the El to 30th Street and walked to the bank. Valerie was a district branch manager for seven Center City bank branches. I just hoped Reuben Carmichael kept all his accounts at PSFS.

She greeted me at the front of the bank, then escorted me back to her office. It was glass-enclosed and looked out into the branch, but with the door closed, no one could tell what we were talking about.

On the telephone, I had played up how much she liked Marie. Then I hit Valerie with a request for help.

"I need this for an important divorce case I'm working on. It involves an innocent person's life."

I took some liberty, since it would be hard to justify Elise as any sort of innocent. But I knew it would take some buttering up because what I was asking my sister to do was in violation of bank policy, and perhaps the law. At the very least, it could get her fired. I certainly didn't want that, not least because Valerie's husband would then make life even more difficult for me.

"I can't believe I'm doing this, Davey," she said, sitting behind her desk. "Tell me what you need or what you're looking for."

I reached into my pocket for the paper with the information. I gave her Elise and Reuben Carmichael's names, plus the numbers of the accounts that I knew of. I asked that she search the bank's system for any accounts with either of their names.

The office filled with a clicking sound as Valerie's fingers flew over the computer keys. Within seconds, the first results appeared on a screen in front of her.

I rose from my chair to walk around the desk to stand behind her, but Valarie stopped me.

"Just stay there. I'll try to turn the screen a little," she said.

Seated in the chair, I leaned forward for a better view, resting my elbows on the desk, my fingers clasped together. The desk pressed uncomfortably across my chest. The screen showed a list of joint accounts and their balances, which were impressive. But then, he was one of the top trust attorneys in the city and she was a big spender.

"These are the accounts you gave me," she said, as she pointed to the screen. "Between all of these and the CDs — see them listed at the bottom — I'm surprised they carry that much in fluid assets, particularly since he's a trust attorney. That's more than three million. Granted these are all interest-bearing accounts, but he could earn more with this much money somewhere else."

"Perhaps he is," I ventured.

"Let me look for accounts under just his name."

There was that clicking sound again. And then something popped up.

"Humm. Interesting," Valerie said.

"What is?"

"Look here. He has a personal checking account without his wife's signature. It was opened two years ago under the name R.J. Carmichael."

"Can you check for activity?"

"Let me see," she said, and there was more typing. The screen quickly provided all the answers. "Humm. Interesting."

"What?"

"Look here," she said, again pointing. "He makes a deposit near the first day of each quarter and soon after wires funds from the account to an offshore account in the Cayman Islands. It appears the money is going to the First Cayman International Bank. I think that's on Grand Cayman Island."

She turned to look at me.

"Is this stuff even legal?" I asked.

"What's illegal about it? He has money here and he can move it to wherever he wants. There's no evidence the money was obtained illegally. But he probably is using it as some sort of tax shelter," she said.

I pulled out a notebook and wrote down the Cayman account number for future reference. "What is he doing with the money after it goes off-shore?"

"No way of knowing that. Banking officials in the Caymans may have some idea, but they're pretty tight-lipped about it down there," she said. "They'd only share it with our government, if really pressured."

Something caught my eye on the list of out-going checks. "What's that?" I asked.

"He's making regular monthly payments to some local company called The Henderson Group," she said. "What's The Henderson Group?"

I considered how much to tell her. In this case, best not to provide too much information.

"I think it's a security company," I said, and quickly steered the conversation in a different direction. "I need you to check on something else. Check to see if PSFS is holding a mortgage for something called Branch Limited, for a property on Rector Street in Manayunk."

"You really are asking a lot of me, you know?"

"Yes, but you love me and will do it anyway." I grinned.

Turning back to the computer screen, she said, "Don't bet your life on it, David."

More clicking, and it showed up.

"Yes. See here. Branch Limited of Philadelphia and, uh, the Cayman Islands, holds two mortgages at that address. One for Unit Four and one for Unit Three. Unit Four is nearly paid off. The payments are automatically paid on or near the first of each month from an account off-shore."

"Is it First Cayman?"

"Not sure, but probably. It's definitely from off-shore."

"How can I find out who owns that account in the Caymans?"

"To confirm it, you'd have to go to the federal government. The bank down there would require lots of identification to open the account but, like I said, they would be reluctant to share that information. The U.S. government wants its tax money, so if anyone knows, it's them."

"Thanks, sis," I said, standing and marching around the desk. I kissed the top of her head and then returned my chair to its rightful place.

"Yeah, right," she said, adding, "Don't let anyone know how you got that information." Then louder, as I was opening the door to her office, she said, "You can do no wrong in Grammy's eyes, now that you have a girlfriend. Too bad there's no telling how long that will last."

I rolled my eyes skyward and left. I didn't close the door.

CHAPTER XX

She collapsed to the floor in a heap.

I passed my local street watcher on the walk from the El to the office. He apparently didn't notice my approach. "Anyone poking around my office, Mookie?"

"It'z da private dick. Nuttin' happenin' taday," Mookie said.

He was in need of some serious dental repair but I guess his entrepreneurship's health plan didn't offer that to employees. I'd bet the only health plan he carried was a 45-caliber under the table. But there wouldn't be any co-pays.

I didn't stop to converse with Mookie after our brief exchange, which I completed while walking. He was a source of information, not a chum. Besides, hunger called. So I stopped in the Chinese takeout downstairs in my building and got beef fried rice in a white cardboard container. It was cheap, would be filling and what I didn't eat at lunch I could take home, though my stomach was saying that wouldn't happen today.

I debated whether to make a call to Thompson in the police department. I knew if I asked a favor, I'd have to give a favor and the only thing I had to exchange was a little information about Stephenson.

Mae was at lunch when I got to the office. I ate a few bites of the tasty rice before I gave in and picked up the phone to make the call. I was lucky. He was at this desk.

"Detective, this is David Blaise."

"Hello, Blaise," he said, a warmth in his voice. "What can I do for you?"

"I'm working a domestic case. A cheating husband. I mentioned that to you before. Apparently, the guy has an off-shore account and is paying his mistress's rent. He's paying her, too, I suppose. But I need some verification as to who owns the off-shore account."

There was a long pause on the other end of the line. "I don't know if I can get that sort of information. The department wouldn't handle anything like that. It's the feds."

"But you're my only hope," I confessed.

"What do I get in return?"

"I'll tell you everything I know about Stephenson."

He laughed. "I knew you were holdin' out on us," he said.

"It's not nearly as much as you might think."

"What do you need to know? And remember, I might not be of any help," Thompson said.

I told him about Branch Limited and provided the account number at the First Cayman International Bank and what I needed verified.

"So, what have you got on Stephenson?" he said.

I outlined all the stuff I had gathered: His apparent interest in a case at Georgia Central University back in the '60s regarding hookers, and that his calendar, which was missing, listed a meeting with someone with the initials LMS. "Any of this mean anything to you?" I asked.

"I'm at a loss," he said. "On that other thing, I'll get you what I can. But don't expect much."

The call ended just as Mae returned. And I was surprised. For once, she wasn't wearing anything one size too small.

She had a soft drink and was switching shoes, taking off sneakers and putting on a pair of black flats when I saw her. I placed both hands on the front of her desk and leaned forward. I didn't look directly at her. I was still thinking.

"Some time ago, you told me you used to, uh, date a guy who worked in the FBI," I finally said, looking at her.

"I did. But it's been a while. I'm not in this business

anymore, remember?" Mae scooted her chair all the way up to the desk, on which she placed both arms. Our faces were only inches apart. I straightened and walked back across the small office to take a chair against the wall opposite her desk.

"There's something I need to have confirmed, and the only option I can think of is with the feds. You think he might be able to help? Can you get in touch with him?"

Mae can be wicked even when she isn't being sexual. She had a wicked twinkle in her eyes as she pulled herself up to her desk. She crossed to the front and leaned back onto the desk. "What you need to know?"

"Hand me a piece of paper," I said. Mae turned and grabbed a pad from her desk and handed it to me. On it I wrote the Carmichael names, plus the name of the Cayman's bank and the account number. Then I handed it back. "I need to know who owns that account and what the account is used for."

"I gotcha," she said, taking the paper without looking at it.

She must have a lot of confidence in her contact to give me that assurance without even knowing what I needed to know. "Thanks, Mae."

I headed back to my office and as soon as I did, Mae was standing behind me in the doorway. "I found something for you."

"A headache?"

There was that wicked, naughty smile again. "You're gonna want to give me a raise for this."

"Only if you tell me something worthwhile. And you'd better tell me fast . . . before I kill you." I sat down behind my desk.

"I found Wilbur Stephenson's ex-wife."

"Oh my goodness," I said, leaping out of my chair. "I doubt I can afford to give you a raise, but a kiss? Definitely."

I went over and planted a smacker on her cheek. "Where is she? Somewhere in the South?"

"Honey Brook, in Chester County."

"Chester County? Pennsylvania?" I said, backing up and propping a hip on my desk. "You sure?"

"Positive. And I got an address and a phone number."

"Where in the world is that? I've never heard of it."

"Somewhere past Exton. I got directions," she said.

"Thanks. How'd you find her?"

"I checked the divorce records in South Jersey. Thought she might have changed back to her maiden name. Oliver. That's not an improvement over Stephenson, but what can I say," Mae said. She walked completely into the office and stood in front of me. "Since I couldn't find her in Jersey, I checked Philadelphia and the Pennsylvania suburbs. And there she was."

"Excellent work. You sure it's the right one?"

"Positive."

A scary thought entered my mind. "You didn't call her or anything, did you?"

"Of course not," she said, backing away, a bit of anger or disappointment in her voice. I wasn't sure which.

"I'm sorry, Mae. I just needed to make sure before I take my next step," I said, trying to smooth things over. "But great work. Thanks."

Mae turned and headed back to her office. Silent but smug, she returned a moment later with the information on Stephenson's ex-wife.

I called the home phone number. I didn't know what I would say, but it wouldn't be that I was a private detective. There was no answer.

I examined the directions to her house. It looked to be quite a haul out to her place. But if I got her, I'd be at least one step ahead of the police. And if I found Stephenson before Gregory, I definitely planned to gloat.

I checked the time. I had dinner plans with Marie after her class and didn't want to break them, or she'd really think I was brushing her off. I'd head up to Honey Brook and if

Stephenson's ex wasn't home, I'd wait until she showed up, if I had the time. With luck, she might have some clue to Stephenson's whereabouts. If I was truly lucky, I might find him hiding out with her. That would be idiotic, but people sometimes did idiotic things.

~*~

Christina Oliver, the former Mrs. Wilbur Stephenson, didn't really live in Honey Brook, wherever that was. She lived in one of five old houses clustered together in extreme Chester County in Wallace Township. It was down the road from a century-old church, and an hour's drive from Center City Philadelphia, including nearly fifteen minutes on the Pennsylvania Turnpike. Once off the turnpike, I hit the back roads, driving past cemeteries, old farmhouses, tranquil fields and the occasional lake. I was so focused on finding Wilbur Stephenson I didn't have time to enjoy the view.

I inadvertently passed Oliver's house, not knowing I had reached it until too late. So I decided a bit of surveillance of the area was in order and turned around at the corner.

It was difficult to gauge the age of the houses. All were two-story, detached homes with a porch. Most of the surrounding area was farmland, but there were these five houses, probably built around the same time. Early twentieth century, was my best guess.

There was no sidewalk in front of the houses, only a small gravel strip where a sidewalk might otherwise be. A late model red Chevy pick-up truck sat in front of the house bearing Oliver's address. I parked — there was plenty of space — and walked up to the front door. I could hear a Helen Reddy song coming from inside the house. I listened for a moment, then knocked on the door and waited.

A woman, perhaps forty and attractive in her own way, opened the front door but left the outer screen door closed. She had an average build with just the beginnings of flab in the middle. And though her dishwater blond hair hung limp past her shoulders, there was still a chance some lonely middle-aged man would take a liking to her. That chance, however, was fading by the minute.

"May I help you," came a sweet Southern drawl from her razor-thin lips, which were painted an unusually bright shade of red.

"My name is David Blaise, ma'am. Are you Christina Oliver?"

"Yes," came the tentative reply. She didn't smile.

"I'm a private investigator from Philadelphia and I'd like to ask you a few questions about your former husband, Wilbur Stephenson."

"What's he done now?" she said, resting her weight against the door jamb to further block me.

"Hasn't anyone . . . the police . . . contacted you?"

Concern raced across her face. It made the lines appear more pronounced, and she looked older.

"No," she said, straightening up. "No one's said anything to me."

"Your ex-husband is missing."

She collapsed to the floor in a heap.

~*~

I stepped in past the door without thinking.

With a degree of difficulty, I was able to lift her into my arms and carry her to a couch in what was a very modest living room. I dampened some paper towels in the kitchen sink and wiped her forehead with them.

In time, her eyes fluttered open and she recoiled when she saw me sitting on the edge of the couch with her. But the panic quickly receded as memory kicked in.

"Are you all right? Would you like me to get you some water?" I asked.

Slowly, she sat up on the couch, straightened her dress and moved her legs to the floor. She was hunched over but shook her head no. Finally, she looked me in the face.

"You said Wil's missing?"

"Yes. It's been over a week."

"Do you know what happened to him?"

I shook my head *no*. "I was hoping you might be able to help me."

She got up and headed for the kitchen. "Maybe I *do* need something to drink."

I stayed put and soon heard water from the faucet filling a glass. She called from the kitchen. "Would you like some water or maybe some sweet tea?"

"No, thank you, ma'am. I'm fine."

When she returned with a glass full of water, she sat in a chair across the room from me, again straightening her dress for modesty's sake. She was quiet for more than a minute. I dared not say anything as she apparently considered what to say next.

"I told that damned fool he was making a mistake. But he's never listened to me about anything."

"A mistake? What mistake?"

"He was trying to make some extra money, saying I was sucking him dry." Looking from one corner of the room to the other, she said, "Does it look like I'm living in the lap of luxury? I don't think so. I can't help it if he blows all his cash down at the shore. I only want what's rightly mine from our marriage."

"How was he going to make extra money?"

"He was doing some freelance security work when he ran into *that* woman," she sneered, scratching her leg just below the knee.

"What woman?" I shifted my weight on the couch and crossed my legs.

"The same hooker he got mixed up with back in college."

"When was that?" I asked, and instantly remembered the newspaper article I took from his dining room table.

"Senior year. I think he's sleeping with her again, and he's gonna try to get some money out of her."

"Who is it?" I asked, hoping I didn't sound too impatient.

"Oh, I almost forgot," Christina said, getting up and walking over to a desk where she pulled a folder out of a drawer. "He told me months ago, if anything ever happened to him, I should go to the police with this."

She handed me the folder and immediately an old black and white picture fell out and onto the floor. Christina picked it up, looked at it with disgust and then handed it to me.

"That's her. Lula Mae Stobe was her real name, though Wil had a sex name for her. I can't remember that, now."

The woman in the clear black-and-white picture was on her knees in the middle of a circle of three white young men that included Stephenson. The men didn't have on any pants and the woman wasn't wearing anything but panties, and those were on her thighs halfway to her knees. It was clear she was about to engage in some sexual activity, and apparently with all three men.

She was shapely, with a thin waist and round, firm breasts that were disproportionately large for a woman with her frame. The face in the photograph was pretty, with fine cheekbones and full lips. She wore her hair in a thick, full Afro, which was in keeping with the style of the time. Unembarrassed, she smiled for the camera.

And, though older now, there was no mistaking Elise Carmichael in the picture.

~*~

I thanked Christina for the information and quickly got on my way, letting her know I'd be in touch if I found Stephenson. My mind was in such turmoil I could barely drive. Again, Elise Carmichael, a.k.a. Lula Mae, had lied to me. She doled out the truth as if it were as scarce as water in the middle of the desert. And she was involved in both major cases I was working. I could barely think of where to go next.

At a pay phone at a gas station on Route 100 just before the entrance to the Turnpike, I called the office. Mae had stayed late and was about to leave. Thompson had not called, but she had talked to her FBI friend.

The account in the Cayman Islands was listed as belonging to a company called Branch Limited, and Branch was solely owned by Reuben Carmichael of Philadelphia, Pennsylvania, U.S.A. The account paid the mortgages on several properties, including the ones in Manayunk, and there was a monthly stipend to an account in First Pennsylvania Bank for Carolyn B. Adams.

She was well taken care of.

By the time I reached the city, it was time for my pizza dinner with Marie. I was still shaken, but seeing Marie's face momentarily erased all thought of the cases.

We went to a pizza joint on Henry Avenue only about a mile from the campus. It was cloudy and warm outside. Rain was in the forecast.

It fit my still sour mood.

We ordered a cheese pizza, but I got sausage and mushrooms on half. I tried to pay attention to her as she discussed her day and the progress of her class, but I had a lot on my mind. Focusing on the present was problematic. I planned to start the next day with a difficult meeting with Elise Carmichael. Where that led would determine what I planned to do after that.

But Clara was also lurking in the back of my mind.

"Am I boring you, David?" Marie asked.

"Uh, no," I said sharply, returning to the conversation. "Sorry. What were you saying?"

"It doesn't matter what I was saying. You aren't interested," Marie said, sounding wounded or maybe sad, I couldn't tell which.

"Marie. I'm truly sorry. I've had one hell of a day and tomorrow promises to be a bear. I know I should leave my worries at the office. I'll do better. I promise."

Marie just looked intently at me.

"David," she said, "I understand. Really. But you can be so myopic. You focus on the task ahead so intently that you miss other equally important information."

She reached forward and took my hands. It was one of the first truly affectionate and personal things she had done. She could be extremely sexual, yes. But emotionally, she was reserved, holding back her true feelings.

I assumed it was because she didn't want to move too fast, to advance to a point beyond our having a lot of good sex. Then there was this one small gesture.

"It was just like when we met. You were so focused . . . first on me, then on finding a telephone. You totally missed that you were being followed. Clear your head and take in other things. You'll be better off for it."

I smiled. She was quite beautiful. And she was right.

"I'll try. I promise," I said. "You want to head over to my apartment after we eat?"

"Won't I be a distraction?" she asked seductively."I hope so. It's a distraction I need."

CHAPTER XXI

"The truth? That's rarely all men want."

I heard someone scream, "No!" and sat up straight in bed. Perspiration beaded my forehead and rolled down my bare chest. At first, I wasn't sure where I was or what time it was. An instant later, two facts settled in my brain. I wasn't alone, and I was the one who had screamed.

It was ten minutes to three in the morning and my bedroom was still dark. I heard rain pelting the windows. Marie was sitting up in bed, apparently keeping a silent vigil over me since before I woke up screaming.

"You all right, David?" she said, moving toward me. She reached for my head. "You're hot."

Though I probably shouldn't have, I shook my head no, brushing aside her concerns without a word. I swung my legs off the bed and headed for the bathroom. In the dark, I turned on the cold water and reached for a wash cloth. I dampened it and wiped the sweat off my body.

When I returned to the bedroom, a bedside lamp was on and I could see Marie sitting cross-legged on the bed wearing my over-sized Sixers jersey.

"I'm sorry. . . ." I couldn't think of anything else to say.

"It's okay." She didn't say anything more for a few seconds, apparently uncertain of what to say or do next. But then a solution must have come to her. "Who's Clara?"

"*Clara*? How . . . how do you know about her?"

"You mumbled her name a lot in your sleep. Then you

shouted and woke up. I thought it must be something about her."

I knew this conversation would likely come sooner or later. I had hoped later.

"She," I said and stopped, searching for the right words. ". . . is part of my past."

"Apparently, not that far in the past, since you're still talking about her in your sleep," Marie said. "She must have been important. Why haven't you mentioned her before?"

The question was a minefield I wasn't ready to enter. This wasn't my first night with Marie and I hoped it wouldn't be the last. But I still wasn't ready to answer the question.

I walked around to the other side of the bed and sat, facing Marie.

"It's complicated," I said.

Marie returned my stare, saying nothing. We both knew the next few moments might determine whether our relationship would continue.

"Whatever you have inside bothering you, David, you can't keep it there forever," Marie said. Reaching behind my head, she pulled me forward and tenderly kissed my forehead. Then she turned and clicked the switch off on the bedside lamp, throwing the bedroom back into darkness.

Marie laid down on her back with the bedding pulled up to her neck, and her hands clasped across her chest, as if she were protecting herself. She didn't speak again and I couldn't tell if her eyes were open or shut. But within five minutes I had my answer. The room filled with the soft, rhythmic sound of her snoring.

I didn't sleep well, and was wide awake listening to the rain pitter-patter against the windows when the alarm went off at seven. In a complete deviation from my normal weekday routine, I decided to go for a run. I nudged Marie awake, not wanting to run out on her without saying something first. She got up and dressed.

"You don't work this morning. You don't have to leave. You should stay and get a little more sleep."

"Well, I have some studying to do and it would be better to do it in my own apartment," she said as she reached the door. "I'll talk to you later."

There wasn't much else I could say. When she closed the door to my apartment I wasn't sure if she was also closing the door on me.

I got my shoes, light running shorts and a t-shirt and hit the pavement. It was seasonably warm but the rain felt cold as it pelted my skin. It was bracing.

I ran down to Penn, through the campus and back. Of course, I was dripping wet from the rain and from sweat when I returned, but my head was clearer. I was beginning to get a handle on my cases and my personal life.

I showered and shaved, made breakfast and ate, then called Elise Carmichael with news that I had information on her case. I found a trail of money to an off-shore account that was transferred back into the country and into accounts she knew nothing about. I thought she'd be happy with the progress in the case, but she balked when I told her I'd be there by ten in the morning.

I stopped by the office for some paperwork then headed up the Lincoln Drive to the Carmichael's house on Sedgwick. When I arrived, Elise opened the door, as stunning as ever. She had on a tight, black, knee-length skirt and a sheer white blouse over a white camisole. She wore a black head band that pulled her dark hair off her face.

What she didn't wear was a smile.

"Come in, Mr. Blaise," was all she said. She apparently decided to display her displeasure with me by adopting a very formal countenance. After all, I had the nerve to call this meeting, not her.

I followed her once again into the library. It looked as it was before, all the way down to the crystal decanter with water and four glasses. She sat in a chair with a small table between us and crossed her legs in a slow, calculated way intended to draw my attention to their shapeliness.

I held a folder on my lap.

"Your husband is having an affair," I said, "but we've covered all that. He owns two condos in the building in Manayunk where Carolyn Adams lives, including, of course, her property. She also gets a monthly stipend from him.

"All the money, it appears, is funneled through an account at the First Cayman International Bank on Grand Cayman Island. After money is transferred from off-shore back to the United States, the mortgage and taxes are paid through an account solely in his name at PSFS. Adams gets money paid directly to an account at First Pennsy."

She sat erect with a smug, superior attitude, although I had just outlined in some detail the failings of her marriage and, by extension, of her personal life. But I was not finished.

"I told you I cannot stomach you lying to me."

I opened the folder and took out the black and white picture I received from Christina Oliver, handing it to Elise. Her eyes went wide when she saw it and the smugness melted away, replaced with shock, then horror.

"But you lied to me, Elise. Or should I call you Lula Mae?" I asked.

"Where did you get this?" she softly demanded, though not giving the picture back. Her body slumped into her chair and she just stared at the photograph.

"Where's not important. What is important is I have it," I said.

"Wilbur Stephenson," she said, without further comment. Though she was shaken, some of her confidence was coming back. She got up and walked around, finally coming to a stop about five feet in front of me. "What do you want from me? Money? Sex?"

Money and sex must be one and the same with her. But I wanted neither, at least not from her.

"All I want is for the lying to stop. I want the truth."

"The truth?" she said, spitting it out. "That's rarely all men want." Elise dropped the picture on the table beside me and she sat again.

Then she told me the story.

CHAPTER XXII

"As a light-skinned black woman, I was popular."

For the first time since I met Elise, she looked tired. Always composed and in control, she seemed confused and unfocused. It was as if she was barely present. When she spoke, I realized she probably wasn't.

"I was fourteen the summer prior to entering high school," she said, her hands on her lap and her feet about a foot apart and flat on the floor. "I lived in Montgomery, Alabama. Daddy worked in the mill. Momma was a domestic. I didn't see her a lot during the week. She stayed in the white folks' house. My older brother was already in the Army by then. He made it a career."

Elise looked at me for the first time, as if she had forgotten I was there. She ran her hand through her hair and continued.

"We had family all over the South . . . on farms and whatnot . . . but a lot of folks moved to Atlanta, including my daddy's younger brother, Otis."

She looked in my direction again. Though she was more composed, I wasn't sure she was talking to me. "Uncle Otis was fine. I mean *really* fine. Uh-wee, he was a glory to the eyes."

Elise held up her hands and examined both the front and back.

"He was light. Had my complexion and skin color. Light brown eyes and was as handsome as he could be. Wore his wavy hair pulled back," she said, finally addressing me again.

"And he was a sharp dresser . . . sharp as a tack . . . and a smooth talker. He could charm the clothes off any woman. And he often did."

Elise reached over and poured herself a glass of water from the decanter on the nearby table. She took a long sip. I assumed it all was a way of stalling. She said, without looking at me, "I don't know why I'm telling you all this."

"You must want to get it all off your chest." I folded my arms and waited. She resigned herself and resumed.

"Daddy and Uncle Otis disagreed a lot, like on how a real man should handle himself. There was tension between them. Daddy believed in hard physical labor and protecting his family . . . Momma, me, my brother. Uncle Otis believed in hustling. But he was so good at it.

"Uncle Otis was about thirty when I was fourteen. He was married to a woman from up North. Her name was Elise Branch," she said.

I had been studying a painting on a far wall but I looked up. "Elise Branch?"

"It's how I got this name," she said. "You already know my birth name."

"Aunt Elise was a brassy, flirtatious woman, just the sort Daddy and Momma hated. Like I said, I was fourteen, and she and Uncle Otis came down from Atlanta to a family picnic. It was in mid-July, as I recall, and it was bright and sunny and warm. The grass on my cousin's farm outside Montgomery was soft under my feet and the air smelled sweet. I had blossomed into a woman's body since I saw Uncle Otis last, which was a couple of years. When he saw me, his jaw dropped."

Elise sat up straight, which tended to force her chest out.

"I finally had developed breasts and I loved the attention I got from the boys and even more so from grown men." It was probably all she could do to keep from running her hands over them. I swallowed hard and kept my hands on my thighs.

"Go on," I said.

"Uncle Otis flirted with me when no one was looking, and I flirted back. He asked if I had a boyfriend and I said 'yes.' And he asked if I had let him do anything to me, like touch me. I giggled, and said a little touching. But I made him promise not to tell my parents."

I squirmed in my seat and could feel blood rushing to my face. I could almost tell what was next, and it would be both personal and embarrassing. "You don't have to do this if it's too painful," I said.

"I never talk about it. That's what makes it painful," Elise said. "Just before it got dark, he asked me if I wanted to make a little money. We were poor and I never had any money, so I said 'yeah.' We went out to the barn when no one was watching and he showed me five bucks.

"'Let me see your tits,' Uncle Otis said. I was surprised because he was so direct. I didn't move at first," Elise said. "But here was this fine, smooth-talking man who just wanted to see something for some cash. I had already let boys see them . . . sometimes even touch them . . . for free. What was the harm? I lifted up my shirt and pulled up my bra."

Elise looked toward the door to the library, as if someone was coming who might hear. I followed her gaze but there was no one. I returned my attention to my client.

"Uncle Otis looked around quickly, then turned back to me and said, 'Take your top and bra off.' And I did. He examined me with a cool detachment I came to better understand later. I wasn't a person to him, just something with breasts."

I alternated between rubbing my forehead for a headache that hadn't developed yet, although I was sure it would, and stroking the beard on my chin, although I was clean-shaven.

"'Nice tits. Better than I thought. Here,' he said, pulling out two fives." Elise said. "He didn't touch me. Didn't even try. He just gave me the money and walked out. Over the next couple of years, he'd give me more money to see my breasts.

"There was a great deal of civil unrest down South back then. Things were particularly nasty in Alabama. Daddy wanted me to get out of Montgomery when I graduated from high school. He said I should attend a small college somewhere else in the South, but I wanted a big city, like Fisk in Nashville or Spelman in Atlanta. He was adamant and said no."

Elise abruptly got up and walked around, aimlessly. The memory must have been difficult.

"Daddy was the head of a local gun club in the NAACP. The club was there to protect us, and he had several guns in the house. My daddy was big and strong and had broad shoulders. The whites down there hated him," she said.

Elise stopped pacing and turned to face me.

"One night my mother was walking home from work and was run over and killed by a drunken white man. He left the scene and left Momma lying in the street. It was only a block from our house," Elise said, hands on her hips. Then her voice rose. "Daddy was incensed. There was a rage I hadn't seen before. It was an accident, but my daddy didn't care. He said the man wouldn't have been so careless if it was in a white neighborhood. So Daddy got his gun, went out, found out who the guy was and shot him."

She stopped. I wanted to say something but couldn't break the silence. Elise stood, motionless.

"The killin' caused an uproar and the police came lookin' for him. They were going to charge him with murder. Daddy hid out somewhere, then left for New York. He said he'd come get me later. But the FBI was after him, too, because he had fled the state. So he escaped to Canada. When the FBI heard he was in Canada, they notified authorities there, and the Mounted Police searched for him, too. He left Canada for Cuba, the only place in this hemisphere where the U.S. government couldn't get him."

She stopped again and grabbed her glass of water. When she put it back with the other three, she said, "He never returned and I never saw him again. He died of cancer in Cuba while I was in college."

Elise walked around again, stopping at the bookshelf and running her finger along the spines of numerous books. She selected one and pulled it out. After checking the front and back covers, she put it back. I wasn't sure which book she picked.

"By the time I finished high school," she said without looking at me, "I was homeless. I lived with neighbors most the time. But I got accepted to Morris Brown in Atlanta and I moved there with Uncle Otis and Aunt Elise, my only family," she said, looking at me again. "What I didn't know was that they were both in the sex trade."

"But you didn't have to do that," I interrupted.

She frowned at me but stayed where she stood. "What choice did I have? I had no past. No place to go. I was homeless. Without them, I'd be on the street. What was I to do?"

Elise walked over to the desk and opened a wooden box. Without offering one to me, which would have been polite even if she was sure I'd decline, Elise took out a cigarette. She used a large, silver cylindrical lighter. She inhaled as deeply as I had ever seen, drawing the smoke into her lungs and exhaling the bluish-gray smoke from both her mouth and nose. It brought to mind a dragon, breathing fire. But it seemed to relax her.

"They lived in Decatur, an upscale area south of downtown Atlanta. As soon as I got there, Uncle Otis wanted to see my tits but he also started touching and feeling them. He said they couldn't afford to support me and I'd have to do something to support myself. He said sex was the way to do it. They ran an elite escort service out of their house and could use another girl, particularly a pretty, light-skinned black girl.

"I wasn't a virgin and it was my way out. I agreed," she said.

Going over to the couch, Elise sat down and crossed her legs, casual and relaxed. Her arm was perched over the side arm of the couch and she held the cigarette in a way that almost dared an ash to drop. She threw her head back and blew out the smoke, which formed a cloud about her head.

Elise spoke as if we were old friends and it was the most mundane of subjects.

"Uncle Otis took me into one of the bedrooms to have sex with me. He didn't rape me or anything like that, but he fucked me for three days straight. He said he was training me in how to satisfy my clients. And Uncle Otis wasn't the only one. Elise slept with me, too, because she was into that sort of thing. It was also her job to teach me how to walk, talk, act and dress like a high-priced call girl."

She leaned forward and flicked ashes from the tip of her cigarette into an ashtray on the coffee table.

"I didn't mind it. I didn't feel degraded. Or used. Or abused. It was a job I decided to take and I learned how to do the job well," she said, again taking a small bit of tobacco from her tongue.

"I always hated the name Lula Mae. In college I introduced myself as Elise Branch. As a sex name, I just used Kitty. Aunt Elise was also light-skinned and her name was Kat. So when we worked together, which we did a lot, we were Kitty Kat.

"There's a lot of money in Atlanta, both black and white. Uncle Otis had white and black clients and started arranging dates for me. I enjoyed it. The attention, the money. I enjoyed turning men on . . . and the occasional woman . . . and satisfying them. Plus, I was paying for my own college education. That required money. I liked school, enjoyed the excitement and the sex, and I really loved the money.

"Despite school, I was quite busy," Elise said. "Next to white women, the black men clients liked light-skinned black women best. And white men who wanted a black woman generally felt threatened by a dark one. So as a light-skinned black woman, I was popular with them, too."

She inhaled the last of the cigarette as if it were the last breath she'd ever take. It was long and deep. Blowing the smoke into the room, Elise rose and went to the desk, where she smashed the cigarette butt in an ashtray. She leaned back onto the desk.

"It went on for a couple of years and I never had any trouble. Not once," she said. "Then, in the spring of my junior year, I was at a fraternity party at Morehouse. There wasn't any sex. It was just a college party. And that's where I met Reuben."

Elise rocked back and forth against the desk, staring up toward the ceiling on the far end of the room, as if a happy memory were coming from there.

"We hit it right off. He was shy and considerate, and he treated me well. Like a person. Most men looked at me and wanted me. It was all about sex. But Reuben was different," she said, finally drawing me back into her attention. "He liked to dance . . . do you like to dance?"

I didn't have a chance to answer before she continued.

"We went a lot to this cheap little restaurant near campus. And he always paid. Wouldn't even let me offer to pay. I had plenty of money, of course, but I couldn't let him know that. He didn't run in the sort of circles that included call girls, so he didn't know that about me."

A harshness returned to her voice. "Uncle Otis thought it was funny that I was dating, and insisted that I not let it interfere with work. That summer, Reuben went home to Philadelphia, but we wrote each other a couple of times a week. We even talked long distance once or twice. And when he got back on campus in the fall, we started seeing each other again. And that's when all hell broke loose."

Elise walked back around to the couch across from me and flopped down, a certain angry resignation to the gesture. She had gotten another cigarette but hadn't lit it.

"Some frat boys over at Georgia Central were trying to help some of the football players. And these good ol' white boys loved black girls, if they weren't too dark. They got in touch with Otis and told him what they wanted. He arranged for a couple of group sex parties at frat houses that fall, and I went to a couple," she said, crossing her legs again. "Plus, I connected with one or two players individually. Privately. I had done that over the years a couple of times without telling Otis or Elise. It was cash and I didn't have to share it. They were my special clients. One of them was Wilbur Stephenson."

I was fascinated and wanted to ask her how she met Stephenson but didn't dare interrupt her. She was now on a roll and I didn't want to knock the train off the tracks. I just listened, my hands a little sweaty for some reason.

"The night everything blew up, I was supposed to be at a frat party but was on a date with Reuben. Everybody got arrested and within a couple of days, police shut down the escort service. Uncle Otis and Aunt Elise got arrested but promised to keep my name out of it. And they did, for the most part.

"They dropped the charges against her. I always suspected it was because she had slept with most of the police and prosecutors, or their wives, and they wanted to avoid the embarrassment. Uncle Otis got out on bail, at which point he skipped town. Elise left, too."

Elise stared into the space between us, as if it somehow would provide some clarity. Once again, I felt invisible to her.

"I had some funds to fall back on after they left, so I survived my last year. And I also did occasional sessions with Stephenson. But after the end of the school year, I told him it was over. He begged me to stay, to keep seeing him. I refused. I had sex with him for the last time the night before I got married. And for once, I didn't charge him."

Finally, she looked at me again. Easing forward, with her arms on her thighs to support her upper body, she said, "I never told Reuben about any of this. No one really knows even to this day. We got married, went on our honeymoon and moved to Philadelphia because he was enrolled at Penn Law School. He graduated with honors, got a good job with a top law firm in the city and we stayed here. I decided to start fresh. I had a college degree, some sophistication and, after Reuben finished law school and got a job, I didn't work. The past was the past and would stay there."

~*~

"So what happened?" I asked, amazed that she had been so forthcoming and intimate. It was a first for her, at least with me it was.

"Nothing happened at first. Reuben and I got along well. But in time, we grew apart. Reuben was working all the time, first trying to make partner, then trying to build up the practice. It got so we hardly communicated."

"And that's when the affair started?"

"No. Perhaps. I don't know," she said in rapid succession as if considering each quickly, and dismissing it.

"Tell me about Wilbur Stephenson."

She got up and walked around the room. It was a delaying tactic, I was sure, allow her to collect her thoughts and check her emotions.

Finally, she faced me again.

"I knew him back in college. He was a jock. We had . . . a thing back then. But it was all over once I finished school and married Reuben. I told him that."

"How'd Stephenson find you here?" I said.

"Totally by accident. By chance. I didn't communicate with him after I left college and moved north. That life was behind me. I don't know if he looked for me, but I assumed he had moved on like I had. He didn't know where I was," Elise said.

She walked over to the books and ran her finger along the shelf as if looking for dust. Another delaying tactic.

She turned back to face me.

"Reuben and I attended a charity event for CHOP . . . Children's Hospital of Philadelphia . . . I don't know when, sometime early last year, I think. Wilbur was handling some security at the event. He saw me and came up to both of us. I had to introduce him as a friend from college because Reuben was standing there. After that, Wil knew I lived in Philadelphia and knew my last name. It didn't take much for him to find me."

"And did he?"

"Yes. A couple of days later. I didn't want to see him but he insisted. I finally agreed. I shouldn't have, but by then I was beginning to starve for attention," she said.

Elise turned her back to me and looked out the window as if doing so would help provide some answers.

I waited.

"So I met him for lunch and then, once when Reuben wasn't around, for dinner. It was then he pressured me for sex. I resisted, said no, but I finally gave in."

"Does your husband know?"

She turned back to me with a fierce expression on her face. "No. He never seems to pay that much attention. And I wouldn't have ended up being blackmailed if he knew."

"Blackmailed?"

"Yes. Wil started asking me for money. A little at first and then more and more. Finally, he threatened to tell my husband, ruin me socially, if I didn't give him money."

"And you did."

"Yes. About ten grand I had been hoarding."

"Your husband didn't know you had that money?"

Elise shook her head. She went back to the chair across the small table from me and slumped back into it. This personal session was taking a toll on her and it was beginning to genuinely show.

"I knew Reuben would find out sooner or later. It was just a matter of time. That's why I came to you."

"*Me*? I don't understand."

"My marriage is already in shambles, headed for divorce. What you learned about Reuben's finances proves he knows it too," Elise said. "I wanted to get something strong on Reuben so I'd have more leverage for a settlement. And I need a settlement, because I haven't worked since Reuben's last year in law school. I have no idea how to support myself."

"You had me look up dirt on your husband, hoping it would mitigate whatever he would get on you?"

"Crass, but true."

I narrowed my eyes and took a deep breath. It got her attention. "There's a problem. Wilbur Stephenson is missing."

Elise looked genuinely surprised, sitting up straight in her chair. "What? When?"

Now it was my turn to be surprised. "You didn't know?"

"How *would* I know?"

I had to remind myself of her propensity for lying. "When was the last time you saw him?"

"Couple of weeks ago. He's always the one who contacts me."

"Where'd you see him?"

She hesitated for a heartbeat and a half before giving a vague answer. "Somewhere in the city."

I stopped to think. Before I was attacked in Stephenson's house, I saw his calendar, which indicated meetings with LMS. Clearly, LMS was Elise Carmichael. But there was something else. There was a missing piece and I was sure she was lying, or at least holding something back.

My throat was dry and I reached for my glass of water when it hit me. There were four water glasses with the decanter. There'd only been three the first time I was at the house, which struck me as odd back then. It was a set and there should have been more glasses.

Then it hit me.

This high-ball glass was among the items I originally saw on Wilbur Stephenson's dining room table. It was the missing glass from this set. It left a water stain on some of his papers, but was gone by the time police arrived.

I looked at her but didn't share any of my thoughts. I could be in the presence of a killer. She had the opportunity to kill Stephenson, and certainly the motive. But I needed the evidence to prove it, and I needed to get it fast.

"The police haven't come to talk to you about Stephenson?"

"No. Why would they?"

"Weren't you listening? He's missing. And you recently saw him. It was near the time of his disappearance," I said.

"But so have lots of other people, I would assume."

"He wasn't blackmailing them," I countered.

There was a silence between us as she considered. She was a cunning and calculating woman. And in some perverse way it was interesting to watch her mentally work out her next move.

"Frankly, I got lucky finding the connection between you and Stephenson, but it won't be luck with the police," I said. "They'll find it just like I did and come to ask you questions. And they'll expect better answers than you've given me."

Again she hesitated. She seemed to quiver with uncertainty. Or was that an act for my benefit?

"I don't know where Wil is. I didn't do anything to him. You have to believe me, David. Please. You have to believe me," she reached out as if to touch my hand. "Will you . . . go to them? Tell them what I've told you? Make that connection for them?"

I hadn't considered it yet. She was a client and there were privacy issues. But I also didn't want to be an accessory to a crime. I certainly didn't want to commit a crime for a client who has lied to me often and who was trying to manipulate me now.

"I can't keep this secret from the police. It might be relevant to an on-going investigation," I said.

She let that sink in for a minute and appeared to reach a decision.

"All right. I'll go to the police. But you have to let me do it in my own way and in my own time."

"Don't take long."

"How long do you think I have?"

"You should go tomorrow."

"Will you go with me?"

"No. But you should take a lawyer with you."

After I left the house, I considered calling Clara to tell her I had made a big breakthrough in finding Stephenson. But I wanted to wait until after Elise went to the police. She promised to do it the next day after sleeping on it overnight.

And I wouldn't wait any longer than that for her to do it.

CHAPTER XXIII

"There's a dead man on your couch!"

I don't do confrontations well. Never have. I can do them, but I don't like them.

I was exhausted from the encounter with Elise Carmichael and wanted nothing more than just to call it a day. I parked on the street at a meter around the corner from the office just to avoid the possibility of encountering Mookie on the street. Besides, I had no intention of staying long in the office.

I walked up the stairs because the elevator wasn't on the ground level. On the second floor, I went into the men's restroom. After splashing water on my face from the wash basin, I stared into the mirror.

What had I gotten myself into? All these women were driving me insane. Marie, Clara, Elise, my secretary, my sister, Grammy Taylor, even Carmichael's mistress — Carolyn B. Adams. It was more than I could take. I reached for a couple of paper towels from the dispenser, dabbed my face dry and headed down the hall to the office.

Mae was typing when I entered. She looked up and was about to speak, but I spoke first.

"I'm closing the office for the rest of the day. Call it a vacation. Call it a personal day. It doesn't matter. But you can have the rest of the day off," I said. "Go home."

She stopped and looked up at me with a quizzical expression. "The day off? Why? You still paying me, aren't you? You ain't out of money, are ya?"

"No, it's not money. I'm just tired. Tired of the cases in the last two weeks, tired of everything," I said.

"You having women problems. I can tell."

I ignored the comment. "Don't you have some arrangements to make with the city? Didn't Mayor Goode say he planned to help all the people affected by the MOVE fire? Get started on it. Go home."

Mae straightened items on her desk in preparation for leaving. I watched as she pressed the 'send' button on her computer and a document came out of the printer across the room. I walked over, picked it up without looking to see what was on it and handed it to her. She placed it in a folder for later action.

"What are you going to do?" she asked.

I scratched my head and sat in a chair. I would have put my feet up on her desk, had the desk and the chair been closer. "I haven't decided. But it won't be work."

She left in short order, and I just sat in the office considering my options.

For the lack of anything better to do, I went down to Independence Hall and took a public tour. I've never been much for history. It was boring, but at the moment I wanted boring. In the room where they debated the Declaration of Independence I contemplated the sun carved into the chair where George Washington sat during some sessions of the Continental Congress.

To my view, the sun was rising, a sign of optimism.

On a whim, I went to see Richard Pryor in "Brewster's Millions," which was playing in the theater behind the Bourse Building across from Independence Hall. It wasn't my favorite Pryor film, but it was light-hearted and didn't require me to think. I didn't want to think. I just wanted to watch and eat buttered popcorn.

I don't remember the drive up to East Falls to see Marie. But for the first time since morning, something got my full attention. Marie had on a long skirt that fit nicely across the hips and a t-shirt that stopped just above her navel. Just before I opened the car door for her, she pulled my head to her mouth and whispered in a low, husky voice, "To save us time, I'm not wearing any panties." Then she kissed my cheek and got in the car.

I had a spring in my step as I sauntered around to the driver's side of the car. We kissed before I started the engine. The kiss was long and satisfying.

"That's just a preview of what's to come," she said.

I got the message and immediately put the car in gear after the engine fired up. There was sexy talk the entire way to my apartment; neither of us could wait to tear the other's clothes off.

For me, it would be the perfect way to end a hard day. I had my arm around her waist as we ascended the stairs in the building. Marie would alternate between nibbling on my ear, saying something sexy and giggling at her own imagination.

I didn't even care about the music coming from the apartment across the hall.

I inserted the key into the lock but the door began opening on its own. That's rarely a good sign. Well, actually, it's never a good sign.

Marie didn't seem to notice, but I stopped her from entering. I held a finger to my lips and she gave me a worried look.

Standing to the right side of the door, I pushed it open and looked inside. It was dark.

"Stay here," I told her.

"You're going in there? *Why*? Shouldn't we call the police?"

"Just stay put."

I eased into the dark apartment and noticed something was different in the living room. It wasn't a mess, but something wasn't as it should be. I hit a switch and the room filled with light. Then I saw it. There was a man on the couch. He wasn't moving. He had a bullet hole in the head.

From behind me, I heard Marie scream. "There's a dead man on your couch!"

Careful not to touch anything, I entered the room and looked around. Nothing else seemed to have been touched or moved.

"Stay here in the hallway," I cautioned Marie.

"Are you crazy? I'm not staying out here."

"Then stay behind me."

I stepped into the living room with Marie on my heels. Leaving her near the front door, I went room to room to make sure everything was safe. Nothing seemed disturbed. Everything seemed normal, except for the dead body on the couch. That was definitely not normal, even for me.

"I want you to go stand over there," I said, pointing toward the kitchen.

Marie held a hand over her mouth. I don't think she had seen a dead body before. The subject had never come up. I hadn't often seen one myself but I needed her to stay calm.

"Don't touch anything." I said.

"Don't worry. I won't. I think that's the guy who was following you."

"It is. Or was," I said. "Simon Balcombe. Remember, don't touch anything while I call the police."

Within thirty minutes, the building, hallway and apartment were all crawling with police officers. The students from across the hall stopped playing loud music and huddled with Mrs. Findley just outside my doorway, whispering to each other. On the street, a crowd gathered as word spread of the shooting and the discovery of a body.

Inside my apartment, the body was still uncovered, and police photographers were taking pictures of everything in the room. Others were dusting everything and looking for other clues.

Officers had Marie in the kitchen and me in the bedroom for initial questioning. And lucky me — I had Thompson and Gregory.

I was sitting on the bed — glad I had made it in the morning — as Thompson leaned against the door and Gregory paced back and forth.

"Let me see if I have this straight. You say you got to the apartment, noticed the door was ajar but entered anyway, where you discovered a dead body on the couch," Gregory said. "Is that it?"

"That's it."

"Where had you been before that?"

"I picked up my friend from her apartment in East Falls and we drove here," I answered.

"And what were you doing before that?"

"I was downtown at a movie. Before that, Independence Hall."

"Can anybody verify that for us?" Gregory's voice was becoming more and more hostile with each question.

"I doubt it. I was alone. I didn't talk to anyone in particular."

The questioning stopped as he jotted down my answers.

Thompson said little and entered the questioning only to fill the void of silence. But he didn't alter his casual attitude.

"How long were you here before you called police?"

"One minute or so. I checked out the rest of the apartment first."

"And did you touch anything? The body? Anything?" Thompson asked.

"No. Neither of us did."

"Did you know him?" Thompson asked.

"Not really. He apparently had been following me for about a week."

"His identification says he's another private investigator. He have any reason to investigate you?" Gregory said.

I felt like screaming at the man. But it surely would do no good. I restrained myself. But I looked him in the eye when I answered.

"You would have to ask him," I said.

"Convenient for you that I can't do that, isn't it. Damned convenient," Gregory said.

I said nothing out of fear of letting the situation get out of control.

Thompson spoke up. "You don't know why he was following you?"

"No, but I think it might have been about the domestic case I have. I'm doing some work for the wife and he could be working for the husband. That's my guess."

"Who's the client?" Gregory said.

"That's really none of your business," I said.

Gregory took a step toward me but Thompson moved to cut him off.

Thompson said, "That you both could be working on opposite sides of a domestic case is reasonable. But why would he be here, waiting for you?"

"Are you asking me?" I asked.

"No, just thinking aloud," Thompson said. "You have a gun? And a permit?"

"Yes. It's in a drawer in my office. The permit, too."

"What caliber?"

"Thirty-eight."

"We're going to need to see it, you understand, to see if it's been fired lately," Thompson said. "Standard procedure."

"We can go tonight to get it, detective. Anything I can do to help out your investigation," I said.

The exchange must have irritated Gregory. He looked down at his notes and stumbled forward, changing the subject. "And this woman, this young woman. What's her name?"

"Marie Toussaint," Thompson and I said together. Gregory looked at his partner then back to me.

"Yes, Marie Toussaint. Why is she with you?"

I couldn't take it anymore. The tension in the room, which was in addition to the tension I had been feeling all day, reached a boiling point. Only through the force of will did I not stand up and confront him.

"Listen, sergeant, ask anything you want about this case. But my personal life is my concern and none of your damned business," I said, raising my voice.

"In this investigation, hotshot, I decide what's my business. And if I decide to haul your ass downtown and charge you with murder and anything else I can think of, I will," Gregory barked. "I'm sick up to here of guys like you," he said, holding his hand up to eye level. "You think you know it all. Getting involved in all sorts of things and messing it up for real working detectives like me. We'd probably solve more crimes without guys like you getting involved. But then, we'd also probably have fewer crimes."

"Ryan," Thompson said, interrupting again. "I think we have all we need here. Come on. Let's go."

Gregory glared at me a little longer, snapped his notebook shut and left the room.

They had loaded Balcombe onto a stretcher and were about to take him out by the time I returned to the living room. I went over to Marie, put my arm around her shoulder and pulled her close. "I'm so sorry about this."

"Do people die in your apartment often?" she asked.

"This is the first time, and I hope it doesn't establish a pattern," I said.

"Me, too. I couldn't handle that."

The implication was clear. If she couldn't handle that, she couldn't handle me, either.

I waited until all the officers were gone and then I took Marie home.

~*~

There is that moment when something that has eluded my conscious mind falls totally into place. Perhaps it's because there were times, such as in the middle of the night when I was sleeping, when all the distractions of the normal day were stripped away. Something that might otherwise seem obvious to me gets lost in the cacophony of sensations I have to deal with constantly during the day. The obvious gets lost in the fog.

I woke up suddenly in the middle of the night and sat upright in bed. The answers were in the papers Valerie had printed out for me from her office.

Though it was nearly two in the morning, hours after I had surrendered my gun to police, I headed back to the office. It was amazing that there was any traffic on Walnut Street heading west at such an hour.

I turned south at 52nd and drove the remaining few blocks to the office. There was no problem finding a place to park directly outside. The only people moving about at that hour were the true night owls, those looking for some sort of action and the police who were looking to prevent it.

Of course, the building was locked at night, once the Chinese merchants downstairs left. But all tenants had a key to the outside door and another key to shut off the security alarm once inside. It wasn't a particularly sophisticated security system, and it often amazed me that thieves didn't just bypass it and break into the building on a nightly basis.

The elevator was turned off, so I took the darkened stairs, glad that there were lights to illuminate the way. There was an eerie quiet to the building at that time of night. I probably wouldn't have entered the empty building alone and unarmed any other time in the last two weeks if it weren't for the fact that my stalker was already dead, shot to death in my apartment. I unlocked the door to my office and switched on the lights. Then I relocked the front door.

No need in being careless. This might be the night thieves bypassed the security system.

I went to my office and to the desk drawers on the right. Sitting, I pulled out the file which I had intended to completely read the day before but hadn't. I opened it and looked through until I found the property ownership records.

And there it was. Why hadn't I seen or thought of it earlier? It didn't matter. I could see it now. I knew who owned the house on Osage where the body was found. And I knew whose body it was and who had killed him.

Getting back to sleep once I got home wasn't that hard at all.

CHAPTER XXIV

"You're on thin ice there, Mr. Blaise.
Slander is a serious charge."

I looked out my office window and onto the street at five minutes to one in the afternoon and saw Mookie moving an orange traffic cone so a shiny black, two-door Mercedes would have a place to park on the street next to the office. Even from my vantage point from the second floor, Elise didn't look happy. But I didn't expect her to be.

She wore tan Capri pants and a matching belted tan jacket that reminded me of a safari top, with over-sized pockets on the chest. Large sunglasses protected her eyes from the strong sunlight and partially hid her face, as if she were some sort of celebrity and didn't want to be recognized. Yet, everything about her outfit screamed, "Look at me."

She marched into the office, passed Mae without acknowledgement and entered my domain without knocking or announcing herself.

"What is this all about, Mr. Blaise? I have a plane to catch this afternoon."

"Perhaps you should sit down, Elise. We're about to have some company. And if I were you, I wouldn't be so sure about catching that flight."

She opened her mouth to say something but I paid that little attention. I heard the front door open again and looked up to see a large man in a dark blue business suit enter. He looked and dressed like a lawyer. But then again, he was one. I had seen him up close before but this would be our first actual meeting. He was accompanied by two other men, a clean-cut older man in another dark lawyer suit, and a fifty-something man in a business casual navy blazer and gray slacks.

"Hello," the first man said to Mae. "My name is Reuben Carmichael and I was told I needed to come here immediately. Who are you and what do you want?"

"Reuben," Elise said, leaving my office. "What are you doing here? What's going on and why is Andrew Strange with you?" To the man in the navy blazer, she said, "And who are you?"

Carmichael addressed his wife. "All I know is I was told to come here and that I should bring my lawyer. I said I *am* a lawyer, but they said bring another one. That's why Andy's here. And this is Angelo De Luca, who's been doing some investigative work for me."

De Luca clarified somewhat. "Ma'am, how do you do? I work for a security firm called The Henderson Group."

Nolan and Clara, and officers Gregory and Thompson entered at the same time and came into my office. The office was then as crowded as I had ever seen it. I was grateful I had enough chairs lined up, although the officers apparently preferred to stand by the door, on either side of the frame.

The reason for that was obvious. No one was getting past them.

I made all the introductions, although I had never met Carmichael, Strange or De Luca. Then I sat on my desk facing everyone.

"What is this all about, Mr. Blaise? I have a business to run," De Luca said.

"I totally understand, Mr. De Luca," I said. "And I plan to get you out of here as quickly as possible. But first let me extend my deepest sympathies at the death of one of your employees last night in my apartment. It's a tragic loss. But I assume you're totally aware that he had been tailing me, and perhaps even threatening me, for the last two weeks at the behest of Mr. Carmichael here."

"You're on thin ice there, Mr. Blaise," Carmichael said. There was a seriousness to his voice with an underlying threat to its tone. "Slander is a serious charge."

"Oh, shut up, Reuben," Elise snapped.

"Yes, it is serious. But before you decide to sue me, I have a little story to tell. Then you can properly decide if it's slander. And you'll have witnesses. Everyone in this room."

There was a brief knock on my office door and a uniformed police officer stuck his head in. Seeing Thompson, he handed him a large, thick manila envelope, closed the door and left.

Thompson turned back to me and said, "Please continue."

Turning to my SEPTA friends, I said, "Clara, Russ, I'm sorry to inform you that Wilbur Stephenson's been found and he's dead. He probably died about two weeks ago, wouldn't you say officers?"

"Yes," Gregory said.

"About two weeks," added Thompson.

Elise reacted to the news, shifting in her seat and looking about, but she said nothing.

Clara looked shocked but also managed to keep her composure. "You found him? Why didn't you tell me? Where was he? How did he die?" The questions rushed out so quickly I imagined Clara was having a hard time figuring out what she wanted most to know.

"His body was found about a week ago, in the debris of a house on Osage Avenue. But it wasn't in the MOVE house. It was in a house down the block. They didn't know whose body it was," I said, checking a couple of faces for any recognition of where I was going. They were all passive. "Has the final positive identification been made yet?"

"We're working on it," Thompson said.

"But you got the dental records from his ex-wife?" I asked.

Both Thompson and Gregory nodded.

"Anyway, Stephenson didn't die in the MOVE fire. He was already dead. Shot twice, in the chest and in the head. Probably was dead two or three days before the bombing, wouldn't you say officers?"

"Yes," Gregory said.

"Russ, your employment records show he last worked on Thursday, May ninth. He missed work the next day, and his neighbors and others definitely don't remember seeing him on Saturday. Plus, before I was attacked while I was in his house last week, I saw a calendar entry where he was to meet someone with the initials LMS on that Friday."

Carmichael, who had barely been listening up until that moment, looked up sharply and turned in his chair to face me. I looked at him and then back to his wife. "See, Elise? He already knows about Lula Mae Stobe . . . about your past. But I'll get to that in a minute."

She looked at Carmichael with surprise but he refused to return her gaze.

"Stephenson was probably killed on that Friday and certainly by Saturday," I said. "My secretary Mae, whom you all met on your way in, lives on the sixty-two-hundred block of Osage and said the police made everyone leave on Saturday. That is, everyone except the people in the MOVE house. Now, I don't know for sure if Stephenson was killed in the house or killed elsewhere and taken there for storage and later removal. Officers?"

"Our guess is he was lured to the house and then killed. It would be the easiest way. And all the evidence points to that," Thompson said. "But we can't be certain at this point. It may take time to determine that conclusively."

"If it can be proven conclusively at all," Gregory chimed in. Thompson said nothing but nodded in agreement.

"Yes. It makes sense that the killing happened there," I said, shifting just slightly on the desk to get a little more comfortable on the solid wood surface. "And there are two other things that make this really interesting. The house where the body was found belonged to the Carmichaels."

There was a slight stirring in the room.

"I have no idea what you are saying, Blaise," Carmichael said.

"Oh, please, Reuben. Don't try and deny it. I've seen the tax and mortgage records," I said. "But that's not all. The other interesting thing is that the same gun killed both men. Stephenson . . . and Balcombe, in my apartment last night. A .38-caliber revolver."

I was nearing the end and I turned to speak directly to Elise. "Tell me, do you have a gun?"

"Uh?" Elise was surprised by the question.

"Do you own a gun? Be careful with your answer," I said. "There are police officers present. And lots of witnesses, in case I get sued later."

She hesitated and appeared to consider how to answer. Then she just blurted out, "Okay. So I own a gun. What about it?"

Thompson stepped forward, reached into the manila envelope and carefully pulled out a revolver, a Smith & Wesson .38-caliber. "Is this the weapon?" he asked Elise.

Elise went wide-eyed and speechless.

"You really don't have to answer," Thompson said. "We served a search warrant on your house this morning. You weren't home. But we found the gun in your bedroom. We immediately had it tested, and this gun is the murder weapon. It was found in your house and it has your fingerprints on it. Yours and only yours."

"Mrs. Carmichael, as your lawyer, I advise you not to say another word," Strange said, speaking for the first time. He had a deep, authoritative, baritone voice.

I smiled and pointed to Elise's husband as I looked at Strange. "I thought you were *his* lawyer. Switching sides, counselor?"

Both lawyers ignored me. No sense of humor!

"Whether she talks or not, she is under arrest for the murders of Wilbur Stephenson and Simon Balcombe," Gregory said.

Elise got up and came to me, nearly falling in my arms. How dramatic. "David, what are you saying? Why are you doing this to me? Please don't do this. Tell them the truth."

Her husband and the two officers grabbed her and sat her down again. Hands to her face, Elise's shoulders rose and fell as she sobbed. It was a good act, though I had seen better.

"This is what I think happened. Reuben, you probably decided some time ago to divorce Lula Mae, here. You probably knew for years about her past but said nothing," I said.

"I don't have to listen to this rubbish," he said and was getting out of his seat before Gregory stopped him.

"Let's just sit down and listen to the story, okay?" Gregory said. It was the first time I was almost thankful for Gregory's presence.

Carmichael quieted down. Besides my voice, the only sounds came from Elise sobbing into her hands and from the passing cars outside.

"Where was I? Oh, yes. Reuben, you started planning, secretly socking away money in the Caymans so you wouldn't have to give it all to her in the divorce settlement. And you had your affair with Carolyn Adams, buying her a condo and giving her money every month. It was only a matter of time before you left Elise and moved into the other condo you own in the building where Adams lives so comfortably.

"With me so far?" I asked, to make sure everyone was up to speed.

"Elise, you knew nothing of this, of course. You were unhappy in your marriage and wanted out, but Reuben was your meal ticket and you planned to keep it. That is, until Wilbur bumped into you. At first, it was okay. You loved the sex, didn't you? You enjoyed getting the attention your husband wasn't giving you . . . attention Reuben was giving his mistress. And you were ultimately paying him back by having sex with someone else, an old flame from back in your college days in Atlanta."

She looked up, eyes red. "No, that's not so. It's not so."

I ignored her. Everyone else did, as well.

"But it all began to change when Wilbur asked for more and more money. And you had to keep paying it because Wilbur threatened to tell Reuben and you thought Reuben would dump you once he knew your past. But there was only so much money you had stored up. Where? In a cookie jar in the kitchen? Doesn't matter. You were running out of time. And that meant a more permanent solution."

The room was silent as a church on a Monday morning. I had everyone's complete attention and I was enjoying it.

"You knew your husband's firm used Henderson for security. You knew Balcombe had done work for your husband. So you privately approached him, offering money and perhaps sex if he'd take care of your little problem with Wilbur Stephenson. You lured poor, unsuspecting Wilbur to the Osage house and shot him. Then Balcombe was to dispose of the body. But before he could, police evacuated the neighborhood and he couldn't get to the body.

"Days later, police bombed the MOVE house and the entire neighborhood burned to the ground. When police were going through the debris, they were completely surprised to find a body on a property where no one was expected. They didn't know whose body it was and couldn't even immediately tell which property it was in, it was such a total mess up there.

"If the body had been disposed of as you originally planned, poor Simon Balcombe would have been implicated in the death, and his guilt might have insured he'd still be alive today. But that didn't happen. After I talked to you yesterday, you knew I was aware of your connection with Stephenson.

You lured Balcombe to my apartment, which you had him search earlier. This time, you told him some of Stephenson's stuff was truly there. You told him I had said so. And that's where you eliminated Balcombe with the same gun used to kill Stephenson."

Elise shook her head but didn't speak.

"You took the gun with you when you left. By killing him in my apartment, you could frame me with Balcombe's death . . . after all, he was stalking me, had threatened me . . . and you eliminated the last direct link back to you in the Stephenson killing. The last link, that is, except for the gun," I said.

"You lied to me again yesterday, Elise. You never planned to go to the police. You couldn't afford to. You were leaving town. For good."

"Elise, how could you?" Carmichael said as he turned to his murderous wife. "I provided for you. No matter what was going to happen with our marriage, you would have been all right, taken care of even in the divorce. I would have made sure. Why this?"

Elise grabbed onto her husband. "Please, Reuben. Don't let them take me. I didn't kill anyone. Please! I still love you. Please, Reuben!" She sobbed, her make-up now running down her face.

The officers came forward, took her arms just under her armpits and lifted her out of her chair. Gregory read Elise her rights.

"Elise. Do not say a word to anyone. We'll handle this. I guarantee it," Carmichael said as they took his wife away.

"Thanks, Blaise," Thompson said.

"Thank you," I said.

Thompson and all the other police officers stationed in my outer office left with their murder suspect. So did Carmichael and Strange, both trying to reassure Elise as she was led away.

"Well, you solved a complicated case, Mr. Blaise. Congratulations," De Luca said, reaching into his jacket pocket and pulling out a business card. "We should talk some time. Perhaps we could find something to work on together. Give me a call."

I doubted that, but instead I said, "That sounds terrific. Thanks." I accepted the business card he offered without actually looking at it.

"Thank you, David," Clara said, giving me a peck on the cheek. "You did good work."

Russ shook my hand as he and Clara left, leaving me alone.

Finally.

I sat in my chair, put my elbows on my desk and applied pressure to my temples. I was still rubbing them when Mae entered.

"You found the bad guy, or gal as it is," she said.

"I did."

"Well, I hope she paid you in advance," Mae said. Her tone was serious. She paused, standing over my desk, and I looked up at her. "I told you she'd be trouble. And I also told you sometimes the money ain't worth the trouble. You should trust me on that."

She turned, walked out of my office and back to her desk, her hips swaying as she went.

CHAPTER XXV

"Well done, big brother."

Marie Toussaint was quite the acrobat in bed. Sexually, she was expert at both giving and receiving, determined to please. And in sleep, she seemed equally as energetic.

When heading to dreamland, like in love-making, she started slowly. As many women do, she liked to cuddle and hold, body pressed against body, arms and hands finding comfortable places and legs intertwined.

Unlike in love-making, she moved away when totally asleep. Back turned and curled up, she hogged the covers quite selfishly. Interestingly, at this stage she held her hands in little balls near her face. As the night wore on, she slept with her arms and legs all over the place. The covers were thrown off with abandon as if she was throwing off all constraint or restraint, physically, sexually, spiritually.

Not yet accustomed to having her spend the night, I slept fitfully and thus was periodically able to watch her metamorphosis throughout the night. At daybreak, she was in her final stage, with her left leg lying across my right, her right leg bent at the knee and her arm hanging off the side of the bed.

Her hair was wild, all over the place, as if she had just walked through a hurricane. Her head was cocked to the right and her mouth was open, though not a sound escaped. She was beautiful, but I knew she'd find her appearance embarrassing. So I'd keep it to myself.

I eased out of bed, found my clothes and headed out quietly. Less than twenty minutes later, I returned to find her still asleep. In the kitchen, I pulled out a never-used serving tray my sister once gave me and placed two cups of hot coffee on it, plus a plate of donuts, a glass of orange juice and a single rose.

"Hey. Wake up," I said as I nudged her. Marie rolled over toward my side of the bed, and rubbed her nose several times with the back of her hand as she opened her eyes.

Seeing the tray, she said, "Oh, wow. Thank you. That's so considerate."

I leaned over and kissed her. "And you could use a little Tic-Tac," I joked. She smiled, punched my shoulder with the palm of her hand and excused herself to go to the bathroom.

"Ahhhh," she screamed a second later from behind the closed door. "I look horrible. How can you look at me like this?"

She returned, still undressed and with her hair somewhat flattened to her head though clearly still uncombed.

"*Don't* look at me. I look so bad," she said as she climbed back into bed.

"No. You look lovely, as always," I corrected and kissed her again. I didn't care about morning breath.

We ate and drank, making small talk. Finally, she asked, "Are you working this afternoon?"

"This afternoon? The Sunday before Memorial Day. Good gracious, no," I said. It appeared she didn't understand.

"Why not?"

"The Indianapolis 500 is today. I always watch the race from beginning to end at my grandmother's house, generally with one of my brothers. Grammy Taylor loves the race. And it's turned into a tradition," I said. "What are you doing?"

"I'm going to see my parents this afternoon and then coming to your grandmother's house for dinner. What time should I be there?"

"You really don't have to do that." I didn't want her to feel obligated.

She pulled back from me and had a serious look on her face. "You don't want me to come?"

I smiled, hoping to reassure her. "Of course I'd like for you to come. I just didn't want you to feel that you have to."

"I enjoy your family, at least the ones I've met. And they seem to enjoy me. It's no obligation," Marie said. "So what time?"

"Be there by six."

I tried not to stare, but she had a little powdered sugar from her donut at the corner of her mouth. "You have a little something, some sugar, on your mouth." I leaned in close and instead of wiping it away with my fingers, I used my tongue.

"Ah-ha. Thank you," she said, looking down. Picking up the crumbs and sugar from a donut, she put some on her neck, just below her left ear. "And do you see any more?"

"I do."

I nibbled her neck and she giggled until she pushed me away. Marie did circles with her fingers around the plate with the remains of the donuts, collecting crumbs and bits of powdered sugar. She traced her fingers down her chest between her breasts and then circled her left nipple.

"And now? Any crumbs?" she asked.

I laid her back on the bed and devoured her body, enjoying one taut nipple and then the other. She arched her back as I continued. Lying across the top of her, I looked up, resting my chin on her chest between her breasts. Our eyes met and we both smiled.

"I think there are lots of crumbs further down," she said, pushing my head down her body. "Oh yeah, Babe. There're lots of crumbs down there."

~*~

Promptly at six, someone knocked on Grammy Taylor's door

and I went to answer it. Standing back, I let Marie in. She was carrying two bottles of sparkling apple cider.

"I thought these might be good as a gift to your grandmother for having me over," Marie said, handing me one bottle.

Grammy Taylor entered and walked over to welcome our guest. "Marie, just like the virgin," Grammy Taylor said as she collected the younger woman in a hug. Marie and I exchanged wide-eyed glances, wondering what Grammy meant. "It's so great to see you again."

Grammy Taylor headed back to the kitchen, passing Allen and Stuart, who were watching television in the living room. I made an introduction.

"Marie, this is my younger brother, Allen. Allen, this is my friend Marie," I said. "And you've met my brother-in-law, Stuart. From last week."

Marie gave a polite "how are you." Allen looked up approvingly to acknowledge Marie, while Stuart merely leered. Again. Steering her away, I made apologies for Stuart when we reached the dining room and were out of earshot.

"Oh, don't worry about it," Marie said.

I intended to get more glasses for the sparkling cider but stopped. For this evening, the table was set with real china instead of less formal dinner plates, and with Grammy Taylor's best silver and crystal stemware, except for where the kids would sit. The setting was for eight. Allen apparently was staying.

"Something special going on tonight?" Marie asked, looking around.

"Beats me," I said as the table drew my full attention. "Looks like it, I guess."

"I see we're having fried chicken. I like that," Marie said.

"Yes," I said, scratching my chin as I stared. "And mashed potatoes, candied yams, green beans, lima beans, corn, rolls. And, of course, sliced tomatoes, cucumbers and onions. We always have those."

"Dessert?"

"Cherry pie this evening. Grammy just made it. It's cooling in the kitchen," Valerie said, bringing out a bowl of food.

"Hummm, I knew I smelled something mouth-watering when I got here," Marie said.

Valerie hugged Marie once she put the food on the table. "Good to see you again," she said. Then, looking at me, "And two weeks in a row. My, my, my. What am I to think of that?" Then she went back into the kitchen.

"Don't mind her," I said, embarrassed.

"Needn't worry," Marie said, following Valerie into the kitchen. "Can I help?"

As the women brought out the food, I poured the bubbly, non-alcoholic cider into everyone's glasses. Then Grammy Taylor called the other men to the table.

As it was the previous week, Stuart and Grammy Taylor sat at opposite ends of the table. Valerie was flanked by Cora and Cody on one side of the table and Marie was flanked by my brother and me on the other. I reached over to grab my grandmother's hand to my right and Marie's hand to my left as Stuart once again offered grace.

"Father God," he said. "We are gathered together here at this table to enjoy your wonderful bounty. Thank you, Father God, for the opportunity to gather again as family and friends to partake in this wonderful meal. I pray that you, Father God, will bless this table and everyone seated here. Now, Father God, please bless this delicious meal and the hands that prepared it. And we will give You all the praise, all the honor and all the glory. In Christ's name . . . let everyone within the sound of my voice say. . . ."

"Amen," we all said.

As she released my hand, Grammy Taylor looked down the table and gave Stuart an approving glance. He was getting better at saying grace.

After the Bible verses, we loaded our plates.

"Who won the race? The Indy 500?" Marie asked, passing me a bowl of mashed potatoes.

"It wasn't Mario Andretti. I wanted him to win," Grammy Taylor said. "Can you pass me the chicken, please?"

"But it was exciting. He led more than half the race," I said.

"And still lost it," Allen offered, reaching for the gravy.

"What happened?" Marie asked.

Not sure how much information to give her, I decided on the Cliff Notes version. But even with as short an explanation as I could give, Marie's eyes glassed over. Thankfully, Valerie changed the subject.

Picking up her cider glass, Valerie said, "Let's have a toast to Davey for solving those murder cases. Here's to Davey."

Everyone clicked glasses and drank. It was a great moment and I felt good.

"So how'd you figure it out, big brother?" Allen said.

"I found out that Elise Carmichael, who originally was my client and who is now accused of murder, knew Wilbur Stephenson, whose badly burned body was found in a house on the same block of the MOVE fire. And I knew he was blackmailing her about her past," I said.

"And that's where I came in, risking my job to help you, by the way," Valerie said, addressing me directly. "I provided you with the information on those off-shore accounts and on the properties that Reuben Carmichael bought."

I winked at Valerie. "Looking at those records, I was able to tie Elise both to the house they owned and to the gun that killed both Stephenson and Simon Balcombe, the guy who was killed in my apartment the other day," I said.

"Well done, big brother," Allen said as he shoveled a forkful of food into his mouth, washing it down with water.

We all ate and for a while enjoyed small talk that didn't involve murder or my job. Allen told the family about his new girl, Renee, to everyone's delight, most especially my grandmother.

But after a while, as we neared the end of the main course, Marie stopped eating, put down her fork and looked directly at me. "I know you've thought of all of this but there's a flaw in your reasoning, your conclusion, at least in how you just outlined it. But I'm sure you already know that, right? The part you didn't explain."

"And what is that?" I asked, trying to keep the irritation out of my voice. This was my moment of triumph in front of my family and she was trying to ruin it.

"Babe, you can tie Elise to the gun. She owns it and her fingerprints are on it. And you can tie the gun to both deaths," Marie said. "But you can't tie her to the house where Stephenson's body was found. That's the flaw."

She now had everyone's attention.

"I told you. They owned that house," I said carefully. "Valerie showed me. We found the property records."

"Yes. I showed him," Valerie piped in with familial support, though she was sounding a little less certain.

"Under the law, yes." Marie said. "They jointly owned it because they're married. But you told me the off-shore accounts and the properties . . . the condos, some properties, among other things . . . were things Reuben never told his wife about. That would include the Osage house, wouldn't it? So how could *she* lure Stephenson to the Osage house, kill him and leave his body in that house . . . a house she didn't *know* she owned? That's the flaw."

You could have heard a pin drop, even on the carpeted floor.

"Is that true, Davey?" Grammy Taylor said.

"Wait a minute. Let me think." I leaned forward, placing my left elbow on the table, and massaged my forehead.

"Elbows," my grandmother sternly reminded me.

"Thanks." I moved back but was still perplexed.

"Looks like you might have royally screwed up, Davey. They might have to pull your private eye's license after this," Stuart said. He sounded gleeful. A glance from Valerie wiped the smile off his face. There was no doubt who was wearing the pants in that household but I didn't have the time to enjoy the fact.

"Her fingerprints are on the gun and the gun killed both men," I said.

"That's not necessarily conclusive. The killer could have planted them on the gun. Happens all the time on television," Valerie said. "I saw it a couple of months ago on Magnum, P.I. I love that show. And that Tom Selleck . . . what a dream."

"I like Higgins, myself. He's sexier," Grammy Taylor said. She ignored the stares.

"Someone could have planted the evidence to frame Elise and hope that no one would notice anything else," Marie said. "I'm sorry, Babe. I thought that was a problem but that you had worked it out. That's why I didn't say anything."

"David Anderson Blaise, are you sending an innocent woman to jail?" Grammy Taylor asked in a stern voice. She rarely used my full and proper name, and hearing it in that tone wasn't a good omen.

"I'm not personally sending anyone to jail. I'm not a police officer," I protested. "And I'm not a judge or jury. They're the only ones who can send someone to prison."

"Semantics, David," Valerie said. Now everyone was using my proper name.

At that moment, Cora tried to reach over her mother and hit her brother with a spoonful of mashed potatoes. It briefly cut the tension.

Valerie slapped her hand away. "You stop that right now or I will send you from the table to eat in the kitchen," she said.

"He started it," Cora said in sheepish defense.

"I don't care who started it. You sit still and eat your

dinner," Valerie said with sternness. And turning to her other child, she said, "And you. I know you probably did it. I got my eyes on Cody. Sit up and be quiet. The adults are talking."

"Let's back track for a minute and see what we know," I said. Everyone was eating but much slower now. "We know Elise knew Stephenson, he was blackmailing her and he's dead."

"That Balcombe is dead is something I know with certainty," Marie said. "I saw the body."

Grammy Taylor looked at her with considerable sympathy. "Sorry about that, my dear. You shouldn't have had to go through that."

Marie smiled. "Thank you, Mrs. Taylor."

"Call me Grammy Taylor. Everyone does," my grandmother said.

Marie smiled again as I took a deep breath.

"And we know which gun killed them both and whose fingerprints are on it. Those are knowns," I said. "It's reasonable to assume that Balcombe was somehow involved with Stephenson's murder. Either he did it or knew who did it."

"I can accept that," Marie said.

"Then who killed Balcombe?" I asked of no one.

"David, you have to clean this up. You can't send an innocent woman to prison," Grammy Taylor said.

I looked at my grandmother and said in all seriousness, "Elise Carmichael is anything but innocent, believe me, Grammy."

"You get my meaning. You find the right person and do it fast. And you get that woman out of prison," Grammy Taylor said, sounding like a judge. She didn't spell out the consequences I'd face if I failed to heed her instructions but I was sure they would not be good. I would fare better with the police.

Before she uttered another word directly to me, she abruptly changed subjects and addressed the entire table. "Now. Who wants some pie?"

She got up and headed for the kitchen.

CHAPTER XXVI

"You'll never get away with this."

Marie and I were standing at her car, which was down the block from mine. My back was to the door and she was leaning into me with her arms around my neck.

"Well, I guess you were right," I said, dejected. Self-pity was making headway. "I'm not that great of a detective."

"Oh, stop that! I was just kidding and you know it. You're a great detective," she said. "But like I told you a couple of nights ago, you get so wrapped up concentrating on one thing that you can miss something else that's obvious. And important."

"It seems obvious to me now," I said in lame defense. My mouth was suddenly dry. I couldn't swallow.

"That's what I mean," Marie said.

"I'm not sure what to do next. How to figure it out."

"But you will. I know it. Truly, you will. I have trust in you. We all do," she said, giving me a kiss. Then she broke away and pulled me from her car. "I have things to do tonight and, more importantly, I don't want to distract you. You have thinking to do."

Marie walked around to the driver side and opened the door. "Now go figure it out." She got in the car, turned on the engine and rolled down the window closest to me. "And as incentive, you get no boo-TAY from me until you figure it out."

"Not much of an incentive," I said and laughed.

She nearly rolled the window up on me, put the car in gear and drove off.

I walked back to my grandmother's house, said my good-byes and headed home. I knew I had missed something but I just didn't know where. Or where to look.

The one thing I wasn't going to do, at least not immediately, was call either Thompson or Gregory. If they arrested the wrong person, on my recommendation, of course, then the real killer was still out there and believed they were getting away. No need, at the moment, to change that perception.

And it wouldn't hurt for Elise Carmichael to spend a couple of days in the pokey. She might not be a murderess, but she was guilty of something, if only of being insufferable.

I went home and cleaned house, straightened my dresser and put my books in order. But there was no inspiration. I thought of calling Marie just to hear her voice and say good-night but decided against it as I reached for the phone. I undressed and got ready for bed, instead.

As happened several nights before, I woke up with inspiration. I still couldn't put my finger on what I had but I knew it was somewhere in the paperwork — the tax records or the bank records. I would have to pour over both.

Again, I got up, dressed and drove to the office. Given that it was a holiday weekend and in the wee hours of the morning, the streets were even more deserted. The building was dark and creepy but I didn't let it bother me.

I got to my office, unlocked the door and went inside.

Back at my desk, I only turned on the desk lamp, then pulled out all the files. Spreading them across my desk, I went over page after page, at first noticing nothing.

But then I saw it.

In almost everything I saw, Carolyn Adams's name never had a middle initial. But on several bank wire transfers from the First Cayman International Bank to First Pennsy in Philadelphia, her middle initial was listed as "B". I looked further and saw the significance. It was in signed documents relating to her account at First Pennsy. She signed her full name, with the middle name spelled out.

Balcombe.

"There, there, there. I got it," I exclaimed.

Though it was the legal holiday, I planned to call the police first thing in the morning. I began organizing things so I could leave but then I heard the first door to my office opening.

"*Damn*, I should have locked that door," I thought.

I pulled open the last bottom drawer on the right and reached for my gun, only to remember too late I had surrendered it to police and hadn't gotten it back yet.

"Bring your hands up slowly, Mr. Blaise," a voice said from the darkness. It was a male voice and I recognized it as belonging to Reuben Carmichael. He walked into what little light there was in the room and I saw the gun in his hand. It was pointed at me. "Do it now. I don't want to shoot you here and now, but I will."

I raised my hands to the top of the desk so he could see them. I heard something else behind him but I couldn't see anything.

"Now get up. Slowly," Carmichael ordered.

"You'll never get away with this," I said, rising from the desk. "The police will realize Elise was framed."

"Perhaps. But not before I'm gone," he said. "I've been preparing this for months. I think we'll get away with it."

"Oh, I know we'll get away with it," said a female voice behind him. Carolyn Adams entered, holding a gun next to Marie's head.

Marie's mouth was taped shut and her hands tied before her. But her eyes were opened wide. There was no mistaking the fear and panic on her face. I doubt she had ever been through what she was going through. I've pissed women off before, but this was beyond anything I had ever involved a woman in.

If we survived, which was questionable, I hoped I'd have a chance to redeem myself with her.

But things didn't look good.

"Step around the desk," Carmichael said, "and keep your hands where I can see them."

"You don't have to do this to her. Let her go and just take me," I said.

"Sorry, but it's much too late for that and you know it, Mr. Blaise. She's our insurance," Adams said. "Let's go. Walk in front of us. And one wrong move, just one, and I shoot her and you watch her die. Then, I shoot you."

I didn't doubt she'd do it. Two people were already dead.

We left the office and Carmichael shut off the lights. I could hear Marie silently weeping as I racked my brain trying to figure out how to get out of this mess.

"Take the stairs," Carmichael said, and we navigated them mostly in the dark.

"Where to now?" I asked as we reached the bottom floor.

"Head for the front door. It's unlocked, and there's a van outside," Carmichael said.

"How did you get in here in the first place?" I asked.

"Please. This old building? It was a snap. Balcombe told me how to get around this primitive security system," Carmichael said. Then, to rub it in, "You should have talked that idiot brother-in-law of yours into spending more money on it. But that's another thing it'll be too late for you to do."

I walked out the front door. Sitting at the curb was a paneled van, its engine running. Even in the middle of the night, that was a stupid thing to do in West Philly. Carmichael yanked open the door and indicated with his gun for us to get inside. Marie entered first and I followed. Adams brought up the rear as Carmichael closed the door and went around to the front, got in and took the wheel.

The van had long benches running along both walls and Marie and I sat on the wall on the driver side, while Adams, always alert to us though she held the gun somewhat casually, sat on the other side just behind the passenger seat. Carmichael drove south on 52nd Street and turned right onto Baltimore Avenue.

"Can I at least take the tape off her mouth?" I asked.

Adams looked quickly at Carmichael, who nodded. "Go ahead. But if either of you make a sound, you're dead. Got it?"

"I understand," I said. Marie had calmed down and seemed resigned to what was happening. She was sitting on my right and I turned to face her. "This might hurt a little, but I have to pull it off fast."

Again her eyes widened just as I reached up and yanked the tape off. "Yow-eee," she said after I yanked, and her eyes filled with tears. But then she turned to Adams.

"Where are you taking us?" Marie asked.

"Sit quietly and don't worry. It'll be your final resting place," Carmichael said.

"What I want to know is why," I said.

"You people are just determined to talk, aren't you?" Adams said. "Why can't you just shut up?"

"Sweetie, maybe we should tell them, as a final gift," Carmichael said, looking into the rearview mirror. "It will be fifteen minutes or so before we get there."

"You tell them, then," Adams said in a biting tone.

Though curious, my goal was to keep them talking and perhaps a tad distracted as I thought of options.

"It's about the money, of course, and not wanting Elise to have any of it," he said as we left Philadelphia city limits and entered Delaware County. "Then Stephenson showed up and provided the means of dealing with her."

"Was it really her gun?" I asked.

"But of course. A while ago, I told her there had been some burglaries in the area and suggested we get a gun to keep around the house for protection. I bought it myself and presented it to her. But then I wiped it clean and never touched it again. So only her prints were on it," Carmichael said.

"She balked at first, but I got her to a shooting range a couple of times so that she was familiar with how to use a gun. That was crucial. The police would have to know she could use a gun, that gun," he said, turning left onto Church Lane and driving over the bridge that spanned the SEPTA railroad tracks.

We were headed into Yeadon but I still had no idea where we'd end up.

"I knew Stephenson needed money and I knew he was getting some from her. So we came up with a plan to eliminate Stephenson with Elise's gun and to frame Elise," Carmichael said.

"Where did Balcombe and the Henderson agency come into play?" I asked.

"When I hired them, I told De Luca I was investigating my wife and I specifically asked for Balcombe. We knew him," Carmichael said, looking briefly back at Adams.

Carmichael stopped talking and Adams didn't jump in to fill the gap. But I already had the answer.

"That's what the 'B' stands for. Balcombe," I said to her. "He's a relative."

"Former relative. A former and late relative," she said.

"*What*?" Marie asked.

Adams looked directly at me and it confirmed what I was thinking. She smiled. She was really enjoying herself now and it annoyed me. "Go ahead. Tell her," Adams said.

"Former, because Balcombe was probably related to her by marriage. Ex-husband, I'd guess. She once had his name and changed it later. I saw it on a couple of documents." I stopped, not wanting to tell Marie the rest of what I suspected because of its implications. But Adams insisted.

"Go on. I'm interested in knowing what you think of the rest. As I was saying, former and late relative," she said, reminding me.

"Late, because she's the one who killed him."

Marie gasped just as we turned right onto MacDade Boulevard. Carmichael picked up the story.

"I got Elise out of the picture on that Friday when Stephenson went to the Osage house thinking he had a meeting with her. Balcombe was there and took care of him with her gun. He planned to remove the body that night and dispose of it but couldn't because of police activity on Osage. They were everywhere and it only got worse as the weekend went on. Then there was the bombing and fire," Carmichael said.

"Can we get this story over with? We're almost there," Adams said, sounding impatient.

"Less than a mile. We turn right on Springfield," he said. "Because of the fire, we couldn't get to the body. Then, immediately after the fire, Balcombe came to me with the news that you were following me and Carolyn. Elise had hired you. But you were also looking into what happened to Stephenson. It was perfect, but we had to come up with a plan to deal with the loose ends," Carmichael said.

"And one of those loose ends was Balcombe," I said.

"Reuben thought killing him in your apartment would be enough to get rid of him and implicate you in the murder, but I never thought it would work," Adams interrupted with contempt. "I knew it wouldn't. And it didn't."

"It got Elise out of the way," Carmichael argued.

"Only until her P-Eye here figured it out. I always said you underestimated him," she said to Carmichael, then turned back to me. "But I didn't. I knew you were smart. You had to be. You managed to steal our wallets right from under our noses just days apart. That was you, wasn't it?"

I didn't answer.

"It was brilliant. And that's when I knew you'd figure it out," she said. "And at some point I'd have to personally deal with you."

We turned onto Springfield Road in Collingdale. There were housing developments nearby and I knew the area. We were passing a cemetery on the left and I realized where we were going. Eden Memorial Cemetery, the oldest African-American-owned cemetery in the country and a perfect place to dump two bodies. We turned left and passed under the stone archway and into the cemetery grounds.

"Turn your lights off," Adams cautioned Carmichael. "You don't want to draw any attention from those houses over there."

Under her breath, I heard her say, "Idiot."

Carmichael apparently missed that. He was a big man, an imposing man. But both his wife and his mistress had him under their thumbs. I wondered how the man ever functioned. Obviously, he was drawn to domineering women.

Gravel crunched under the van's tires as we went deeper onto the property. It was flat and open, but at some distance from the road it would be impossible to see the van in the darkness, let alone see any people.

Adams was looking out the front and said, "This is it. Head to the left about forty feet and stop."

Carmichael turned and then stopped. We waited as he walked around and opened the van door, showing he was still holding a gun. Adams waved her gun, indicating for us to go first.

"Do you see that hole in the ground over there? Walk over there to it," she said.

Marie was weeping again as she tripped over a loose piece of ground, falling on her face.

"Get up, get up," Adams angrily barked.

I grabbed Marie by her forearms because her hands were still tied behind her back and helped her up. When she was on her feet, Adams slapped her so hard across the face, Marie fell back onto her butt.

"Don't fuck with me, you ignorant bitch. Now get up and get walking." And to me, she said, "And don't you help her again, either."

With difficulty, Marie got to her feet and we completed our short walk to a partially dug grave. There were shovels in mounds of dirt where someone had labored by hand.

I wished there was something I could say to reassure Marie but I couldn't think of anything. If I had, I would have said it to myself first.

"Reuben, why don't you cut her hands free. She's going to have to dig a little," Adams said, now clearly the one in charge. Pulling a small knife hidden from somewhere in his clothes, Carmichael cut Marie's hands free. She massaged her wrists.

"The circulation will start to come back when you start digging," Adams said to Marie. Then, to her partner, she said, "Did you leave the keys in the van, Reuben?"

"Yes. Just like we planned."

"Good. Time to tie up another loose end," Adams said. From five feet away, she pointed the gun and fired.

Pop, pop, pop.

The shooting surprised Marie and she jumped back. It was too dark to tell if Carmichael was shocked when he was hit. He fell to the ground and didn't move. Shot at such close range, I was sure he was dead.

Keeping an eye on us, Adams said, "Back up." She walked around to retrieve Carmichael's gun.

"You see, I really don't need him. Not any more than I needed my ex-husband. Poor Reuben," Adams said, looking down at the dead body. "He was so pussy-whipped by that hussy he married he never saw this coming. Now I keep the condo and all the money in the Caymans. And I don't have to put up with him."

"Now what?" I asked, though I was getting the picture. One last stall for time.

"Now I will shoot you and plant one gun on you and one on him. It'll look like you mortally wounded each other. Two problems taken care of," she said. "The police will realize that Reuben's hussy is innocent and will think you figured out that he was behind it all. You confronted him, but he brought you out here where you shot each other. End of story."

"What about Marie?"

"Don't you worry about her. I'll deal with her after you're gone," she said.

"But why did you involve her in the first place?"

"Like I said, she's the insurance we needed to get you out here," she said. Then to Marie, "Over here near me. I want you to see his face when he dies."

Marie cautiously moved toward Adams, who was keeping an eye on us both. But Adams didn't notice a shovel on the ground as she backed up. She stepped on the blade of the shovel and it popped up and nearly hit her. Adams lost her balance and dropped her guard.

I was on the opposite side of the grave with poor dead Reuben Carmichael between us, and too far away to take advantage of the situation. But Marie lunged at Adams and they both fell to the ground, rolling around. When they got to their feet, neither had a gun.

Adams swung and hit Marie with an open hand but she hit like a little girl and it barely seemed to phase Marie. Adams might be willing to kill, but she didn't do it with her bare hands.

Marie was in a fighter's stance and responded with a solid right to the face that nearly knocked Adams off her feet. "Let's see how bad you are without a gun, you crazy bitch," Marie said, and followed it with two more solid strikes to her face.

I thought I heard a nose break before Adams went down. She rolled to her right and apparently saw the gun. She reached for it and was about to get up but it was too little too late. Marie had the shovel.

As Adams turned with the gun in hand, Marie swung with all her might, expelling the air from her lungs in a primal scream of fear, anger and rage. A huge clang, much like the sound of a church bell being rung, rode the air, caused by the full force of the shovel striking Adams' head. She dropped back on the ground and didn't move.

When I reached Adams, I was amazed her head was still attached to her body. Marie, her chest heaving with each breath, was standing over Adams, ready to swing again. If Adams wasn't already dead, I knew Marie would kill her if she as much as moved.

I retrieved both guns and turned to Marie. Her lip was busted and bleeding. I held her shoulders, steadying them and forcing her attention to me. "Calm down, calm down, okay? Breathe. It's over."

Marie nodded and dropped the shovel. Then she threw herself into my arms. I didn't want to let go but I needed her to focus. I pushed her to arm's length from me.

"Listen to me, Marie. Are you listening?"

Again she nodded, apparently still unable to talk.

"This is what I need you to do. See those houses over there?" I pointed at rooftops visible in the distance. "I need you to go to one of those houses, bang on the door and get someone to call the police. This is the Eden Cemetery. Can you do that?"

She was still breathing heavily but she managed to say yes.

"I'll stay here and watch over things until you get back. I have a gun in case something happens. But I need you to go, okay? Just walk carefully around the graves," I said.

Marie kissed me quickly on the lips. "I'll go now," she said. "Get help." She was shaken but was beginning to collect herself.

"Good. I'll be safe, but you should go now."

CHAPTER XXVII

I'd make it home another way.

The sun was coming up and I was still sitting at the desk of Detective Thompson of the Philadelphia Police Department, being interviewed. Marie was nearby, at the desk of Sgt. Gregory. Though the crime scene was in a neighboring suburban county, the authorities there were allowing Philly officials to take the lead at the moment. After all, it was Memorial Day, a day when the detectives in small suburban departments took off. And besides, Philadelphia police had already done the lion's share of the preliminary investigative work.

If Gregory or Thompson was terribly upset about being called out of bed at an ungodly hour on a national holiday to handle a case they effectively thought was over, they didn't show it.

Marie looked tired and drained. Her hair still had pieces of twigs and bits of dirt in it. Her clothes were dirty and her arms had little scratches. She didn't appear to have any other physical injuries except a busted lip. But I was sure she had untold psychological ones. After all, Marie had been kidnapped at gunpoint from her apartment, threatened with death, hit, knocked down, saw a man standing next to her get shot dead, had a fight-to-the-death with her would-be assassin and put Adams into the intensive care ward with head injuries that could be mortal.

She had experienced a lot in the last few hours.

"You about finished with me?" I asked Thompson.

Nodding my head in the general direction of the other desk, I added, "Mind if I go check on her?"

Thompson smiled before he said, "Go ahead."

I walked over, knelt beside her and picked bits of tree from her hair, dropping them into Gregory's wastebasket. Her shoulders slumped from the heavy weight of the night's events and because she hadn't had any sleep. But she was composed.

"How you holding up, kiddo?" I asked cheerfully.

"I'm okay," she said. "Could use some coffee, though."

I looked at Gregory and he said there was a pot on a hot plate on a table on the other side of the vast room.

"I'll get you some and be right back," I said. And to Gregory I said, "Sergeant?"

"I'm fine, thanks."

Away I went and returned with coffee.

"And you hit her in the head with a shovel," Gregory was saying to Marie as he continued taking down her statement. "I'm impressed."

I pulled up a chair and sat down. Gregory looked up from his typewriter and acknowledged me and then went back to typing up the report.

"How did you figure it out?" he asked me.

"Marie actually put me onto it. She said Elise Carmichael couldn't have known about the house on Osage, though we knew Balcombe had a connection there," I said. "Searching back through the records, I saw where Adams' married name was Balcombe and thus she was the connection. She must have dropped the name Balcombe after she divorced him, and only used the 'B'."

"How'd they know you were going to be in your office at that hour of the night?" Gregory asked.

"They didn't." It was Marie who spoke. And I had been wondering the same thing. "After they grabbed me from my apartment as insurance, they headed over to David's apartment to kidnap him, using me as bait," she said in a matter-the-fact sort of way. "They arrived just as he was leaving and followed him to the office."

I touched Marie's shoulders to comfort her and myself. There was no telling what might have happened to her if Carmichael and Adams had gotten to my apartment *after* I'd left.

"Don't forget to tell him about what happened on our first date," Marie interjected.

A raised eyebrow showed Gregory thought that should be an interesting topic. "What happened on your first date?"

"We ate at a restaurant on Main Street in Manayunk across the street from Adams' condo, and I'm pretty sure now that I saw Balcombe enter the building. I already knew he was the guy who had been following me," I said.

Thompson walked over and stood in front of his partner.

"You about done?" Thompson asked Gregory.

"Yeah. Just a couple more details," he said, then turned his attention back to me. "So Carmichael planned to dump his wife all along?"

"That's my guess," I said. "He knew about her past and decided to change things, once Adams entered the picture."

"Where'd Balcombe come in?" Gregory asked.

"Carmichael's law firm uses the Henderson Group, but using Balcombe was probably Adams' suggestion, since she had a past with him. He was an element she thought she could control. And he was the one who did all the legwork."

"I think if we look through all the paper work, we'll see that Adams controlled or had access to some of, if not all of, the money Carmichael was hiding in overseas accounts," Thompson said.

"That's probably right," I said. "She handled framing Elise for Stephenson's murder. She killed Carmichael to get all of his money and planned to frame me in the deaths of both Carmichael and Balcombe. And she, of course, killed Balcombe. Neat trick."

"Can prosecutors prove it all?" Marie asked.

The officers looked at each other but neither spoke. I filled the void.

"Assuming Adams lives, probably. But it may be a couple of days before we know if she lives." Turning to Marie, I said, "You hit her pretty hard."

"I didn't mean to, I don't think," she said.

Oh, at the time, I'm sure you did, I thought. To the officers, I said, "And as for the evidence, a lot of it is circumstantial, but it's overwhelming. And she'll certainly be convicted for killing Reuben Carmichael. We both witnessed that. Plus, there'll be kidnapping, assault, attempted murder and weapons charges."

"What about Elise Carmichael?" Marie said. "She should be let out. She's not guilty."

"Well, not guilty of this," I said. "Not guilty of murder."

"It's a bit early now, but in a couple of hours we'll contact the DA's office and see about getting Mrs. Carmichael out on bail, pending the outcome of this case," Gregory said. "That shouldn't be a problem, since it appears she didn't kill anyone. They should drop the charges fast."

I was tired and ready to leave. "You think you have everything? Both of us are a bit tired. It's been a long night," I said to the officers.

"I'll bet it has been," Thompson said.

"Yes. We're done here," Gregory said, turning away from the typewriter. He grabbed our attention again as we rose. "But we may have some additional questions at a later date."

"That's fine. Just not today," I said.

"I'll have a car take you home," Thompson said. Then with a smile and a wink to me, he said, "But try to stay out of trouble, Blaise, at least today. It's a holiday."

I asked the officer driving us to drop Marie off at her apartment first. It was mostly quiet in the car, with each of us seeking the solitude of our own thoughts.

When we arrived at Marie's apartment and she was about to get out, she pulled on my arm. "Can you come in with me for a while? I'm still . . . a little . . . scared."

What a dick I was. I hadn't even considered that since she was kidnapped from her own apartment hours earlier, Marie might be a little uncomfortable going back there, particularly alone.

We got out of the car together and I thanked the driver, telling him I'd make it home another way.

"Certainly," I assured Marie. "I'll stay as long as you like."

THE END

About the Author

Photo by Jay Alley

MB Dabney is an award-winning former journalist with several published short story mysteries to his credit. He is also the co-editor of "Decades of Dirt" and "Murder 20/20," both anthology publications of the Speed City chapter of Sisters in Crime. An Untidy Affair is his debut novel. The father of two adult daughters, he lives in Indiana with his wife, Angela.

Made in the USA
Middletown, DE
03 September 2021